AMISH MIDWIVES

AMISH MIDWIVES

THREE STORIES

AMY CLIPSTON

SHELLEY SHEPARD GRAY

KELLY LONG

 ZONDERVAN®

ZONDERVAN

Amish Midwives

Bundles of Blessing Copyright © 2021 by Amy Clipston
A Midwife for Susie Copyright © 2021 by Shelley Sabga
Christmas Cradles Copyright © 2009 by Kelly Long

Requests for information should be addressed to:

Zondervan, *3900 Sparks Dr. SE, Grand Rapids, Michigan 49546*

ISBN 978-0-310-36324-8 (downloadable audio)

Library of Congress Cataloging-in-Publication Data
Names: Clipston, Amy, 1972- Bundles of blessing. | Gray, Shelley Shepard. A midwife for Susie. |
   Long, Kelly. Christmas cradles.
Title: Amish midwives / Amy Clipston, Shelley Shepard Gray, Kelly Long.
Description: Nashville : Zondervan, [2021] | Summary: "From bestselling authors of Amish Fiction
   come three sweet stories about new life, hope, and romance"-- Provided by publisher.
Identifiers: LCCN 2020044565 (print) | LCCN 2020044566 (ebook) | ISBN 9780310363224
   (paperback) | ISBN 9780310363231 (epub) | ISBN 9780310363248
Subjects: LCSH: Amish--Fiction. | Christian fiction, American.
Classification: LCC PS648.A45 A46 2021 (print) | LCC PS648.A45 (ebook) | DDC
   813/.08508--dc23
LC record available at https://lccn.loc.gov/2020044565
LC ebook record available at https://lccn.loc.gov/2020044566

Zondervan titles may be purchased in bulk for educational, business, fundraising, or sales
promotional use. For information, please email SpecialMarkets@Zondervan.com.

Printed in the United States of America

21 22 23 24 25 LSC 10 9 8 7 6 5 4 3 2 1

CONTENTS

GLOSSARY

ach: oh
ack: oh, no
aenti: aunt
appeditlich: delicious
bedauerlich: sad
boppli: baby
bopplin: babies
bruder: brother
bruders: brothers
bu: boy
Budget, The: newspaper
Daadihaus/dawdi haus: grandparents' house
danki/danke: thank you
dat/daed: dad
dawdi: grandfather
Derr Herr: the Lord
dochder: daughter
doktah: doctor

dummkopp: moron

Englisher/Englisch/Englischer: person from outside the Amish community; non-Amish person

fraa/frau: wife

freind: friend

freinden: friends

froh: happy

gern gschehne: you're welcome

grossmuder: grandmother

Gude mariye: Good morning

gut: good

Gut nacht: Good night

haus: house

Ich liebe dich: I love you

jah: yes

kaffi: coffee

kapp: prayer covering or cap

kind: child

kinner: children

kocha: cook

kuche: cake

liewe: love, a term of endearment

maedel: young woman

mamm: mom

mammi: grandmother

mann: man/husband

mei: my

naerfich: nervous

narrisch: foolish

naut: night

nee: no

nohma: name

Plain: Amish way of life

rumspringa/rumschpringe: "running around" period for teenagers

schee: pretty

schweschder/shveshtah: sister

sohn: son

Was en der welt?: What in the world?

Was iss letz?: What's wrong?

Wie geht's: How do you do? or Good day!

wunderbaar: wonderful

ya: yes

BUNDLES OF BLESSING

AMY CLIPSTON

With love and hugs for my super-cool sons, Zac and Matt. I'm so blessed to be your mom!

FEATURED CHARACTERS

JACOB (DECEASED) M. VERNAY (DECEASED) SWAREY
Kristina m. Lester Byler (deceased)
Marlena m. Richard Lapp

MARLENA M. RICHARD LAPP
Katy
Betsie Lin

FREDA M. PHARES SMOKER
Aidan
Lydia Ruth m. Thomas "Tommy" Zook

LYDIA RUTH M. THOMAS "TOMMY" ZOOK
Thomas Jr.

ONE

~~⊷∽⊶~~

The alarm clock buzzed, the sound reminding Kristina
Byler of bleating sheep. With a yawn, she rolled over and
smacked the Off button. She rubbed her eyes and then
looked over toward the large window, where sunlight
peeked in past the green shades.

Kristina pushed herself up and dangled her legs off the
side of the bed. After a stretch and another yawn, she stood
and hurried down the short hallway to the bathroom.
Then she returned to her room and began to dress. As
she pulled on her favorite blue dress and a black apron,
she heard a little voice start to sing next door. A smile
overtook Kristina's lips. Her little niece, Betsie Lin, was
awake.

"I'll be there soon, *mei liewe*," Kristina called.

How she loved living with her sister and her family!
Seeing her two nieces every day was a blessing.

After twisting her thick, long, blonde hair up in a bun
and pulling on her prayer covering, she slipped her cell

7

phone into the pocket of her apron and then hurried across the hallway to Betsie Lin's room.

Kristina grinned as she knocked on the door. "Hello? Is anyone home?"

"*Aenti!*"

Kristina pushed the door open and found Betsie Lin standing in her crib with her arms outstretched. "*Gude mariye, mei liewe!*"

The fifteen-month-old laughed and squealed. With her light-blonde hair and hazel eyes, she reminded Kristina of a painting of an angel she'd once seen in one of the little gift shops in nearby downtown Bird-in-Hand, Pennsylvania. Betsie Lin had inherited her pretty hazel eyes from her father.

"*Aenti* Kissy!" Betsie Lin said as she reached for her.

"I love being your *Aenti* Kissy." Kristina's heart warmed at the sound of the nickname Katy, Betsie Lin's sister, had given her when she was a toddler.

Lifting her niece from her crib, Kristina carried her over to the changing table. Betsie Lin sang nonsense songs and made noises while Kristina changed her diaper and put a yellow dress on her.

"Let's go help your *mamm* make breakfast." Kristina carried her down the stairs and into the large kitchen, where the smells of breakfast and coffee filled her senses.

"*Gude mariye!*" Kristina announced, placing Betsie Lin in her high chair.

"Hi!" Katy called as she sat in her booster seat. She

waved a buttered roll in the air and then leaned over toward her sister and touched her hand as Betsie Lin squealed with delight. With her blonde hair and bright-blue eyes, Katy was the spitting image of her mother when she was her age.

Marlena stepped away from the stove, where bacon sizzled in one skillet and eggs fried in another one. At twenty-eight, Marlena was two years younger than Kristina, and with her dirty-blonde hair and blue eyes, she reminded Kristina of their mother. She sliced homemade rolls and buttered them before walking over to where Betsie Lin sat in her high chair. Kristina's eyes moved to Marlena's abdomen, which seemed to distend a little more today. Her third child was due in early June, which meant that Kristina would have a new niece or nephew in approximately three months. She couldn't wait!

"How are you this morning?" Marlena kissed her toddler on the top of her head and then handed her a buttered roll before looking over at Kristina. "Did you get in late last night? Richard and I never heard you come in."

"*Ya*, I did." Kristina cupped her hand over her mouth to cover another yawn. "Sara Beth Fisher had a long delivery."

"*Ach* no. Is she okay?"

"*Ya*, of course. If it had gotten too complicated, I would have called the rescue squad. But everything went fine. She had a baby *bu*. Eight pounds and three ounces. They named him Michael."

"I'm so glad. When did you get home?"

"I think around twelve-thirty."

Marlena clucked her tongue. "Why didn't you sleep in later then?"

"Because I wanted to help you." Kristina walked over to the stove and began scooping the fried eggs onto a platter. "I need to earn my keep around here."

"Please," Marlena snorted. "You're a second *mamm* to these girls. Plus, my pantry in the basement is stocked with canned goods because of you."

"Well, it's because you all are my only family. Of course I want to share with you." She tried to ignore the sadness that swirled in her chest as she forced a smile.

Had it not been for her sister and brother-in-law's generosity, Kristina would be living alone in the home she'd shared with her husband, Lester, before he had unexpectedly died in an accident four years ago.

She shoved away the thoughts and placed the platter of eggs on the middle of the table. Then she began scraping a small amount onto each of her niece's plastic plates.

"What are your plans for today?" Kristina asked her sister.

"Probably cleaning and sewing." Marlena set the crispy bacon onto the table and nodded over at her older daughter. "Katy is outgrowing her dresses faster than I can sew them."

"I can help you with that." Kristina moved around the table, making room for the rest of the dishes. "Of course,

I can do the cleaning if you're not feeling up to it. How did you sleep last night?"

Marlena sighed and touched her abdomen. "I couldn't get comfortable, but I feel fine." She broke up a piece of bacon and handed it to Katy and then did the same for Betsie Lin before she started toward the door. "But hold that thought. I need to call Richard in for breakfast."

"I'll pour the coffee." Kristina reached toward the cabinet with the mugs just as her cell phone rang. She pulled it from her pocket and found Tommy and Lydia Ruth Zook's number on the screen. Her stomach gave a little flutter.

Marlena stopped and faced her. "Who is it?"

"Lydia Ruth must be in labor." Kristina answered the phone. "Hello?"

"Kristina!" Tommy sounded out of breath. "Lydia Ruth started having contractions a few hours ago. She thought it was false labor since she's not due for some time, but her water just broke."

"Do your best to keep her comfortable with the methods I told you about. I'm on my way."

"*Danki*," Tommy said before disconnecting.

"Lydia Ruth's water broke—it's time!" Kristina slipped the cell phone back into her apron pocket, grateful she had charged it with her deep cycle battery last night. Then she picked up her calendar from the counter. She flipped to March and shook her head. "She's nearly two weeks early, which is unusual for a first baby, according to the books I've been reading."

Just then, the back door opened and closed as Richard walked into the kitchen. His dark hair was mussed as if he had just removed his straw hat. He grinned as he looked over at his daughters.

"*Dat! Dat! Dat!*" Betsie Lin lifted a handful of scrambled eggs into the air and then dropped them onto the high chair tray.

"Hi, Betsie." Richard gave a little chuckle as he kissed Betsie Lin's cheek and then touched Katy's nose. "Hi, Katy." Then he gave his wife a special smile. "Breakfast smells *appeditlich*."

"Tommy Zook just called. Lydia Ruth is having her *boppli*," Marlena told her husband.

"Oh." His hazel eyes rounded as he looked over at Kristina. "I'll get your horse and buggy ready."

"*Danki*." Kristina hurried toward the stairs. "I'm sorry to run, but I need to get my supplies."

"I'll make you some breakfast to eat in the buggy," Marlena called after her.

"*Danki*!" Kristina jogged up the stairs to her bedroom, where she grabbed her supply bag, which was always packed and ready to go.

When Kristina reentered the kitchen, Marlena held up a thermos and a plastic container. "*Kaffi* and an egg and bacon sandwich."

"*Danki*." Kristina kissed her nieces on their heads. "See you later, girls!" Then she headed for the mudroom, where she pulled on her shoes and sweater.

"Be safe and give my love to Lydia Ruth and Tommy."

"I will." Kristina shouldered her bag, then took the sandwich and thermos from her sister's hands before stepping out into the crisp, early March morning.

She shivered as she hurried down the back porch steps to where Richard finished hitching up the horse and buggy. She always appreciated how her brother-in-law not only took good care of Marlena and their children but also went out of his way to help Kristina. He had welcomed her into his home after Lester died and never once seemed to resent her presence. He was a good man with a giving heart, and she was grateful he had married her sister.

"*Danki* for helping me get ready," she told him.

"Of course." Richard pulled open the door. "Give Tommy and Lydia Ruth our regards."

"I will." She climbed up into the buggy and then guided her horse down the rock driveway toward the road.

Kristina managed to eat most of her breakfast sandwich and sipped some coffee during the short ride to the Zook farm. When she arrived, she tied her horse to the fence and then scooted up the back porch steps. A familiar happiness settled over her as she knocked on the door. It was time for her to help deliver another baby!

She was certain this was what the Lord had called her to do after she'd lost Lester. Kristina had helped deliver Katy during an unexpected snowstorm that prevented the ambulance from arriving in time. After helping to bring Katy into the world, Kristina was convinced it was her calling.

"Kristina!" Tommy's brown eyes were wide as he pushed open the door. "I'm so glad you're here. Lydia Ruth is miserable, and I have no idea what I'm doing."

"I'm sure you're doing just fine." She smiled up at him. "Let's go deliver your *boppli*."

Kristina sat down on the edge of the bed next to Lydia Ruth as they stared down at her baby boy later that evening. "He's beautiful, Lydia Ruth. And I think Thomas Jr. is the perfect name."

The labor had taken most of the day. And after the baby was born, Kristina cleaned him up before taking care of the rest of the room. Then she talked to Lydia Ruth about breastfeeding, sharing what she'd read in the mountain of library books she frequently studied. Now Lydia Ruth rested against a few pillows and stared down at her son, who was swaddled in a blanket as he slept.

Kristina glanced up at Tommy and spotted tears pooling in his dark eyes. "You have been blessed."

"We have." Lydia Ruth touched the shock of dark hair on the baby's head and then looked up at her husband. "He has your dark hair."

"And your chin." Tommy leaned down.

Kristina stood up. "Since my job here is done, time for me to go!"

Lydia Ruth smiled up at her. "Kristina, you're a blessing to our community."

Kristina felt her cheeks heat. "*Danki*. I'm really just a mother's assistant. You did all the work. And I'm honored you trusted me to help."

"Our parents should be here soon. I'll make *kaffi* and pull out that chocolate *kuche* you baked yesterday." Tommy kissed Lydia Ruth's cheek. "I'll be back soon." He glanced over at Kristina. "I'll put the box of canned fruits and vegetables in your buggy and get your horse from the barn." He had stowed her horse and fed it earlier in the afternoon.

"I appreciate it."

Lydia Ruth smiled up at her husband as he walked out of the room and then stared down at her son once again. "I can't believe he's here." Her voice wobbled. "Tommy and I have prayed for a *kind* since we were married three years ago. I'm so *froh*."

Kristina nodded as she packed up her bag. Her heart squeezed as she recalled also praying for a child, but the Lord had other plans for her. She was meant to help Amish children enter the world instead of raising children of her own. And she was grateful!

"I can't wait for *mei mamm* to get here," Lydia Ruth continued, her gaze still focused on her child. "She is going to be so excited to meet her first grandchild."

Kristina stopped packing her bag and looked over at Lydia Ruth. "Thomas is her first grandchild?"

Tilting her head, Lydia Ruth looked over at Kristina. "*Ya,* of course."

Kristina's throat dried as a vision of Aidan Smoker, who was not only Lydia Ruth's older *bruder,* but also Kristina's ex-boyfriend, filled her mind. Last Kristina had heard, Aidan had moved to Ohio eight years ago to marry a pen pal. "Aidan and his *fraa* haven't had a child?"

"Aidan never married."

Speechless, Kristina tried to ignore the strange mix of shock and curiosity that whipped through her. Why hadn't Aidan married? She wondered what had happened to him.

Shoving away her thoughts of the man who had broken her heart nearly a decade ago, Kristina picked up her bag. "Call me if you need anything."

"I will." Lydia Ruth smiled over at her. "*Danki,* Kristina."

Excited voices floated up from the downstairs.

"It sounds like you have company," Kristina said.

"If *mei mamm* is here, would you please send her up?"

"Of course." Kristina stepped out of Lydia Ruth's bedroom and headed down the stairs.

The aroma of coffee filled her senses and caused her mouth to water. She hadn't eaten since she'd had a turkey sandwich nearly three hours ago.

When she stepped into the kitchen, Freda Smoker,

Lydia Ruth's mother, nearly knocked Kristina over as she hugged her. "I can't wait to meet my grandson!"

"He's beautiful, Freda." Kristina gestured toward the staircase. "Lydia Ruth is waiting for you."

Freda rubbed her hands together. "I'm so excited to hold him."

"Enjoy him." Kristina smiled and then continued toward the door.

She entered the mudroom, set down her bag, and pulled on her sweater. As she buttoned it up, she heard the sound of male voices drifting in from the porch. After hefting her bag up on her shoulder, she pushed open the back door.

Then she stepped out onto the porch and came face-to-face with Aidan.

Her heart jumped into her throat, and she froze in her tracks, her feet cemented to the porch as she looked up into his cerulean eyes.

TWO

⁂

Kristina's nerves spiked as she stared up into the face of the man she'd once believed she would marry. Her mind spun like a cyclone, and for a moment she was certain she was dreaming. Yet there Aidan stood, staring at her with an expression that appeared as baffled as she felt.

Behind him the sun had begun to set, sending vivid bursts of orange, red, and yellow across the sky. A crisp breeze reminded her that the temperature had dropped, and she shivered.

"Kristina," Aidan finally said, his voice the same warm, rich sound that had once reminded her of chocolate pudding. "What a surprise." A hesitant smile overtook his lips, and the signature dimple on his right cheek made its grand appearance.

"*Ya*." She fiddled with the strap of her bag and tried to swallow past the swelling ball of emotion clogging her throat.

Aidan looked good—really good. His dark hair was still the perfect contrast to his sky-blue eyes, and he was several inches taller than she was. His shoulders were broad while his arms looked muscular and defined under his long-sleeved, dark-blue shirt. She took in his angular, clean-shaven jaw—the evidence confirming for her that he'd never married.

But why he'd never married was none of her business or concern. After all, Aidan had destroyed her trust, and she would be better off to walk away from him and not allow him back into her life.

"Kristina is the most sought-after midwife in the Lancaster community," Tommy said.

Kristina turned toward Tommy and blinked. For a moment, she'd forgotten that he and Phares, Aidan's father, still stood nearby.

Aidan seemed to study her as if she were an intricate puzzle. "When did you become a midwife?"

"After Lester died."

Something unreadable flashed in Aidan's eyes when she mentioned her late husband, who had been Aidan's best friend since they were in school together. Perhaps he missed Lester. No, he couldn't possibly. After all, he hadn't come home from Ohio to attend Lester's funeral.

At the memory of his absence, resentment filled her.

"How long are you in town visiting?" She worked to keep her tone even.

Aidan leaned back against the porch railing and crossed his arms over his wide chest. "I'm back for *gut*, actually. I just got here on Monday."

"Oh?" Kristina hoped her expression remained casual despite her mounting shock.

"It's all my fault." Phares patted Aidan's shoulder. "I decided it's time to retire, so I asked Aidan if he wanted to move back here and take over my dairy farm. After all, Aidan is a still a bachelor, so nothing's keeping him in Ohio. It was time for him to come home."

Aidan glanced over at his father and sighed before looking back at Kristina.

She shifted her weight on her feet. "Well, welcome home." She lifted her chin. "I'll see you all at church on Sunday." Then she met Tommy's gaze. "Congratulations again. Call me if you need anything."

"I will." Tommy nodded toward her waiting horse and buggy. "I put the box of canned goods in the back for you."

"*Danki*." Kristina said good night and then headed down the porch steps.

"Take care," Aidan called after her.

She was certain she could feel Aidan's eyes burning into her back as she made her way to the buggy.

As she guided her horse down the long, rock driveway, her mind began to wander with memories of Aidan and their two-year relationship. Her thoughts brought awareness to something that still sat hard and cold over her heart as she recalled how much Aidan had meant to her.

She had known Aidan and Lester since she started school in first grade. They were all acquaintances in school and church, but they grew closer when she joined their youth group at sixteen. Even though Aidan and Lester were two years older than she was, she quickly became good friends with them.

Shortly after she'd started attending youth group gatherings, Kristina developed a crush on Aidan. She was drawn to his lopsided smile, contagious laugh, and rugged good looks. She was certain she had fallen in love with him when she was only sixteen years old. And when he asked her to date him when she was eighteen, she was just as certain she was going to marry him.

Then everything changed when he'd destroyed her trust and shattered her life. She broke off their relationship, and Lester was there waiting for her, ready to dry her tears and console her. Lester won her heart with his sympathetic ear, easy sense of humor, and sunny personality. Soon after she became engaged to him, Aidan moved to Ohio.

Kristina took a ragged breath as tears filled her eyes. Oh, how she missed Lester! He'd been her rock when she needed him most. Her relationship with him was always easy. They rarely argued.

Her relationship with Aidan had been the opposite. She recalled how she and Aidan always seemed to have a fire burning between them. Their relationship was complicated and intense, and she could still recognize that intensity in his blue eyes. And now he was back, meaning she'd have to see him at church and around town.

She clenched her teeth and grasped the reins tighter in her hands. Somehow she'd have to ignore him and dismiss the heartache she couldn't seem to forget.

Aidan leaned forward on the porch railing and folded his hands as he watched Kristina climb into her buggy. He'd nearly fallen over when she stepped out onto the porch. She was the last person he'd expected to see today.

After nearly a decade away, Kristina was still the most beautiful woman he'd ever known, with her hair that reminded him of sunshine, her gorgeous, cornflower-blue eyes, and her bright smile—although she hadn't blessed him with a smile. Instead, she'd just stared at him as if she was trying to figure out if she should talk to him or flee.

Kristina had been the love of his life, the woman he wanted to marry and with whom he'd hoped to raise a family. Although they had a rocky relationship at times, he loved her with his whole heart, and he'd planned to ask his parents if he could build a little house on their farm for him and Kristina to live in. But so much for that plan. Before long, she'd broken up with him and destroyed him and his dreams.

He knew he'd run into Kristina eventually, but he hadn't expected to see her only three days after he'd arrived back in Gordonville. Then she appeared on his sister's porch, and Aidan was tongue-tied when she looked up at him. He worked hard to keep a calm demeanor, hoping his nervousness didn't expose him.

When she mentioned Lester, he almost lost his cool. Lester had been Aidan's best friend nearly his whole life and then he'd betrayed Aidan when he quickly swooped in and grabbed hold of Kristina after she broke up with him.

In a matter of a month, the two people he trusted most had stabbed him in the back, and he had no choice but to leave Gordonville and move to Ohio to try to start over. His cousin Fannie had written him to tell him about her friend Louise, and he hoped he could possibly plan a future with her. But then those plans faltered too.

Aidan swiped his hand down his face, hoping to erase the ache that radiated through him.

"I'm going to see how Lydia Ruth and the *boppli* are doing. I have *kaffi* on, and there's a chocolate *kuche* on the table," Tommy announced before heading into the house.

Aidan cleared his throat and turned to face his father. As much as he longed to forget Kristina and the pain she'd caused him, he also couldn't fight back his curiosity. He craved to know more about what he had missed in her life.

"Kristina is a midwife now, huh?" Aidan worked to keep his voice casual. "How did that happen?"

Dat sank down into a rocker and rubbed a hand over his dark-brown beard that now boasted flecks of gray. "From what I understand, she delivered her *schweschder's* first *boppli* and then decided to become a midwife."

"Oh." Aidan nodded, but he was still flummoxed. He

never imagined her working outside the home. Did that mean she hadn't remarried?

He pursed his lips. Why did he care? It wasn't any of his business.

"Has she remarried?" He heard himself ask the question and did a mental head slap.

"No. She's living with her *schweschder* and her family. She lost her *mamm* right after you left and then her *dat* passed away about five years ago."

Aidan frowned. "I heard. So *bedauerlich*."

"I suppose after she lost Lester she felt completely alone, so she moved in with Marlena and Richard."

"Richard Lapp?"

"That's right."

"He's a *gut* guy." Aidan stood up straight. He and Richard had been good friends in school and in youth group.

Dat studied him, and Aidan suddenly felt itchy under his stare. "You and Kristina dated a long time ago, and that's ancient history now. There's no reason why you can't be *freinden*. I know she hurt you, but that was nearly a decade ago."

Aidan swallowed a snort. Just seeing her around the community would be difficult enough. The idea of trying to be her friend was impossible. *Lord, give me strength!* "You make that sound much easier than it is, *Dat*."

"It's our way to forgive, Aidan."

"I know that." Aidan needed to change the subject.

He gestured toward the house. "Why don't we go meet your new grandchild?"

Dat grinned as he stood. "That's a great idea."

Warmth filled Aidan as he redirected his thoughts toward his new nephew and his sister's happiness.

As he climbed the steep steps to the second floor, he found himself wondering if he would ever have a family of his own. He was thirty-two now, which meant finding a mate might be more difficult. Could he possibly find a woman who would love him and settle down with him?

He shoved the thoughts away and then moved to the doorway to his sister's bedroom. He smiled as he watched his brother-in-law hold his newborn while his sister and parents gazed adoringly at the tiny baby.

Aidan couldn't stop the tears that filled his eyes. *God is good.*

Kristina yawned as she stepped into the mudroom after stowing her horse and buggy in the barn. All of her muscles and bones ached after her long day, but she couldn't stop her smile. With God's help, she'd assisted with another beautiful birth. Oh, how she loved her job!

She set her bag and the box of canned goods on the bench in the mudroom and then shucked her sweater and shoes. She entered the kitchen and the faint aroma of meatloaf filled her senses, causing her stomach to rumble.

She found Marlena sitting at the table drinking a cup of tea while reading a novel.

Marlena looked up from a book. "How did it go?"

"Lydia Ruth has a healthy *boppli bu*."

"*Wunderbaar.* I saved you some supper." Marlena stood and pointed toward the stairs. "Get changed, and I'll warm it up for you."

"*Danki.*" Kristina's stomach growled, loudly this time, as she made her way up the steps.

She peeked into her nieces' bedrooms where they slept and smiled at them before heading into the bathroom. She took a quick shower and then slipped on a nightgown and robe, twisting her hair into a tight bun and covering it with a scarf.

When she reentered the kitchen, she found a place set for her, including a cup of tea, along with a plate of meatloaf, green beans, and mashed potatoes.

"You're a lifesaver, Marlena. I feel as though I haven't eaten in a week." She sank down into the chair and breathed in the delicious food.

"Did you have lunch?" Marlena sat down across from her.

"*Ya*, but I think that was yesterday."

Marlena chuckled.

After a silent prayer, Kristina dug into the food.

"I'm sure Lydia Ruth and Tommy were *froh*, *ya*?" Marlena asked.

"*Ya*. The labor was long, and she pushed for quite a

while. But Thomas Jr. is healthy. He weighs seven pounds and eight ounces. Once Lydia Ruth was settled, Tommy called both of their parents." She felt her smile wobble as she recalled her brief encounter with Aidan.

"What is it?" Marlena leaned forward as if anticipating a juicy piece of gossip.

"Lydia Ruth's parents came to see her and the *boppli*."

Marlena gave her a palms up. "And . . . ?"

"And Aidan was with them."

Marlena gasped. "Is he visiting?"

"No, he moved back. He's taking over Phares's farm, so Phares can retire. And . . . he's not married."

Marlena's mouth dropped open. "He's not married?"

Kristina shook her head and scooped more mashed potatoes into her mouth. A strange feeling overcame her as she recalled Aidan once again. Why did she still feel that strong tie to him? It couldn't be attraction. Not after the way he'd hurt her.

"Wait a minute." Marlena held her hand up. "Didn't he go to Ohio to be with that *maedel* his cousin had told to write him?"

"Her name was Louise." She nearly spat the words.

Surely Kristina couldn't still be envious of this woman. After all, Aidan had left and she married Lester, who gave her a happy life for as long as the Lord had allowed. Why should she care that Aidan chose Louise over her? "Apparently, he didn't marry her."

"That's a twist."

Kristina guffawed. "You could say that again."

Marlena rested her elbow on the table and her chin on her palm. "Aidan was so handsome. And you two were so in love."

Kristina scowled. "Stop."

"I remember how he used to come over at night, and you'd sit on the porch and talk for hours. And he looked at you like you were the only *maedel* in the world."

"Marlena, please." Kristina's appetite suddenly evaporated. "That was a long time ago."

"But he's back now, and you're both single." Marlena's pretty blue eyes rounded. "Maybe it's a sign from God!"

Kristina set her fork down on her plate beside her half-eaten piece of meatloaf. "If we were meant to be together, it would have worked out years ago. I love my life and my job." She gestured around the kitchen. "I'm *froh* here. I don't need to worry about finding a new husband. I have a purpose."

Marlena nodded, but her expression told Kristina that she wasn't convinced. "You're telling me that you've given up on having a family of your own?"

Pushing back her chair, Kristina stood and carried her plate and utensils to the counter. After scraping her leftover food into the trash can, she began filling one side of the sink with hot, soapy water. "I've just accepted that this is my life."

Marlena joined her at the sink. "Everyone is entitled to find someone to love them."

"I had that with Lester. God decided it was his time, and I have accepted that too."

Marlena gave her a sad smile, and Kristina turned her attention back to the sink.

"I'm fine. Stop worrying about me."

"You and Aidan are older now. You're more mature. Maybe you could work things out."

"There's nothing to work out." She rinsed the dish, and Marlena began drying it. "I've forgiven him, but I could never trust him. Besides, I'm happy with my life."

Kristina ignored how Marlena shook her head. Her sister was wrong. Not everyone needed to be married. Some people were better off on their own.

If only she could stop her heart from feeling so lonely.

THREE

Aidan plastered a smile on his face as he shook another old friend's hand on Sunday morning. He stood with the other men in the congregation outside of the Glick family's barn.

He silently marveled at how most of his old friends were still members of the congregation, but they all sported beards now, which meant they were all married. And most of them smiled while they shared stories about their children. The only story Aidan could share was that he was back and still single. His shoulders sagged.

He glanced over to where families walked from their parked buggies toward the house and barn, and he felt a strange stirring in his chest when he spotted Kristina carrying a toddler as she and Marlena ambled toward the house. Marlena held the hand of another little girl who looked to be three or four.

He blinked and took in Kristina's beauty as she smiled at something her sister said. He studied the child in her arms. With her blonde hair and bright smile, she could pass for Kristina's child, but that wouldn't be possible since Lester had been dead for four years now. And he felt sure that news would have reached him in Ohio. No, the toddler had to be one of her nieces. He couldn't pull his eyes away from Kristina as she continued toward the house and then disappeared through the back door to meet with the other women in the kitchen.

"Aidan. It's been a long time."

Turning, Aidan found Richard Lapp holding out his hand in greeting. "Rich. It's so *gut* to see you."

"You too." Richard shook his hand. "I heard you were back, and I was so surprised. How nice that you're taking over your *dat's* farm."

So Kristina had told her family all about his return to Gordonville. What else had she said about him? "*Danki.* I hear you and Marlena have two little ones."

"*Ya.*" Richard grinned. "Katy is three, and Betsie Lin is fifteen months. We're also expecting our third in early June."

"Wow. You're blessed."

"I am." Richard leaned back on a fence post. "Marlena and I married almost five years ago. We're hoping the Lord will bless us with a large family. Did you know that Kristina lives with us?"

"*Ya, mei dat* mentioned it."

"She's been a great help with the *kinner.* I don't know what Marlena would do without her."

Aidan glanced toward the kitchen. Questions swirled through his mind. Was Kristina dating anyone? Would she remarry and have a family of her own? He shouldn't even care after the way she broke his heart and then married his best friend.

"What about you?"

Aidan faced Richard's curious stare. "What do you mean?"

"What kind of work did you do in Ohio?"

"I had a dairy farm. I sold it before I came back."

Richard shook his head. "It's tough work."

Aidan chuckled. "That is an understatement. I almost considered telling *mei dat* no and looking for another profession, but the land has been in our family for generations. I couldn't just let him sell it."

"I understand."

Aidan and Richard fell into an easy conversation about their farms. Soon it was nine o'clock and time to file into the barn for the service. Aidan found his way to the unmarried men's section and sat down between two young men who looked familiar. He nodded hello and then picked up his hymnal. Quiet conversations swirled around him, and the rest of the congregation filed into the barn and found their seats.

He looked over toward the married men's section and spotted Richard sitting with other men he recalled from his youth group days. Aidan felt out of place, like a fish out of water, looking over at his former friends who

32

all wore beards. He glanced around and surmised that he was one of the oldest bachelors in his congregation. What had he done wrong to wind up alone at the age of thirty-two?

The married women made their way in, and Kristina sat with her younger niece on her lap. She leaned down beside her and whispered something to her older niece, who had climbed up on the bench between Kristina and Marlena. He took in Kristina's pretty face, her long neck, and her pink lips. She had somehow become more beautiful than he recalled—or maybe she had always been a stunning beauty, and he hadn't truly appreciated her.

To his surprise, Kristina met his gaze, and his throat dried as she gave him a hesitant smile. He returned the smile, and suddenly he felt transported back in time to a decade ago when he and Lester would sit together in church. During the services he would steal glances over at Kristina, who would offer him a shy smile before turning her attention back to the ministers.

Oh, how he missed those days! Life seemed simpler back then. He had his best friend, Lester, and his beautiful girlfriend. He was certain that he would marry Kristina and raise a family with her while Lester also settled down with another woman. Then the two couples would remain close as they raised their children in the same community.

But everything fell apart, and they both betrayed him.

That familiar anger and resentment that had haunted him for nearly a decade boiled beneath his skin. Why did he miss the two people who had hurt him the most? It just didn't make sense!

Guilt suddenly clutched his chest. He shouldn't harbor any ill feelings toward Lester. After all, Lester was gone now, and there was no way Aidan could set things right between them.

Aidan looked down at the hymnal in hopes that the song leader would begin the first hymn soon. He needed a break from his confusing thoughts.

When the service started, Aidan tried to focus on worshipping the Lord instead of on his swirling emotions. He did his best to keep his attention on the minister, but his eyes frequently roamed over to Kristina, where she spent her time whispering to her nieces, watching the ministers, or looking down at her lap. She hadn't once looked over at him. And again he pondered why his heart seemed to long for Kristina's attention.

Aidan helped the other men convert the benches into tables for the noon meal when the service was over. Then he followed his father over to one of the tables and sat down beside him.

Tommy and Richard joined them, sitting across from Aidan and his father as the women carried platters of food to the tables.

"How are you feeling, Tommy?" Richard asked him.

"Okay." Tommy nodded. "Lydia Ruth stayed home with the *boppli* today, but she insisted I come to church." He cupped his hand to his mouth to cover a yawn.

Dat chuckled. "Tired, eh?"

Tommy gave a little laugh. "*Ya.*"

"A child changes everything," Richard said.

"That's true." Tommy picked up a pretzel from his plate and ate it.

"And the changes are worth every moment," *Dat* added.

Aidan swallowed a sigh as he once again wondered if he would be destined to spend the rest of his life alone. He peered across the barn to where Kristina smiled and chatted as she filled coffee cups. He was overwhelmed with the urge to talk to her.

But how could there be anything left to say after the way their relationship had ended?

He dropped a pile of pretzels onto his plate and then smothered a piece of bread with peanut butter spread while Richard, Tommy, and *Dat* continued to talk about children. Aidan smiled and nodded, still pondering if he would always be the odd man out.

When lunch was over, Aidan headed toward the barn exit as the women filed in to take their turn to eat. He spotted Kristina walking into the barn with Marlena, and he picked up speed, hoping to talk to her. When a hand touched his arm, he stopped.

"Aidan."

He turned toward Rosetta King smiling up at him. He recalled her from school and youth group, but they hadn't been much more than acquaintances. "Rosetta. Hi."

She gave him a warm smile. He'd always thought she was attractive, with her dark hair and eyes and her petite figure.

"I'm so *froh* you're finally back." She leaned in closer. "I was wondering if I could possibly bring you a meal sometime. Would you like that?" Her expression was eager as if a negative response might shatter her. Maybe he could let her down easy.

"I appreciate the offer, but I'm still getting settled in right now." He kept a friendly smile on his face as he spoke, in hopes she wouldn't feel too disappointed.

"Maybe in a couple weeks?"

"Sure."

"*Wunderbaar*! I look forward to it. Have a *gut* week." Then she turned on her heel and headed toward a nearby table, where she scooted in and sat down.

Aidan glanced across the barn to Kristina sitting with her sister. He'd missed his chance to talk to her, but it was just as well. He didn't know what he would say anyway.

Dat sidled up to Aidan when he stepped outside into the cool afternoon air. "What did Rosetta want?"

"She asked me if she could bring a meal over sometime."

Dat grinned. "Sounds like you won't have any trouble finding a girlfriend."

Aidan shook his head. "I don't really know her that well, *Dat*. Besides, I'm not looking for a girlfriend right now."

"Why not?" *Dat's* forehead creased. "You're not getting any younger. Rosetta is a nice *maedel*. I never understood why she didn't marry."

"Probably for the same reason I didn't—because I was hurt and betrayed."

Dat jammed a finger in Aidan's chest. "Which is exactly why Rosetta might be the one for you. Let her bring you a meal, and *that's* how you'll get to know her."

Aidan shook his head. "I'm going home. I'll see you at the *haus*."

As he headed toward his buggy, Aidan looked back toward the barn and wondered if he would always feel awkward around his church family.

Kristina sat at Anna Marie Esh's kitchen table Friday afternoon. She looked down at her journal, which included Anna Marie's measurements and notes about her pregnancy, and then smiled up at her. "I think you're right on track to deliver in late April. How are you feeling?"

"*Gut*." Anna Marie lifted her mug of tea. "I'm a little sore, but it's to be expected."

Kristina took notes. "Are you having any contractions?"

"Sometimes, but I had that with the other three." She gazed over at her three sons, all under the age of six, as they scampered around the kitchen, playing with blocks and toy cars. "Hard to believe we'll be a family of six soon."

Kristina smiled as she watched the three boys. Each of them had their father's dark hair and their mother's golden-brown eyes. Then she turned to Anna Marie. "Do you have a feeling if it's a *bu* or a *maedel*?"

Anna Marie laughed. "I thought each of them was a *maedel*, so only God knows." She pushed her glasses up on her small nose and then grinned. "By the way . . . I saw Aidan Smoker at church on Sunday, and Greta Yoder told me he's back for *gut*."

Kristina hoped her shrug was casual. "That's what I heard too."

Anna Marie leaned across the table toward her. "Didn't you date Aidan?"

"I did." Kristina looked down and wrote more notes to avoid Anna Marie's curious expression.

"And wasn't he Lester's best *freind*?"

Kristina swallowed a sigh. She liked Anna Marie, but she was a bit of a gossip. She knew that anything she shared with Anna Marie would be repeated to Greta before it spread across the community like wildfire. "*Ya*, he was."

"Whatever happened between you and Aidan?"

Kristina fastened a bright smile on her face. "We broke up."

"And then you married Lester."

"Right." Kristina looked down at her journal. "Should we schedule our next appointment?"

"Do you think you and Aidan will get back together?

After all, you're both still single, and you're young enough to get married and have a family."

Kristina clutched her pen with such a force she was almost certain she'd break it in half and send ink spewing across the table. Perhaps this was what all of the women had been gossiping about since they saw Aidan at church on Sunday. Irritation filtered through her.

She silently counted to five and then looked up at Anna Marie's eager grin. "No, I don't think so."

"Why not? He is awfully handsome, and I'm sure you'd like to have a family of your own instead of only delivering *bopplin* for everyone else."

Kristina leveled her gaze with Anna Marie. "I'm very *froh* with my job and my life. And Lester gave me enough love to last a lifetime."

Anna Marie lifted a suspicious eyebrow. She opened her mouth to say something, but Kristina cut her off.

"How about I come back a week from Friday?"

"*Ya*, that sounds *gut*." Anna Marie pushed herself away from the table and walked slowly toward her calendar hanging on the wall. She picked up a pen and then made note of the appointment while rubbing her protruding belly with her free hand. "Same time?" she asked over her shoulder.

"*Ya*, that works for me." Kristina wrote the appointment down before stowing her journal and her planner in her tote bag.

Then Anna Marie faced her and smiled again. "So,

about Aidan. Greta and I were discussing how *wunderbaar* it would be if you and Aidan mended fences and got back together."

Kristina opened her mouth to protest just as a crash sounded, followed by a screech and a sob.

"*Ach*, Saul." Anna Marie hurried over to the toddler who had fallen down onto a pile of blocks. His *bruders* gathered around him, their eyes filling with tears as they watched Anna Marie pick up the sobbing boy and console him.

"You're fine." Anna Marie looked down at his hands and feet and then said, "No scratches. No cuts. You just fell down and went boom." Saul snuggled against his mother, rubbing his face into her neck as he continued to cry.

Kristina smiled at the tenderness. How she loved watching mothers with their babies. If only she could experience that too.

She stood, pulled on her sweater, and lifted her bag onto her shoulder. She gave Anna Marie a wave. "I'll see you soon." Then she headed for the door.

"Kristina," Anna Marie called.

"*Ya?*" Kristina glanced back.

"Give Aidan a chance," she said while rubbing a sniffling Saul's back. "You might be glad you did."

Kristina nodded and then wrenched open the door.

FOUR

Kristina retrieved her grocery list from her apron pocket and then guided her horse down Anna Marie's driveway and toward the road. She tried in vain to erase Anna Marie's comments about Aidan from her mind as she focused on the road ahead. Still, her instructions to give Aidan a chance burned a little, and her mind latched on to it.

But why should she give Aidan a chance? And what did Anna Marie mean exactly? After all, he picked his pen pal in Ohio over Kristina. His choice had been clear, and he'd left Kristina behind without a glance backward.

And Lester.

Kristina swallowed back her threatening grief as their little one-story, brick house came into view at the end of Anna Marie's road. She halted the horse and stared over at the home she and Lester had bought shortly after they were married eight years ago. With its three little bedrooms, one-and-a-half bathrooms, small kitchen, and small family room, it wasn't extravagant, but it was Kristina and Lester's world where they had planned to build a life.

She wiped at her stinging eyes as she recalled how Lester had borrowed money from his parents to not only buy the house but also to start his own roofing business.

They struggled financially in the beginning, but they kept praying the business would take off. And after two years, it did. Lester not only had plenty of clients, but he also had three crews working for him.

Soon they found themselves living a comfortable life, but one thing was missing—children. They had prayed and prayed, and she held on to the hope that God would bless them in his time.

But she never had the opportunity to be a mother.

And then four years ago, she lost everything.

Kristina squeezed her eyes shut, trying to block out the memories of the day her world had completely fallen apart.

Sitting up straight, she directed the horse back onto the road and toward the grocery in Bird-in-Hand. She tied her horse up in the parking lot beside a row of horses and buggies. Then, holding her list, she walked into the store, found a shopping cart, and began moving through the aisles. Once her cart was full and her items were crossed off her list, she headed toward the row of cashiers.

"Kristina."

Turning, she froze when she found Aidan watching her while leaning on a shopping cart. She took in his warm smile and adorable dimple, and a strange flutter started in her stomach.

For a brief moment she found herself comparing Aidan with Lester. Both Aidan and Lester were tall, but Aidan was slightly taller than her late husband. And while Lester was blessed with sandy-blond hair and light-blue eyes, Aidan's dark hair was a stark contrast to his eyes that somehow looked bluer today—or maybe it was due to the fluorescent lights buzzing above them.

Lester seemed to always have an easy smile and silly joke for her. In fact, Kristina could probably count on one hand the times that Lester had been sad, worried, angry, or upset. Yet Aidan was serious and intense. He reminded her of a blazing fire while Lester was a warm, sunny day.

And now Aidan stood in front of her, watching her with those intense eyes. Her throat dried.

"I didn't mean to startle you." He stood up to his full height as he pointed to her shopping cart. "I see you're shopping too."

"*Ya*. I . . . I guess that's what one does in a grocery store." She moved her cart out of the way as a young Amish mother with three children walked past them.

Color rose to his cheeks. "I suppose you're right about that. All the same, I had to run out for some supplies, so *mei mamm* gave me her shopping list." He held up a small, lined piece of paper. "She always has her list."

"*Ya*." Kristina grasped the cart and glanced toward the cashiers.

Aidan cleared his throat. "I had hoped to talk to you at church, but I couldn't get to you before you started eating lunch."

"I'm sure you were busy getting caught up with some folks." She felt her shoulders tense as she recalled how Rosetta had caught his ear. And why should she care? She wasn't jealous of Rosetta. Or was she?

He gave a little laugh and then rubbed his clean-shaven chin. "Everyone wanted to know why I've come back."

Kristina looked toward the cashiers and spotted an open line. "I should really get going. It was nice—"

"Wait." He held his hand up, and she stilled. "Have you had lunch?"

She blinked and then looked toward the clock on the wall. It was after one. "No, I haven't."

"Do you want to grab something? My treat." His eyes were wide and hopeful, which confused her.

She pursed her lips as Anna Marie's words echoed in her mind: *give Aidan a chance.*

If she gave Aidan another chance, perhaps they could be friends again. At the least, maybe they could work things out to the point where seeing each other at church or around the community wouldn't be so awkward. Maybe then the rumors would stop.

"Okay," she heard herself say.

"Great." He looked relieved. Then he pointed to the items in her cart. "Your groceries will be okay?"

"*Ya*. I keep a cooler in my buggy so that I can stow my groceries when I meet with clients."

He nodded and seemed intrigued.

"Well, let's go pay." She pushed her cart toward the cashier, and he followed close behind her.

They reached the register, and he walked around his cart and began helping her load her items onto the conveyor. When she peeked up at him, she found him smiling at her, and she felt her heart come to life for the first time since she'd lost Lester.

And at that moment, she knew her heart was doomed.

Aidan sat down in a booth across from Kristina at the Bird-in-Hand Family Restaurant. He picked up his menu and tried to force his eyes to read it, but they kept defying him and darting toward Kristina.

He still couldn't believe she had agreed to have lunch with him. He'd detected the hesitation in her eyes, and when her forehead puckered, he was certain she was debating her answer. He'd seen that puzzled expression hundreds of times when they were a couple.

But now her expression seemed relaxed as her bright-blue eyes focused on the menu. He once again felt transported back in time. They had frequented this restaurant, as well as many others, with friends and alone.

And now he felt awkward and out of place sitting with her. Would that feeling ever go away?

"I think I'll have the tuna melt," she suddenly said. "How about you?" She looked up at him.

"Oh. I haven't looked yet." He opened the menu.

"You used to always get the Bird-in-Hand Club."

His eyes flitted to hers, and she bit her lip. "You remember that?"

"Why would I forget?" Her expression almost seemed to challenge him, and his pulse ticked up. "I remember everything."

"I do too." He blew out a puff of air and considered asking her why she'd felt the need to dump him without any explanation, but he bit back the retort. Right now, his goal was to get her to talk to him, not make her want to flee. He recalled how stubborn and set in her ways she was. He had to tread lightly to compel her to open up to him. So he smiled. "The club sounds like a great choice."

A young woman who looked to be in her early twenties stopped by for their orders and then took the menus before disappearing again.

Once she was gone, Kristina folded her hands on the table and looked over at him.

"So, you've been working as a midwife for about four years now, right?" Aidan asked.

"Three, actually." She held up three fingers. "The first *boppli* I delivered was my niece."

"Was that planned?"

"No." She gave a little laugh and shook her head, causing the ties to her *kapp* to bounce off her slight shoulders. "Katy decided to come in the middle of a snowstorm, and we had no choice but to deliver her before the ambulance arrived."

"That had to be scary."

"Yes and no." She tilted her head. "I was *naerfich*, but I just sort of knew what to do. You might not believe it, but I felt as if God were guiding me. I stayed calm, and somehow kept Marlena and Richard calm too. When the EMTs arrived, they told me I'd done a great job. Then I had an epiphany that I should keep working as a midwife since many Amish women prefer to give birth at home when they can. I started studying all of the books I could find along with working with another midwife who doesn't live too far from here. Since I'm not a professional, I just help women when it's possible. If I know the expectant mother is high-risk, or if something goes wrong, I try to help the family prepare for the hospital or a birthing center."

He grinned. "I never imagined you would become a midwife. What do you like about it?"

She looked down at the wooden tabletop and absently drew circles with her finger. "I love helping mothers and babies. I feel as if it's my gift, and it's also my way to contribute to the household. My clients barter with fruits and vegetables they've canned or by doing my sewing.

They can't pay me with money since I'm not a professional midwife, but I share my earnings with Marlena and her family."

He nodded, fascinated with this new side of her. "That's great."

She looked up again. "Lester owned his own roofing company before he died, and I didn't have the first clue about running it. After the accident, I sold our little *haus* and the company and then moved in with Marlena. By then, both of my parents were gone, and Marlena insisted I not live on my own." She winced, and her cheeks flushed pink. "There I go, talking about myself too much."

"You're not." *I'm enjoying it, actually.* He felt his smile fade. "I'm sorry about your parents and Lester."

She shrugged, then lifted her glass of water and took a long drink. Soon the waitress appeared and set their sandwiches in front of them.

After bowing their heads in silent prayer, they began to eat, and an awkward silence fell over the table. Aidan racked his mind for something to say, but he drew a blank. It seemed like only yesterday conversation flowed freely between them, but that was before their breakup.

"How does it feel to be back?"

Aidan looked over at her as she studied him.

"It feels . . ." He struggled to find the right word. "Odd."

"Why?"

He set his sandwich on the plate and sighed. "It feels

strange to be one of the oldest bachelors in the unmarried men's section at church."

She nodded as understanding flashed in her eyes. "I know what you mean. It feels strange to be the youngest widow in the married women's section." Then she looked pained. "I'm sorry. I'm taking over the conversation again."

"No, no." He shook his head. "Go ahead."

"No, you talk now." She took another bite of her tuna melt.

"I'm sorry I missed Lester's funeral. If I had known sooner, I would have tried to come back in time, but *mei dat* told me after everything was over."

"I wouldn't have expected you to come back." She picked up a potato chip and popped it into her mouth.

"What happened to him? *Mei dat* only spoke briefly of an accident and couldn't bring himself to talk about the specifics."

She frowned. "He was carrying a box of shingles up a ladder to a roof. He lost his balance, fell, and broke his neck on impact."

"I'm so sorry."

"I had wanted him to stay home that day, but I didn't tell him. I just had this feeling that I can't explain." She sniffed and her eyes filled with tears. "You'd think I'd be over it by now, but grief is an unpredictable thing." She wiped at the tears hanging from her long lashes and then ate another chip.

Aidan swallowed a bite of his sandwich as silence once again fell over them.

"Do you miss Ohio?"

He shrugged. "I miss some of *mei freinden*."

She picked up a chip and paused to study him. She hesitated only briefly before leaning forward. "Whatever happened with Louise?"

He was almost certain he detected resentment in her voice. "It just didn't work out between us."

Her forehead furrowed and then relaxed. He longed to ask her what she was thinking, what the look on her face was concealing.

"I didn't feel a strong connection to my community in Ohio, so it made sense to come back when *mei dat* offered me the farm," he continued. "My parents are talking about moving into the *daadihaus* and giving me the *haus*, but I told them it's not necessary. I didn't bring much with me, and I'm fine living in my old room."

"Did you get rid of all of those mystery novels you used to collect?"

He paused, surprised by the question. "*Ya*, I left them when I moved to Ohio, and *mei mamm* donated them to the library. I didn't buy too many books in Ohio, and I donated the ones I had before I moved."

"I'm surprised you parted with them. I remember what a voracious reader you were."

He shrugged. "*Ya*, that's true. I plan to visit the library soon, but I'm sure I won't need a whole *haus* for my things."

"I understand. I've actually thought about asking Richard to build me a *daadihaus*," she said. "I feel like I'm in the way sometimes. And with their third *boppli* coming in June, they'll have even less room. Marlena insists that I'm a big help, but I still worry."

She looked down at her half-eaten sandwich. "On my way to the grocery store, I stopped by the little *haus* Lester and I bought. The memories were overwhelming." She paused and picked at her paper napkin. "I never thought I'd be thirty and a widow, but I'm *froh* to have my sister's family."

"I thought I'd be married and have a family by now too."

She looked up at him, and their eyes locked for a heartbeat. Questions swirled through his mind. If they had stayed together, how different would their lives have been? Would they have been happy?

Was there any chance they could work through their differences and start over?

He dismissed the last thought, shaking his head as if to dislodge the wild notion.

They spent the remainder of their lunch talking about old friends. Once their plates were clean, he paid the bill, and then they walked outside together, crossing the parking lot to their waiting horses and buggies.

"*Danki* for lunch," she said as they stood by her buggy. "I'll see you at church."

"Be safe going home."

"You too." She waved goodbye and then climbed in.

As he walked away, he once again wondered what could have been.

But he put the thought out of his mind as he climbed into his buggy and started down the road. Kristina would only ever be his friend. If he could only convince his heart to believe that.

FIVE

Marlena hurried down the porch steps and met Kristina at her buggy. "You're finally home. I asked Richard to check the messages to see if you'd left word. I thought maybe you'd been called out to deliver another *boppli*."

Kristina opened the back of the buggy and yanked on the cooler. "No, I got delayed at the grocery store."

"Delayed?" Marlena asked as they lifted the cooler together.

"I ran into Aidan."

"Really?" Marlena's grin was wide as they set the cooler down on the ground.

Kristina ignored her sister's excitement and closed the back of the buggy.

"Well, what happened?" Marlena asked, joining Kristina and picking up her end of the cooler to bring it into the house.

"We talked, and then he asked me to have lunch with him."

"And you went to lunch?" Marlena's eyes sparkled in the afternoon sun.

"I did."

They reached the porch, and Kristina freed one hand to yank open the door. They entered the house one at a time and then set the cooler down on the kitchen table with a *thunk*.

"Kristina, you need to tell me exactly what happened."

"It's not a big deal!" Kristina opened the cooler and began pulling out produce. "We had lunch and then went our separate ways." She crossed to the propane-powered refrigerator and stowed the produce.

"You're infuriating."

Kristina faced her sister, who frowned at her, her forehead wrinkled. "Now why do you say that?"

Marlena wagged a finger at her. "You just had lunch with your ex-boyfriend, and you're acting like it was just an ordinary day."

Kristina paused what she was doing and moved her hands to her hips. "I'm telling you that *nothing* happened. I talked about Lester, and he talked about how strange it felt to be back in the community. Then he paid for my lunch, and we left." She shrugged. "See? *No big deal*."

But that wasn't exactly the truth. Kristina couldn't believe how she'd poured her deepest emotions out to Aidan. What was it about him that made her feel so comfortable? Perhaps he was manipulating her into trusting him only to hurt her again. Or maybe she was just lonely and desperate for a man's attention. She swallowed a groan.

"That *is* a big deal!" Marlena took Kristina's hand. "He's reaching out to you. Maybe he wants to try again?"

Kristina pulled away from her and began unloading packets of lunch meat into the refrigerator. "I seriously doubt that."

"Why?"

Kristina pivoted toward her again. "Because I wasn't *gut* enough for him ten years ago. Why would that have changed by now?"

Marlena blinked at her. "Why do you think you weren't *gut* enough for him?"

"Don't you remember what happened? Aidan and I were together for two years, and we planned to get married. Then he wrote Louise and told her he was going to break up with me and move to Ohio for her. He betrayed me." With her hands trembling, Kristina returned to the cooler and pulled out the rolls and bags of pasta she'd purchased.

Marlena worked in silence beside her, putting the cans of soup away.

"Kris," Marlena finally began, "have you ever considered that maybe God led Aidan back here to give you both another chance at love?"

Looking over at her sister, Kristina guffawed. "You honestly believe that?"

"Why not?" Marlena looked confused.

Kristina rested her hand on her hip. "I already had a wonderful love with Lester. I don't need to get married again." When her sister opened her mouth to respond, Kristina held up her hand. "Don't tell me I'm too young to be alone. I'm fine."

Marlena gently took hold of her arm. "But you *are* too young, Kris. Just think about Marian Ebersole. She was twenty-seven when her husband died. She remarried, and now she has three *kinner*. Don't you want your own *kinner*?"

After taking in a deep breath, Kristina forced her lips into a smile. "Let's put away these groceries before the chicken and beef defrost." She pivoted back toward the cooler and pulled out the frozen meat.

As she rearranged the freezer to make room for her purchases, her thoughts churned with memories of her conversation with Aidan. What had he meant when he said it hadn't worked out with Louise? Perhaps he cheated on her too.

Her frustration simmered, and she tried to push all thoughts of him out of her mind. But his handsome face and radiant smile lingered there, taunting her. She had to find a way to kick him out of her mind permanently.

But it seemed an impossible task.

The chattering of the sewing machine sounded above Aidan as he stored the groceries he had picked up for *Mamm*. After placing the loaf of bread in the bread box, he made his way up the stairs to the sewing room, located beside his bedroom. He found *Mamm* hunched over the machine, working on a new dress.

"I put all of the groceries away," he said, and she gasped with a start.

Placing her hand on her chest, *Mamm* took a deep breath as she faced him, her light-blue eyes round behind her reading glasses. "You and your *dat* love to sneak up on me. It's a wonder I haven't had a heart attack yet."

Aidan felt his lips twitch as he held his hands up in surrender. "I'm sorry. I thought you heard me on the stairs. You always say I'm heavy-footed."

"What do I owe you for the groceries?"

"Nothing. I told you I want to contribute too."

"*Danki*. Would you like me to make you some lunch?"

"No thanks. I ate." He shook his head and then recalled his lunch visit with Kristina.

Their conversation had been strained but also personal. And he felt like a *dummkopp* for sharing his deepest secrets with her. At the same time, he had a feeling that she had shared some very personal things with him too.

He bit his lip and looked down at the floor. Why was his heart so stuck on Kristina?

"Is something on your mind, Aidan?"

He glanced up and found *Mamm* staring at him. He leaned on the door frame. "I had lunch with Kristina."

"Really?" *Mamm's* grin was wide, making him regret he shared the news.

"Yes, I saw her at the grocery store and asked her to have lunch with me."

"That is *wunderbaar.*" She rubbed her hands together. "I don't think she's dating anyone."

He held his hand up. "Both Kristina and Louise broke my heart, and I'm not ready to face that again." He gestured around the room. "I have this farm to run, which is a lot of responsibility. I don't need to add more stress to the mix."

"Having a family would help with the stress. If you had a *fraa*, she would be by your side, helping you with your responsibilities. And *kinner* are the greatest blessing of all, Aidan. Your *dat* and I prayed for more *kinner*, but we were grateful God blessed us with you and your *schweschder.*"

Aidan stood up straight. "I need to get back out to the barn." He stepped into the hall and then stopped when she called his name. He stuck his head in the doorway "*Ya?*"

"God has the perfect plan for you."

He tapped the door frame and then headed back downstairs, through the kitchen and mudroom, and out the back door into the cool afternoon.

His boots crunched down the rock path toward the barn, and he looked at the cloudless sky. As he stepped into the barn, he tried to push away all thoughts of Kristina. But she lingered there at the edge of his mind.

"What are you trying to tell me, Lord?" Aidan whispered. "Am I imagining this strong connection to Kristina? Are you trying to show me something? Please lead me down the right path."

On Sunday, a little over a week later, Kristina walked with Marlena toward the kitchen at the Bontragers' house to meet with the women before the church service began. She carried Betsie Lin in her arms while Katy walked beside her, holding her mother's hand.

Kristina glanced over toward the barn, where men were gathering, and her eyes immediately found Aidan. He looked handsome dressed in his Sunday black-and-white suit as he stood beside Tommy and nodded at something he said.

She studied his face and recalled the Sunday afternoons they used to spend with their friends—laughing as they played volleyball or picnicking by a lake. They had so many good memories, and then it was all ruined.

Aidan met her gaze, and when he smiled and nodded, her cheeks flamed. She turned toward the house.

"Let's go see if Lydia Ruth made it here today." Kristina picked up her pace. "You can meet her *boppli*, Katy."

"I love *bopplin*!" Katy announced as Betsie Lin squealed in agreement.

Kristina walked into the kitchen, where she nodded

greetings to the other women in the congregation. She spotted Lydia Ruth standing on the other side of the room holding her newborn against her chest. She excused herself as she made her way through the knot of women to Lydia Ruth.

"*Gude mariye,*" Kristina said. "How are you and Thomas?"

"We're doing just fine." Lydia Ruth beamed as she tilted the baby so that Kristina could see his face. "We're tired, but we're eating well."

"Oh, let me see." Marlena came up beside Lydia Ruth. "You look fantastic."

Lydia Ruth chuckled. "You can't see the dark circles under my eyes?"

Marlena laughed, too, and then looked down at Katy. "Do you see the *boppli*?"

"*Boppli!*" Betsie Lin reached for the baby.

Kristina swiveled to move Betsie Lin out of reach. "Don't touch."

Katy's eyes widened as she looked up at the newborn.

"How are you feeling?" Lydia Ruth nodded toward Marlena's abdomen.

Marlena touched her protruding belly. "Sore. But excited."

"I'm sure you are." Lydia Ruth looked past Marlena. "Hi, *Mamm*."

Freda sidled up to Kristina and smiled at her and Marlena. "Isn't my new grandson handsome?"

"*Ya*, he is," Kristina agreed.

Marlena smiled. "You must be very *froh*."

"Oh, I am." Freda reached for the baby, and Lydia Ruth passed him over. "I just can't get enough of him." She gazed down at Thomas as Marlena and Lydia Ruth moved on to other conversations. Then she looked up at Kristina. "Are you dating anyone?"

Kristina blinked, surprised by the blunt question. "No. Why?"

"I was just wondering." Freda shrugged. "It's *gut* to know you're single." Then she looked back down at the baby.

Puzzled, Kristina turned toward Marlena, but found her talking to another member of the congregation.

Kristina's curiosity about Freda's question followed her as she walked into the barn and sat with her sister. When the service began, she pulled out a small container of Cheerios and gave a handful to Katy before feeding a few to Betsie Lin.

When the opening hymn began, Kristina balanced the hymnal in her hand while holding Betsie Lin on her lap. Betsie Lin wiggled down to the ground and moaned as she pointed to a spot on the bench between Kristina and Katy. After getting Betsie Lin situated and eating Cheerios with her sister, Kristina turned her attention back to the hymnal.

She felt the sensation of someone's eyes on her, and she glanced across the barn. There sat Aidan, smiling at her. Dizziness overcame her when her eyes met his, and she nodded in acknowledgment. Then she forced her eyes downward to focus on the hymnal.

Her mind raced with new questions. She could remember what it felt like to love Aidan, but she had been so happily married to Lester, it was hard to imagine being as happy with anyone else. How could she even consider living a new life with Aidan? Why was she even wasting her thoughts on him?

She closed her eyes and took a deep breath as she opened up her confused heart to God:

Lord, when I see Aidan, I feel myself falling for him—and I'm afraid he'll hurt me again. Even more, I'm scared I'm not strong enough to stop myself from allowing him back into my life. Please lead me, dear Lord. Show me where you want me to go.

Then she opened her eyes and began to sing again.

SIX

Aidan lingered outside of the Bontrager family's barn after church and waited for Kristina to finish eating lunch. His gaze seemed to gravitate to her throughout the service, and he'd caught her watching him a couple of times too.

While he had tried to concentrate on the minister's holy words, he couldn't control his wandering thoughts. He felt as if an invisible thread were drawing him to Kristina, and he had to know if she felt it too.

He scrubbed his hand down his face. Surely he was losing his mind!

"Aidan!" He looked up to see Rosetta walking toward him carrying a tray stacked with empty serving platters.

"Hi, Rosetta." He took in her pretty smile and eager expression.

She adjusted the tray in her hands. "Did you have a *gut* week?"

"I did." He leaned back on the barn wall. "It's starting to feel like home again. How was your week?"

"Our bulk foods store stays busy during the day. At

night I'm working on some quilts to sell at an upcoming auction."

Aidan smiled as she talked on about the quilts—their colors, patterns, and sizes.

"Do you think I can bring you and your parents a meal this week?" she suddenly asked.

Aidan stood up straighter, surprised by the subject change. "Sure," he said. "I don't see why not."

Her smile seemed as bright as the afternoon sun. "Great! Then how about Thursday?" They agreed on a time and then she nodded toward the house. "Well, I'd better bring these platters to the kitchen."

As Aidan watched Rosetta walk away, worry settled over him. He hoped he hadn't given her the wrong idea by agreeing to supper. The last thing he needed was her expecting him to ask her to be his girlfriend. Although Rosetta was a sweet and kind *maedel*, he wasn't certain he was ready for another commitment. Not to mention his confusing thoughts about Kristina.

But maybe his father was right that he and Rosetta could forge a lasting relationship. He just had to get to know her and see where God led them.

He let that thought settle as he turned back toward the barn. Just then, Kristina walked out carrying two coffee carafes.

"Kristina," Aidan said, taking a step toward her. But when he took in the dark circles under her eyes, alarm gripped him. "Is everything all right?"

She tilted her head. "*Ya.* Why?"

"You look exhausted."

"I had a late night. I delivered a *boppli* over in White Horse, and I got home after one."

"Did everything go okay with the birth?"

"*Ya.*" She nodded. "It was her first, and first *bopplin* usually take longer. But the *boppli* girl and *mamm* are fine."

"*Gut.*" He nodded and they both stared at each other for a moment. His mind again whirled with what-ifs. If they had married, would God have blessed them with children of their own by now?

She held up the coffee carafes. "Well, I should get back to it. The kitchen isn't going to clean itself."

"Maybe we can have lunch again sometime."

"*Ya.* Maybe." When she smiled at him, his insides warmed.

As she walked away, he felt his heart ache for her friendship and possibly even more. But deep down, fear cornered him. If he tried to get close to her, she could tear his soul apart yet again.

"*Gude mariye!*" Aidan announced Thursday morning when he stepped into the kitchen, the delicious aromas of coffee, eggs, bacon, and freshly baked biscuits causing his stomach to growl. How he enjoyed his mother's breakfasts more than his usual bland morning meal of oatmeal and a banana.

His parents echoed the greeting as he sat down between them. They bowed their heads in silent prayer before filling their plates with the scrumptious food.

"Let's make a supply run today," *Dat* said, buttering a biscuit. "I have a list over there." He pointed his knife toward the counter.

"Sounds *gut*. I can call our driver after breakfast. I'd like to stop at the library, too, if we have time. I want to pick up a few books." Aidan scooped some egg into his mouth.

"I was thinking of making a pot roast tonight," *Mamm* said.

"Oh. I forgot to tell you that Rosetta is bringing us a meal tonight." Aidan snapped his fingers. "She left a message yesterday confirming she'll be here around five thirty."

"Really?" *Mamm* held her mug suspended in the air. She shared a shocked expression with *Dat*.

"Isn't that nice," *Dat* said.

"She offered at my first service since being back, and I told her I was just settling in. When she asked this past Sunday, I couldn't bring myself to say no. I thought it would be nice to have a *freind*."

Mamm reached over and touched Aidan's hand. "See, I told you it would be *gut* to come home. And now you're back less than a month, and you're already dating."

"Oh no, that's not what this is about!" Aidan shook his head.

"You never know," *Dat* said. "Your *mamm* and I were *freinden* first."

Mamm nodded. "She's a sweet *maedel*, and she'd be *gut* for you."

Aidan lifted his mug. It was useless to try to argue with his parents. He buttered a biscuit and took a bite. Oh, his mother made the best biscuits!

"You should definitely give Rosetta a chance," *Mamm* continued between bites of bacon. "I don't think she's dated much, but she's a lovely *maedel*."

Dat picked up his mug as he turned toward Aidan. "It's unhealthy to be alone. Plus, you're not getting any younger. You need to find a *fraa* and settle down. I told you we'll move into the *daadihaus*, and you and your new bride can fill the *haus* with *kinner*."

"That would be *wunderbaar*." *Mamm* touched her chest.

"Hold on now." Aidan held up his hand. "This is just a friendly supper. Please don't start planning my wedding or making *bopplin* clothes."

"You never know." *Mamm* sang the words.

Aidan bit back a groan as he chewed a piece of bacon.

They ate in silence for several moments before *Mamm's* expression suddenly brightened. "Oh, I forgot to tell you that I talked to Kristina on Sunday before the service. I found out she's not dating anyone."

Mortified, Aidan gasped as he leaned forward on the table. "You asked her?"

"You weren't going to, so I asked for you." She pointed at him.

"*Mamm*," he began slowly, "tell me you didn't mention me when you asked her."

"Why would I mention you?"

Dat studied Aidan over his coffee mug. "Are you interested in dating Kristina again?"

Aidan shook his head. "If it didn't work out the first time, what would make the second time around any different?"

Dat nodded and then took a sip of coffee.

As Aidan turned his attention back to his breakfast, he recalled how happy he and Kristina had once been. Could they ever find that happiness again?

If not, could he possibly find that happiness with Rosetta?

Aidan met Rosetta at the back door at five thirty. He had showered, freshened up, and changed into clean trousers and a crisp, blue shirt before she arrived.

Now he stood on the back porch and smiled at her as she balanced a casserole dish and a portable pie plate in her hands while her driver backed his van down the rock driveway.

"May I help you with something?" The delicious smell of lasagna wafted over him as he took the casserole dish from her.

She looked pretty in a red dress that complemented her dark eyes and hair. "*Danki*. I hope you like lasagna."

"It's my favorite."

"Oh, *gut*." Her smile brightened. "And I made peanut butter pie for dessert."

He gave her a mock look of suspicion. "Have you been spying on me?"

Her smiled faded, and her face clouded with concern. "No."

"I'm teasing you. Peanut butter pie is my favorite too."

"Oh!" She gave a little laugh that sounded nervous. "I remembered how much you liked peanut butter when we were in youth group. Kristina used to always pack you peanut butter sandwiches when we went to the lake."

Aidan was struck by that. Rosetta had been paying attention to his preferences—and as far back as their youth group days? What did *that* mean? He shook off the thought and opened the door wide. "Please come in."

"*Danki*." She stepped into the mudroom, and he took the pie plate from her as she pulled off her sweater and hung it on the hook.

Then Aidan followed her into the kitchen, where *Mamm* set four drinking glasses on the table beside the plates.

"Hi, Rosetta," *Mamm* said.

"It's nice to see you, Freda. Do you need any help?"

"Oh, no," *Mamm* said. "You've already done the hard work of bringing us a meal. Go ahead and make yourself at home."

Dat crossed to the sink to wash his hands. "Hello, Rosetta."

Rosetta gave him a wave and then lingered by the table as if unsure of where to sit.

"Rosetta brought us a lasagna casserole and a peanut butter pie," Aidan said as he set them on the table.

"Oh, you brought Aidan's favorites. How thoughtful." *Mamm* glanced over at Aidan and winked.

"Sounds *appeditlich*." *Dat* sat in his usual spot.

Aidan gestured toward a chair. "Rosetta, would you like to sit across from me?"

"*Danki,*" she said, settling into her seat.

Aidan and *Mamm* also sat, and after a silent prayer, *Dat* cut into the casserole and then passed the dish around the table.

"This is fantastic," Aidan said.

Rosetta's cheeks flushed bright pink as she looked down at her plate. "I hope you like it."

"How are your folks?" *Mamm* asked.

"They're well. We're all busy at the bulk foods store."

"Rosetta is working on quilts to sell at auction," Aidan announced.

Aidan enjoyed his meal while his mother asked Rosetta

questions about the quilts. With a nervous smile on her face, Rosetta responded between bites of casserole.

Once their plates were clean, *Mamm* cut the peanut butter pie and served the slices, along with mugs of coffee.

"My, my, my, this pie is *wunderbaar*," *Dat* announced.

"It's just sweet enough," Aidan agreed.

Rosetta gave Aidan a warm smile that seemed to hold a promise. "I'm so glad you like it."

A wave of panic overtook Aidan as he studied Rosetta's pretty face. At that moment, he could feel how much she cared for him, but he wasn't certain he could ever like her in the same way.

But his parents' words from earlier suddenly filled his mind. Perhaps he should give Rosetta a chance, as *Mamm* had suggested. And *Dat* was right when he said Aidan wasn't getting any younger. The idea of spending the rest of his life alone terrified him. Maybe Rosetta was the woman God had intended for him to marry.

"Did you know how much Aidan loves peanut butter?" *Mamm* asked.

"I remember how often he ate it at youth gatherings," Rosetta said.

"Is that so?" *Mamm* gave Aidan a pointed look.

Aidan shrugged. "It's true. I love peanut butter."

"I never forgot that." Rosetta's expression became intense. "I remember a lot from those days."

Aidan nodded, but questions filled him. If she had paid so much attention to him and his preferences, was it because she had nursed feelings for him all of these years? Or were her memories of the other young men from their youth group just as strong?

After they finished the pie, Rosetta helped wash the dishes before following Aidan out to the porch. He shivered in the cool, early April evening air as they sat down beside each other on the swing.

"It's colder out here than I thought." He pushed the swing into motion. "Do you want to go back inside?"

She shook her head. "I love the smell of the evening air."

"I do too." Aidan breathed in the fresh scent of moist earth and the animals nearby just as a dog barked somewhere in the distance. "Do you like working at your parents' store?"

She pushed the ties from her prayer covering over her shoulder. "I enjoy helping the customers. I meet nice people every day, and we have interesting conversations."

"That sounds fun. The cows don't say much." He grinned.

She laughed a little too loud and too long, and then she turned toward him. "I hope this doesn't sound forward, but I'm so glad you're back. I was *bedauerlich* you left."

He blinked at her, shocked by this new information. "*Danki*."

Rosetta looked down at her lap. "You never noticed me when you were with Kristina, but I always noticed you."

Aidan bit his lower lip as guilt swamped him. "I'm so sorry."

"It's okay. I'm here now, and I would love to be *freinden* with you."

"I would like that too." And it was the truth. A friend was just what he needed right now. "I'm not ready to date yet, but I'd like to get to know you."

Her smile was warm and inviting. "That sounds perfect."

He settled back on the swing as a vision of Kristina filled his mind. He wondered what she was doing tonight, but then guilt nipped at him. If Rosetta knew where his thoughts were, it would break her heart. And he didn't want to hurt Rosetta the way Kristina had hurt him.

Later that evening, Aidan and Rosetta sat together in his buggy as he took her home. Aidan smiled over at her, and a strange feeling took hold of him. It had been a long time since he'd sat beside a woman in his buggy.

When they arrived at her parents' two-story redbrick house, he halted the horse and then turned toward her. "*Danki* for the *appeditlich* meal. I had a lovely time."

"*Gern gschehne*. I did too." She picked up the serving dishes from the floor of the buggy. "I've always dreamt of having supper with you, and I'm grateful that it finally happened. Maybe we can do it again sometime?"

"That would be nice."

"*Wunderbaar*." She hesitated for a moment as if expecting something and then she wrenched the buggy door open. "*Gut nacht*."

"*Gut nacht*," he echoed before she pushed the buggy door closed and walked up the back porch steps.

As Aidan guided his horse home, he smiled. It felt great to have a friend.

But when the horse turned onto the road that led to his farm, his thoughts wandered back to Kristina. Why was a woman like her single? Why wouldn't she want to find a husband to care for her?

Then guilt plagued him once more. Why did his heart still worry about Kristina, the woman who had crushed his heart, when sweet Rosetta obviously cared for him? It wasn't fair of him to encourage Rosetta when he knew to the depth of his soul that his heart was still stuck on someone else.

But at the same time, he longed to see if his relationship with Rosetta could be something real that wouldn't end in heartache.

He blew out a deep gush of air and glanced up at the sky as the sun began to set, sending an explosion of orange, red, and yellow above him.

"Lead me on the right path, Lord," he whispered. "And guide my heart. I don't want to hurt or use Rosetta when I know I still care for Kristina. Help my heart find its true course—the direction you will it to go."

SEVEN

Kristina sat in Anna Marie's kitchen the following Tuesday while Anna Marie's three sons played with toy cars, rolling them around on the worn, off-white linoleum floor.

After pulling her supplies from her tote bag, Kristina turned to a new page in her journal. "How are you feeling?"

"The same." Anna Marie sighed and then rested her hands on her protruding belly. "I'm not sleeping well because I can't get comfortable, but that's how it is at this stage." She turned to the boys. "Do you think I'll deliver earlier than my due date since they were all early too?"

Kristina nodded as she made notes. "It's possible!"

"I heard something that might interest you," Anna Marie said.

"Oh?" Kristina continued to write in her journal.

"Rosetta King brought Aidan supper last week."

Kristina froze and then swallowed as she looked up at Anna Marie's wide smile. "Who told you that?"

"Lydia Ruth told me when I saw her at the grocery store yesterday. She said Freda told her that Rosetta brought over a lasagna casserole and a peanut butter pie for supper last Thursday."

"Peanut butter is his favorite," Kristina whispered as memories welled up and dragged her down like an undertow. She recalled the hundreds of times she'd made him peanut butter sandwiches and pies when they went on picnics. The pen in her hand shook.

"What else did Lydia Ruth say?" She regretted the question as soon as it leapt from her lips. She didn't want details, but at the same time, she couldn't help herself. What was wrong with her?

"They ate supper and had pie and coffee with his parents before they went out to sit on the porch swing together. Then he took her home." Anna Marie's face glowed as if she loved every morsel of the gossip she shared. "Lydia Ruth said Freda thinks they got along well. Aidan's parents are encouraging him to get to know her. After all, he's thirty-two and still not married. Can you believe that? As handsome as he is, he should have found a *fraa* by now."

Jealousy coiled like a snake in Kristina's belly. But she had no right to be jealous of Rosetta. After all, Rosetta and Aidan made sense together. They would make a great couple.

Kristina pressed her lips together as she tried to suffocate the feelings warring inside her. But the regret lingered there, a sick feeling sweeping through her.

"Isn't church at your *haus* on Sunday?" Anna Marie asked. The sudden subject change nearly gave Kristina whiplash.

"*Ya*, it is. I have to work in the garden, and then Marlena and I need to get some cleaning done." Kristina closed her journal and set her pen on top of it.

"It is a lot of work to host church."

"That's true." Kristina glanced over at the three boys as they continued to push their cars around the floor. She couldn't erase the image of Aidan and Rosetta on the porch swing together.

Did they hold hands? Did he kiss her? Did he ask her to be his girlfriend?

Stop it!

"Should we set another appointment?" Anna Marie asked.

"*Ya*, that sounds *gut*." Kristina and Anna Marie agreed on a date, and then Kristina said goodbye to the boys before walking to the door. "I'll see you on Sunday."

As Kristina walked toward her buggy, she took a deep breath. She had to remove all thoughts of Aidan from her mind. He was her past and nothing more. Never again would they be more than friends.

And for some reason, that reality hurt even more than the news that he liked Rosetta.

Aidan felt someone watching him during the church service on Sunday morning in Richard and Marlena's barn. When his eyes moved toward the unmarried women's section, he found Rosetta smiling over at him. He nodded, and Rosetta blushed before looking down at her apron and yellow dress.

When Aidan peeked over at Kristina, she quickly looked away. Was she avoiding his gaze? He hadn't had a chance to speak with her this morning, and he was almost certain she had deliberately moved away from him when he walked toward her. Her sudden frosty demeanor confused him.

After the service, Aidan helped the other men convert the benches into tables for the noon meal. As he worked, Richard made his way over to him.

"*Wie geht's*?" Richard rubbed his hands together. "Lunch doesn't seem to last long enough on Sundays. I was telling Marlena that we should have you over for supper so we'd have more time to talk."

"I'd like that." Aidan couldn't stop his smile. Not only did he enjoy Richard's company, but having supper with Richard and his family would give Aidan a chance to see Kristina.

"Great. I'll talk to Marlena about choosing an evening."

Aidan turned just as Kristina walked by with Betsie Lin in her arms. He opened his mouth to say hello, but she offered him a dismissive wave and kept moving. He frowned and again wondered why Kristina was suddenly avoiding him.

"Would you please take this *kaffi* out to the barn?" Kristina handed two carafes to Mary, one of the teenagers in the church district.

"*Ya*, of course." Mary took the carafes and started toward the kitchen door.

"What can I do?" Emma, another teenager, asked.

"Take these." Kristina handed a stack of plates and cups to her. "*Danki*."

Then Kristina turned toward the counter and found the plates of food that needed to be delivered to the men waiting in the barn. She spun toward the group of women standing in the middle of the kitchen talking.

"Hello," she announced with a smile, and the women turned to face her. "Would you all please start taking the food into the barn?"

The women complied, gathering up the plates of lunch meat, bread, pretzels, and peanut butter spread. Once the food was gone, Kristina leaned against the counter and released a long breath.

"It's all going to be fine." Marlena smiled as she handed Betsie Lin a piece of cheese while the toddler sat in her high chair. "Soon the meal will be over, and we can eat and relax."

"After the kitchen is clean. I'll be back. I need to check on everyone." Kristina walked outside and then into the barn to survey the long tables of men sitting and eating lunch.

When she spotted Aidan next to Tommy and across

from Richard and Phares, her breath caught in her chest. He looked so handsome today, possibly more handsome than usual. But her lips pressed together when Rosetta came around and filled his cup with coffee, a bright smile on her face. Aidan looked up at her and laughed at something she said.

Once again, she considered how perfect they would be together and scowled at the thought. She just hoped Aidan would treat Rosetta better than he had treated her.

"Kristina," Freda said as she walked over to her. "We need two more bowls of peanut butter spread."

"I'll get them." Grateful for the task, Kristina headed back outside and toward the kitchen.

Later, Kristina filled the sink with hot, soapy water while the rest of the women carried the empty trays and serving platters into the kitchen. Her stomach gurgled as she glanced up at the clock on the wall.

It was after one. Soon the older members of the congregation would head home to rest while the teenagers gathered together to spend the day playing games and enjoying the early spring day.

"I'll wash," Rosetta said as she walked over to Kristina.

"*Danki*." Kristina smiled at her and then turned her attention to Marlena, who was lifting Betsie Lin from her high chair. "Do you need any help?"

Marlena balanced Betsie Lin on her hip and then took Katy's hand. "No, *danki*. I'm going to put them down for a nap."

"Okay." Kristina grabbed a washrag and began to wipe down the kitchen table, where some of the women had eaten their lunch.

She craned her neck and looked over her shoulder at Rosetta working at the sink. She longed to ask her about her relationship with Aidan. But what would she even say? She didn't truly want to hear about how happy they were when her heart felt so fragile today.

Besides, Aidan's relationship was none of her business.

A group of women came in and dropped the used disposable plates and cups into a large trash bag before saying goodbye. Kristina waved at them and then moved to the sink, where she dried the serving platters that Rosetta had washed.

"Hi, Kristina," Aidan's mother, Freda, said as she walked over to the sink. When Kristina nodded, she turned toward Rosetta. "Rosetta! I haven't had a chance to talk to you today."

Rosetta beamed at her. "Hi, Freda. Did you like the butterscotch pie I dropped by on Thursday?"

"I did!" Freda gasped. "It was even better than the lemon meringue pie you sent on Monday."

"Did Aidan like it?"

"Of course! You know how *mei sohn* loves his pies." Freda laughed.

Kristina tried to maintain a neutral face as nausea reached her stomach. Perhaps she should escape this conversation—maybe go to the barn and talk to the other women there. She dried a coffee carafe and tried to push away her threatening jealousy.

"How do you make the butterscotch pie, Rosetta?" Freda picked up a carafe and began drying it. "Mine always comes out too sweet."

"I'll share my recipe." Rosetta turned toward Kristina. "And if you like, I'll share it with you too. *Mei mammi* gave me one of her cookbooks, and I've found the best pie recipes in there. The pecan pie might be my favorite."

Freda leaned back against the counter. "Phares and Aidan like pecan pie. Would you pass that recipe along too?"

Rosetta beamed. "I can bring the book over sometime!"

"I would like that." Freda's eyes shone with eagerness, and Kristina imagined her planning Aidan's wedding with his new girlfriend.

In an instant, the room felt as if it was closing in on Kristina.

"Excuse me," she mumbled, dropping the utensils into the drawer and making a beeline for the back door. She needed fresh air, to get outside before her feelings swallowed her whole.

Kristina welcomed the chilly air as it filled her lungs. She leaned forward on the porch railing and watched families climb into their buggies to head home. A line of buggies snaked down the driveway and headed toward the main road, resembling a troop of ants marching away.

When she saw Anna Marie walking with her husband

and sons, Kristina headed down the porch steps and sidled up to her. "How are you feeling?"

"Crampy." Anna Marie frowned as she touched her
belly. "I think it will be soon."

"I'll be ready when it's time." Kristina touched Anna
Marie's arm.

"We'll call you when we know." Danny, Anna Marie's
husband, spoke to Kristina but looked down at Anna
Marie with a warm and encouraging gaze.

Kristina then started toward the house. She glanced up
at the trees, taking in their bright-green leaves. It finally
felt like spring—her favorite time of year. She glanced
over at the colorful flowers that seemed to wave back at
her from Marlena's garden.

"Kristina?"

She turned and gulped in a breath at the sight of Aidan
walking toward her. His expression seemed hopeful, but
she felt a hollow ache radiate through her. Maybe he was
going to ask her if she'd seen his girlfriend.

He reached up and touched his hat. "I've been trying
to talk to you, but every time I see you, you hurry away
from me."

Kristina crossed her arms over her apron. "Oh, I've
been busy all day." She motioned around the farm. "You
know how it is to host the service."

His eyes roved around her face, as if to assess her. She
hugged her arms closer to her chest, a shield for her heart.

"Have you had any more late deliveries?"

She squinted, trying to comprehend him. "What do you mean?"

"You delivered a *boppli* late the night before the last service."

"Oh." She nodded. "*Ya.* I've had a few more, and I think Anna Marie will be next. But who knows what time of day the *boppli* will decide to come."

"I see." He cleared his throat as an awkward silence fell between them like a great chasm.

She wanted to ask if he was dating Rosetta—longed to hear him say with his own lips that he wasn't interested in anyone else. But Kristina held her tongue. She had no right to ask such questions. She looked up into Aidan's eyes and squeezed her arms tightly against her, wondering about the thoughts rolling through his mind.

"Aidan!"

Kristina turned and saw Rosetta hurrying down the porch steps and toward them. "There you two are," she said. "Freda and I finished the dishes, Kristina."

"*Danki.*"

"*Gern gschehne.*" Rosetta looked at Aidan with adoration in her eyes. "Would you please give me a ride home?" When she touched Aidan's arm, Kristina's skin prickled.

"Sure. I was just walking to my buggy." Aidan's smile seemed forced, and his eyes didn't mirror the joy shining in Rosetta's.

"Great." Rosetta looked like she might burst with excitement.

Aidan looked over at Kristina. "Have a *gut* week."

"You too."

Aidan nodded, but he seemed reluctant to walk away. He stood a beat too long before finally turning back toward Rosetta.

EIGHT

A strange sound tore through the dark bedroom early Wednesday morning. Kristina awoke with a gasp, rolled over, and smacked at her alarm clock as the large, green numbers boasted 5:09. But the digital song continued, and Kristina woke up fully.

Her cell phone was ringing, not the alarm clock.

Sitting up, she snatched the phone off her nightstand and read Anna Marie's name on her screen.

"Hello?" Her voice was hoarse.

"Kristina!" Danny sounded frantic. "Anna Marie is in labor!"

Kristina jumped out of bed and pulled out a dress and apron from her closet. "Keep her comfortable and tell her I'll be there soon."

"*Danki*," Danny said before disconnecting.

Kristina zipped around the room, dressing and winding her hair up before pulling on her *kapp*. She grabbed her bag of supplies and then hurried down the stairs.

After leaving a note for Marlena, she grabbed a flashlight and made her way out to the barn. She hitched up her horse and buggy and was on the road.

"Please, God, help me be a blessing to Anna Marie. Please help this *boppli* come into the world safely," she whispered as she guided the horse toward Anna Marie's house.

Later that afternoon, after many long hours of labor, Kristina placed a squealing baby girl in her mother's arms. "Isn't she *schee*? Just like her *mamm*."

"Oh my goodness!" Danny's brown eyes misted over as he touched the baby's hand. "A *dochder*."

Anna Marie kissed the baby's head.

"What are we going to name her?" Danny asked.

Anna Marie smiled. "How about Kristina?"

Danny nodded, barely holding back his tears. "*Ya*, Kristina it is."

Kristina shook her head as her cheeks heated. "No, no, no. Don't name her after me." She tried to hide her face and the tears that were welling up in her eyes as she began packing up her supplies.

"What about Faith Kristina?" Anna Marie studied her baby girl.

Danny's smile was wide. "I love it." He touched his baby's cheek. "You are Faith Kristina."

Kristina's throat thickened as her tears flowed freely now. "What an honor. *Danki.*"

"No," Anna Marie said. "Thank *you.*"

"Call me if you need me," she said.

"I put the box of canned goods in your buggy earlier when I took care of your horse," Danny said.

"*Danki.*" Kristina finished packing up her supplies and then headed downstairs to where Anna Marie's parents sat on the sofa and the three little boys played. She greeted them before hurrying out to her waiting horse and buggy.

She climbed into the buggy and then blew out a deep breath as her heart warmed. She had successfully delivered another baby. Oh, how blessed she was.

As she guided the horse toward the road, she looked up at the sky and whispered, "*Danki*, God, for giving me this gift to share. All the glory to you."

She led the horse down the street and then halted it at a light. While waiting for the light to turn green, her phone began to ring again. She pulled it out of her apron pocket, and excitement filled her when she found Maranda Blank's name on the screen.

"Hello?" she said.

"Kristina!" Maranda's husband, Joey, yelled into the phone. "It's time! Can you come now?"

Kristina smiled to herself. Two births in one day? "Of course, Joey. I'm on the way. I'll be there in twenty minutes."

Aidan climbed Richard's porch steps later that evening. He looked down at the butterscotch pie his mother had baked and smiled.

He was surprised when Richard called him earlier in the day and invited him to come for supper. Kristina had been on his mind all day while he worked in the barn, and the phone call had seemed like a gift from God. The idea of seeing her sent a jolt of excitement zipping through him.

He squared his shoulders and then knocked on the back door. Heavy footsteps sounded from somewhere in the house and then the door opened, revealing Richard.

"Hi, Aidan. We're so glad you could join us tonight."

"*Danki* for inviting me."

Aidan followed Richard into the kitchen, where Marlena set a platter of roast beef on the table beside a bowl of mashed potatoes, a basket of rolls, and a bowl of green beans. Katy sat on a booster seat at the table beside Betsie Lin in her high chair. The little girls waved at him, and he grinned.

"Hi, Aidan." Marlena greeted him from where she stood, rubbing her lower back.

He couldn't help but notice that her abdomen seemed to have gotten larger since he'd seen her at church. Feeling embarrassed for staring, he quickly looked up at her smile.

She pointed at the pie plate. "What have you got there?"

"*Mei mamm* made a butterscotch pie. She wanted to try a new recipe." He handed it to her.

"Oh how nice." She smiled at her husband. "We love butterscotch pie, don't we?"

"We sure do." Richard rubbed his hands together.

"Why don't you wash up and then we'll eat?"

After scrubbing his hands, Aidan sat down across from Katy. It was at that moment that he realized the table was only set for five. After the silent prayer, he looked at Marlena. "Where's Kristina?"

Marlena lifted her fork. "She's had an exciting day. She left at five this morning to deliver Anna Marie Esh's *boppli*. And then, when she left Anna Marie's *haus*, Joey Blank called to tell her that Maranda was in labor."

"Wow. So she's still with Maranda?" Aidan scooped a pile of mashed potatoes onto his plate.

"That's right," Marlena said. "She left us a message shortly after twelve, so I guess the labor is going on five hours now."

"Do they normally take that long?" Aidan asked.

"Longer sometimes." Richard pointed his fork at Katy. "I think she was twenty-four hours."

Aidan grimaced as disappointment weighed down on his shoulders. "So she might not be home until tomorrow."

"Possibly, though I'm hoping sooner," Marlena said.

I am too. Aidan added green beans to his plate and chided himself. Even if Kristina had been there, the two of them still hadn't reconciled officially. What was he getting his hopes up about?

"How's the farm?" Richard asked.

Aidan and Richard settled into an easy conversation about farming for the remainder of dinner. He enjoyed talking with Richard and Marlena, and he laughed at how Katy and Betsie Lin kept each other entertained while they ate their meals.

Once supper was over, Marlena brought the pie to the table and Richard poured three cups of coffee. Betsie Lin and Katy enjoyed small pieces with cups of milk. Aidan tried to imagine a third child joining their family, and a strange longing clenched him.

"How's Rosetta?"

Aidan's gaze darted to Marlena, who smiled at him.

"What do you mean?" Aidan asked.

Richard shot a glare toward Marlena.

"What?" Marlena gave him a palms up. "It's common knowledge that Aidan and Rosetta are dating."

"Actually, Rosetta and I are just *freinden*," Aidan said.

Marlena gave Richard a knowing smile. "That's how the best marriages start."

"I'm serious. We're just *freinden*." Aidan lifted his coffee cup.

"Do you think you'll ever get married?" Marlena asked, and Richard gave her a warning look.

Aidan opened his mouth to respond, but then he closed

it. The truth was that he wasn't sure he'd ever get married. But he was certain he didn't want to marry Rosetta, even though she was pretty and sweet. Over the past two weeks she had visited him and delivered pies to his house, and it was obvious she'd cared for him for a long time. Still, he couldn't see himself as her husband. Why wasn't she the one he wanted when she was so willing?

Maybe he was losing his mind.

After they finished their pieces of pie, Marlena set Betsie Lin in her play yard and Katy sat nearby with a toy. Then Marlena started to clean the kitchen while Richard led Aidan out to the porch.

"It truly feels like spring," Aidan commented as he sank into a rocker. He breathed in the warm April air.

"Is your *dat* serious about retiring?" Richard asked.

Aidan pushed the rocker into motion. "He is."

"Are you ready to take over the farm?"

"I don't think I have much choice."

Richard laughed and Aidan stared out toward the driveway, hoping to see Kristina's horse and buggy heading toward them soon.

Kristina yawned as she guided the horse toward her brother-in-law's farm. It was nearly seven in the evening, and every muscle in her body ached. While she was grateful both of her deliveries had been successful, she felt like she could sleep for a week. But first, she desperately needed a shower.

She guided the horse up the rock driveway and was surprised to see two lanterns glowing on the back porch along with the silhouette of two figures sitting on the rocking chairs.

She led the horse to the barn and then hopped out. Richard walked over to her, the beam of his flashlight bumping along the ground while guiding his way.

"How did it go?" Richard asked and reached for her supply bag.

"As well as I could've hoped." She cupped her hand to her mouth as a yawn overtook her.

"You must be exhausted." Richard nodded toward the house. "Marlena made roast beef. Go get some."

"*Danki*. There are two boxes of canned goods in the back. Would you please grab them?"

"Of course."

"I appreciate it." She took the bag from him and lifted it onto her shoulder before padding toward the porch. She stopped when she realized that the silhouette on the porch was a man. She looked over at Richard, who had begun unhitching the horse. "Do we have company?"

"Aidan came for supper," Richard called out to her.

Kristina's entire body went rigid at the sound of his name. This was the worst night for Aidan to come for supper. Not only was she too tired to be social, but she was also a mess. She needed a shower, a meal, and then a good night's sleep.

No, she wasn't in the mood to talk to anyone—especially not Aidan.

Squaring her shoulders, she marched toward the house. She would be pleasant to him and then excuse herself.

She climbed the back porch steps and found Aidan rocking in a chair. He smiled up at her. "Long day, Kristina?"

She snorted. "I feel like I could fall over."

He pointed to the chair beside him. "Sit and tell me all about it. I'll get you a drink. Have you eaten? I can get you food too."

"*Danki*, but no." She shook her head. "I need a shower and then some sleep."

The storm door opened with a squeak, and Marlena peeked out. "How did it go?"

Kristina cupped her hand to her forehead. "Anna Marie was easy, but Maranda's took much longer. They're all fine, though. Anna Marie had a girl, and Maranda had a *bu*." She smiled as she recalled how Anna Marie and Danny had decided to name their baby after her. Oh, how blessed she was!

"I was trying to get her to sit with me, but she insists she needs to shower and go to bed." Aidan smiled at her again, and when his charming dimple materialized, Kristina felt a chill dance down her neck.

Marlena pointed toward the rocking chair. "Sit, if

only for a little while. I'll bring you a piece of pie and a cup of *kaffi*."

Kristina cringed. "I really need a shower."

"Why don't you take some time to relax first?" Marlena shot her a warning look. "The pie will fill you up, and the *kaffi* will give you some strength." She held out her hand. "Give me your bag."

Kristina sighed, then handed her sister the bag. She swiped her hands down her sweater and apron, hoping she looked presentable, then sat down beside Aidan.

"It's a lovely night," Aidan said.

Kristina nodded.

After briefly stepping indoors, Marlena returned to the porch and handed Kristina a mug of *kaffi* and a piece of pie. Then she winked before disappearing.

Kristina frowned as her irritation flared. Hopefully, Marlena hadn't invited Aidan over as a way to try to get them back together.

She set the mug of coffee down on the small table beside her and then ate a forkful of pie.

Butterscotch.

It was delicious—heavenly even—but the conversation she'd overheard between Rosetta and Freda filled her mind. Had Rosetta made the pie for Aidan? Her irritation transformed into jealousy and disappointment.

Silence stretched between them as she sipped some coffee. A breeze blew through the porch, and Kristina inhaled Aidan's familiar scent—soap, sandalwood, and something that was just uniquely him. Why could she still recall his smell after all of these years?

"So today has been quite busy," Aidan finally said.

"You could say that." Kristina sipped more coffee.

Aidan rested his elbows on the arm of the chair and smiled over at her. "You're a popular midwife."

"I do my best." She forked more pie, trying not to meet his eyes.

Richard loped up the porch steps balancing the two boxes of canned goods in his arms. "The pie is *gut*, isn't it?"

Kristina nodded. "*Danki* for taking care of my horse and buggy and those boxes."

"*Gern gschehne*." Richard set the boxes on the porch railing. He opened his mouth to say something just as the storm door squeaked open again.

"Richard, I need your help in here," Marlena said, her words measured.

A look passed between the married couple, and Kristina pursed her lips. So her sister *was* playing matchmaker, and it infuriated her. Why wouldn't Marlena just let Kristina enjoy being single?

Richard stood up straight. "I'll see you two later."

Kristina finished the pie and set the plate and fork on the table before picking up her mug.

"Did you like the pie?" Aidan asked.

"It was *appeditlich*." Kristina studied him, her heart racing. Before she knew it, the question was falling out of her mouth. "Did Rosetta make it?"

NINE

Aidan's brow puckered. "No, *mei mamm* made it."

"Oh." She looked out toward the barn and silently prayed for God to take away her jealousy before it ate her alive.

"Why are you asking about Rosetta?"

She faced him again. "I heard you're dating her." The words tasted bitter on her tongue. "The other day after service, I heard her talking to your *mamm* about butterscotch pie. Then you gave her a ride home afterward."

To her surprise, Aidan sighed and rested his head back on the chair. "We're just getting to know each other. And to be honest, I'm not looking for a girlfriend."

Feeling confused, she tilted her head and watched his expression. "Why aren't you looking?"

"I'm not ready to get hurt again."

She angled her body toward him, and they stared at each other. Her mouth dried as questions swirled in her mind. "Did Louise hurt you, Aidan?"

"That's part of it." He rubbed his chin. "Louise not

only changed her mind about me, but she also left me for an *Englisher*. It was humiliating, so I've only told a handful of people about it. I'm not prepared to have my heart broken like that again."

Kristina clasped her mug. "You didn't cheat on her?"

"Cheat on her?" Aidan gave a humorless laugh. "No."

An awkward silence filled the porch again. A car horn tooted in the distance and the low murmur of voices sounded from inside the house. Kristina's mind continued to roar with more questions, but she couldn't form the words to ask them.

"Rosetta is sweet, and she even hinted that she has liked me since we were teenagers. I can tell she really cares for me. In fact, I think she might even love me." Aidan's voice was soft, almost reverent.

Kristina sucked in a breath. She looked over at him and found him fiddling with a loose piece of wood on the arm of the rocking chair.

"I'm just not ready for that kind of commitment." He met her gaze and something unreadable flashed over his face. "I don't feel a connection with her. She tells me everything, but I don't feel like I can share things with her. I haven't even told her what really happened with Louise."

Kristina felt a muscle flex in her jaw as she let his words sink in. Why was he confiding in her when he hadn't yet confided in Rosetta?

Aidan cleared his throat. "But enough about me. Why aren't you dating?"

Kristina looked down at her mug. "Over the years, some men have been interested in me, but I turned them down."

"Why?" His voice was laced with a certain eagerness, and a shiver trilled along her spine.

She looked up, and when she met his intense stare, her blood pounded through her veins.

"I guess I've stayed single for the same reason you have. I don't want to wind up hurt. Plus, I don't want to lose another husband the way I lost Lester." She swallowed and licked her lips. "I'm afraid I'll never again have a relationship like I had with him. He was kind, giving, and thoughtful. He put me first, and he took *gut* care of me."

Her hand trembled as she set her mug on the table, the desire to tell Aidan everything in her heart overcoming her. "I'm convinced I lost my chance at happiness and having a family. That dream died with Lester, so now I'm focused on helping other families grow. That's why God gave me the gift of being a midwife."

He shook his head. "You're too young to give up on love."

She felt her lips lift into a smile as she pointed at him. "You, sir, don't get to say that!"

To her surprise, he laughed, and the sound was sweet music to her ears. How she'd missed that laugh!

"I suppose you're right." He folded his arms over his wide chest.

Silence stretched between them again, but this time

Kristina eased into it. She stared out toward the silhouette of the barn against the pasture and lost herself in delicate memories. She finished her coffee and then glanced over at his handsome profile, wondering if it was safe to ask him the question that had haunted her for ten years. Why had he chosen Louise over her?

He turned toward her and cocked his head to the side. "What's on your mind?"

"Nothing." She shook her head and looked back over at the barn. *You're a coward, Kristina!*

"I think about Lester often, you know. We had such great times together, especially when we went camping."

Kristina snorted. "Remember when we went hiking, and we all wound up with poison ivy? I was never so itchy in my life."

"How could I forget?" He groaned as he touched his forehead. "That was pure torture. I made sure to learn how to spot poison ivy after that trip!"

They shared more stories of their youth, and soon she had to wipe her eyes from laughing so hard.

"We had some *gut* times," Aidan said.

"We did." She looked over at him, and her chest clenched. *Why did you give up on me?*

"I miss those days," Aidan said, his voice as soft as velvet. "I miss Lester."

Kristina nodded as she recalled the two births she'd witnessed today. The miracle of life was so wonderful and precious. She imagined it was bittersweet for parents to have the joy of watching their children grow up, get married, and start a family of their own. At least, for those who were blessed to live a full life and see their children become parents. But she and Lester never had that opportunity. She took a deep breath as her thoughts turned to Lester—his smile, his laugh, his warm hugs.

Then grief hit her fast and hard, and she gasped as her eyes filled with tears and then spilled over. She covered her face with her hands, feeling a mix of humiliation and anguish.

"I'm sorry." Aidan's voice sent a tremor straight to her bones. "I didn't mean to upset you."

She sniffed and tried to get ahold of herself, but the tears continued to pour from her eyes. When she set her hand on the arm of the chair, Aidan covered it with his. The contact sent a spark dancing up her arm, and she pulled her hand away.

"I'm truly sorry for your loss."

"*Danki,*" she managed to whisper, her voice raspy.

He swallowed and then his expression seemed almost sad. "Kristina, I have to ask—why did you pick Lester over me? Was I not *gut* enough for you?"

Kristina winced as if he'd struck her, and anger replaced her grief. How could Aidan say such a thing? "You're the one who started writing another woman while we were dating."

He shook his head and looked incredulous. "I wrote her *one* letter to tell her I wasn't interested. That's all it was!"

"That's *not* true! I read a letter she wrote back to you, and I could tell you had chosen her over me." Her voice sounded thin and reedy. "It was obvious from her words that she was the one you decided you wanted, even though we'd been dating for two years!"

His eyebrows formed a *V* shape. "What are you talking about?"

"I found a letter on my porch that Louise had written to you. It must have fallen out of your pocket after you visited me one night. In the letter, Louise implied you didn't want to be with me anymore—that she wanted you to come to Ohio to meet her because you were planning to break up with me."

"I never said that." His eyes narrowed. "I wrote to her and told her that I wasn't interested in a relationship with her, and she wrote back saying she understood that I *didn't* want to meet her because I loved *you*."

"You're lying. You chose Louise over me. And I want to know why. What did I do wrong?"

He gritted his teeth. "I never chose anyone over you. You must have imagined that because I told Louise I only wanted *you*." He pointed at her.

"Why are you lying to me after all these years? I saw the letter with my own eyes." She stared at him as confusion and aggravation poured through her.

Aidan looked perplexed as he gave her a palms up. "I don't know what letter you mean. When I wrote her, I told her you and I were planning to get married. I didn't lead her on." Then he pointed at her. "You destroyed *my* heart when you broke up with me without giving me a chance to explain myself and then you started dating my best *freind* all because of an innocent letter."

She turned toward him as every cell in her body vibrated with anger. "You cheated on me."

"Cheated on you?" His voice rose. "How do you figure that? None of this was my fault. My cousin Fannie wanted to set me up with Louise. I told her I was *froh* and planning a future with you, but she gave Louise my address anyway. I only wrote Louise back to tell her that I *wasn't* interested, which was all *mei mamm's* idea. She told me to write her back so that I didn't appear rude. I wanted to let her down gently. I never in a million years planned on pursuing her."

Kristina sniffed as more tears filled her eyes. Shaking her head in disbelief, she was unsure how to respond.

Seeming equally as lost, Aidan's expression fell as if his anger had fizzled out, and he looked drained. "You were *everything* to me." He dropped back against the chair, the fight gone out of him. "After breaking up with me, you started dating my best *freind* as if I never existed. That's why I went to Ohio. I couldn't stand the idea of staying here and watching you build a life with Lester or any other man. I thought I could start over there and forget all of my heartache, and I thought maybe I could build a life with Louise since she had been so interested before." He looked over at her and his eyes seemed to plead with her. "Did you even love me at all, Krissy?"

She sucked in a breath when he called her by her nickname. "I loved you, Aidan." *I think I still do!*

"Did you love Lester?"

She nodded and wiped at her eyes. "*Ya*, but I had prayed for a future with you from the time I was sixteen until you broke my heart."

He looked pained as they stared at each other.

Kristina suddenly felt off balance as the past rushed back to her. Had she made a mistake when they broke up? Should she have married Aidan instead of Lester?

Her lip trembled as she stood. She'd already been too emotional with him. She had to go inside before she made an even bigger mess.

"It's been a long day. It's late, and I'm clearly very tired."

Aidan stood. "Me too. I should get going."

Kristina's body shook with confusion as she lumbered into the kitchen and found Marlena and Richard sitting at the table. She crossed to the sink and began washing her mug, plate, and fork.

"*Danki* for supper," Aidan said from the doorway.

"*Gern gschehne,*" Marlena told him. "We're so *froh* you could come."

"Kristina," Aidan said.

She stopped scrubbing the plate and turned toward him.

"I hope to see you again soon."

She nodded as he gave her a look that seemed to be only for her. "Be safe going home."

Richard stood. "I'll walk you to your buggy."

"Thanks," Aidan said.

Kristina held her breath until the two men were gone, and then she turned to her sister, who smirked. "Were you trying to set me up with Aidan?"

"*Ya*, did it work?" Marlena rubbed her hands together.

"No!" Kristina pointed at her. "I told you I don't want to get married again. Besides, Rosetta is interested in him."

Marlena shook her head. "They're not dating."

"I need you to stop meddling," Kristina worked to keep her voice calm. "We missed our chance when we broke up all those years ago. Please stop. Okay?"

Marlena's smile flattened. "I didn't mean to upset you."

"It's okay."

Then Marlena's smile was back. "But you two were out there for a long time. Did you have a nice conversation?"

"We did. We reminisced some."

"*Gut.*"

"But then we discussed what happened between us, and it got confusing. We each have a different view of the past. It seemed like he truly believed what he told me, but that's not what I remember at all. I don't understand why he would lie to me." She cupped her hand to her forehead as a dull throb began behind her eyes. "It's all so jumbled up."

"Maybe you two can talk about it again another time and clear the air. You look like you're going to fall over.

Go take a shower and get to bed." Marlena pointed to the sink. "I'll clean this up."

"*Danki*." Kristina yawned again. "*Gut nacht*."

After a long, hot shower, Kristina dressed in her nightgown and then crawled into bed. As she closed her eyes, she recalled again how her body had reacted when Aidan touched her hand. She still had feelings for him, which put her in peril all over again.

"Lord," she whispered. "Please guide and protect my heart."

Then she rolled over and let sleep find her.

Aidan felt as if he were stuck in a fog of confusion as he guided his horse home. His mind kept replaying their conversation—how he'd opened up to her and how she'd seemed to open up to him. Their conversation flowed so easily, and he felt comfortable with her—more comfortable than he'd ever felt with Louise or Rosetta. Why did he still trust her after all of these years?

But some of the things she'd said to him didn't make sense. She insisted that Aidan had broken her heart, and the pain in her eyes when she told him had nearly destroyed him. How could she say that he'd hurt her when she was the one who ended their relationship?

For the past ten years, Aidan had believed she'd broken up with him without good cause. But what if he had hurt her? He felt as if the world were spinning out of control. Everything he'd believed seemed to be out of focus and reversed. He longed to turn the horse around and go back to finish the conversation. How could he have betrayed her?

He groaned as he recalled the letter he had written to Louise. It had been brief as he'd explained that he was dating Kristina and planned to marry her. Why had he allowed Kristina to doubt his intentions? And the letter from Louise never said the things Kristina repeated to him. It was as if she'd read a completely different letter. How was that even possible?

But if Kristina felt betrayed, then why did she jump so quickly into a relationship with Lester?

Aidan bit down on his lower lip as he let out an exasperated growl. If only he could turn back time and fix things! He may be confused about the past, but he was certain about one thing—he needed to see Kristina again. His soul craved her, and he needed to talk this through with her.

And he knew to the depth of his bones that he didn't feel the same way about Rosetta.

"Lord, please help me sift through these confusing feelings. And give me the strength to be honest with Rosetta when I see her again. And if it's your will, please help me work everything out with Kristina."

Calm settled over his soul. With God's help, he would find a way to get Kristina back in his life.

TEN

Kristina carried a coffee carafe as she walked toward the Yoder family's barn on Sunday, a week and a half later. The warm May sun kissed her cheeks as she breathed in the spring air and smiled at the sound of birds singing in the trees.

She peered over at the barn door just as Aidan walked out, and her pulse ratcheted up. She'd spent the past ten days analyzing their conversation on her sister's porch, and she felt unsettled. She longed to talk to him about the past and understand what had truly gone wrong between them. Perhaps if she spoke with him today, they could make plans to talk in private.

She picked up her pace as she approached Aidan, but she stopped when Rosetta appeared and touched his arm. He looked down at her and smiled, and Kristina felt her heart crack open. Once again, she'd set her hopes on Aidan, and he had crushed them.

The truth stood in front of her—Aidan had lied when

he said he only considered Rosetta a friend. He looked at her with such fondness, it was obvious they cared for each other.

Holding her head high, Kristina moved past them, but they didn't seem to notice. She made her way to the long tables and began filling cups. She smiled and nodded at the men who were ready for lunch, but inside, her soul deflated.

Once again, Aidan had betrayed Kristina, and now she had to find a way to live with the pain as Rosetta and Aidan planned a future together. How would she face them every Sunday at church?

This time Kristina's heart might not recover.

After lunch, Aidan rushed out of the barn after Kristina as she walked toward the house. "Kristina! Wait!"

She spun to face him, and her eyes narrowed as she stared at him.

He slowed his pace and felt his brow wrinkle. "*Was iss letz?*"

"Nothing." She lifted her chin. "I'm just tired."

"I was hoping we could talk. Could I possibly visit with you this afternoon?"

She shook her head. "I had a long week, and I really need to rest."

Aidan took in her expression and was sure she was

lying to him. Why had she put up a wall after opening up to him last week on the porch?

Rosetta sidled up to him, and he resisted the urge to ask her to leave.

"Hi, Kristina," she said before turning to Aidan. "Could I get a ride home today?"

He hesitated and then nodded. "Sure."

As much as he wanted to talk to Kristina, it was time for him to tell Rosetta the truth about his feelings. He'd spent the past couple of weeks praying and thinking, and he needed to be honest with Rosetta before he tried to work things out with Kristina.

"You two have a *gut* afternoon." Kristina's voice was as sharp and cold as glass as she glared at Aidan. Before he could respond, she spun on her heel and marched toward the kitchen.

Aidan looked over at Rosetta. "I'll give you a ride, but I can't visit today."

"Oh. Okay." She looked confused. "Should we get going then?"

Aidan and Rosetta walked to the buggy together, and he opened the passenger side door for her. Once inside, they began the short trip to her house. He stared at the road ahead and silently prayed for the right words to let her down without breaking her heart.

"I'm sorry I haven't seen you the past week," she began. "I've been busy with my parents' store."

He nodded and listened as she discussed the store for

the remainder of the ride. When they reached her house, he led the horse up the rock driveway and then halted it at the top.

"I would like to bring you another meal. Maybe this week?" Her expression was eager.

Aidan took a deep breath. "Rosetta, I need to be honest with you. I care for you as a *freind*, but I don't think I'll ever feel more than that for you."

Her lip trembled, and tears sparkled in her dark eyes. "But we're still getting to know each other. You don't see the possibility of us being more than *freinden*?"

"I'm so sorry, but I'm afraid I don't. You're a sweet and *schee maedel*, and I'm sure you'll find the right man someday. Unfortunately, I don't think that man is me."

"Kristina could never love you like I do." Rosetta spoke so low, Aidan almost wasn't sure he heard her right. "That's why I had to break you two apart all those years ago."

He gasped. Surely he hadn't heard her correctly. "What do you mean, Rosetta?"

"I found a letter you received from Louise after you told her you weren't interested in her. So I wrote a completely different one as if I were Louise, making it seem as if you two were in love. Then I planted the letter on Kristina's porch so she'd think you'd dropped it. When she broke up with you, I thought I finally had my chance."

"You *forged* a letter?" Suddenly all of the pieces came together in his mind, and then something inside of him broke apart. "You had no right! Kristina and I had a future planned!"

"No, you belonged with *me*! But you never noticed me. And my plan backfired because you weren't supposed to leave. Now that you're back, it's my turn. I can make you *froh*."

She began counting off on her fingers. "I will keep your home, cook for you, and make a *gut* Amish *fraa*. Kristina cares more about being a midwife. She'll always put that first."

"No, Rosetta. You're wrong about everything." Aidan's hands clenched into fists as fury tore through his veins. "I have always cared for Kristina, and her love for helping mothers is one of the things I admire most about her. You need to get out of my buggy now. What you did was wrong, and I would never, ever choose you. Especially not now."

She hiccuped before a sob escaped her mouth. Then she pushed the buggy door open, jogged up the back steps, and disappeared into the house.

Aidan's body vibrated with anger as he stalked into the house and found his father sitting in his favorite recliner in the family room while reading a book. He sat down across from him. "Could I talk to you, *Dat*?"

"Of course." *Dat* took off his reading glasses and peered over at him.

"Where's *Mamm*?"

"Napping. What's on your mind?"

"I need some advice." He explained how he took Rosetta home and learned about her deceptions. "I'm in shock. I can't believe she broke us up. I've spent all of these years thinking Kristina and Lester stabbed me in the back, when really, Kristina believed she'd been betrayed by me."

Dat's eyes narrowed as his brow pinched. "That's terrible. What are you going to do?"

Aidan leaned back in the wing chair and blew out a deep sigh. "I'm still in love with Kristina. In fact, I don't think I ever stopped loving her."

"Have you told her yet?"

"No." Aidan rubbed at a knot in his shoulder. "I don't know how."

"Pray about it. Ask God to lead you to the right words and then have faith. If it's God's will for you to spend your life with Kristina, he'll lead you to her."

Aidan nodded as hope took root in his chest. *I'm listening, God. Lead me.*

"Kristina! Kristina!"

"Huh?" Kristina rolled over and rubbed her eyes. It was Tuesday morning, and her bedroom was still cloaked in darkness. Her clock read 4:10. Had she dreamt that someone called her name?

"Kristina!" Richard's voiced echoed in the hallway before a knock sounded on her door. "Marlena's water broke."

She was wide-awake in a flash. "I'll be down in a minute."

She quickly dressed and put a scarf over her hair before hustling downstairs to Marlena and Richard's bedroom. She found Marlena propped up in bed taking deep breaths.

"Are you ready?" Kristina smiled as she touched Marlena's arm.

Marlena shook her head. "I don't know, Kristina."

"We'll get through this." Then Kristina turned to Richard. "Let's have this *boppli*."

After a few hours of hard labor, Marlena's baby was born. "It's a *bu*!" Kristina exclaimed, taking in his tiny fingers and toes. She cleaned him off and weighed him before turning to face her sister. "Do you want to hold him?"

But Marlena didn't answer. Kristina came closer to her sister, whose skin seemed pale and gray. Marlena's eyes were open, but only just.

"Is something wrong with Marlena?" Richard said.

"I'm not sure." Kristina handed the baby to Richard, and she set to examining her sister. "There's a lot of blood here—more than usual. I—I think you need to go call 911, Richard. Tell them to send an ambulance."

Richard's eyes were big as plates when he placed the baby in the bassinet and sprinted out the back door toward the phone in the barn.

"Marlena, Marlena, stay with me!" Kristina remained by her sister's side, running a cool rag over her forehead. Was she losing consciousness? Were her breaths slowing?

Please, God! Help my sister!

It seemed like an eternity before the EMTs arrived. They strapped Marlena to a gurney and took her and the baby out the back door, with Kristina and Richard behind them.

"Will you stay with the *kinner*?" Richard wrung his hands as they watched the EMTs load Marlena into the ambulance. "They should be waking up soon."

"Of course. Call me as soon as you talk to a doctor."

"I will," Richard said before climbing into the back of the ambulance.

As the ambulance sped away, Kristina dissolved into tears.

"I'm going to Richard's *haus* today," Aidan told his parents as he walked through the kitchen later that morning. "I'll be back soon, and then I'll finish the chores."

He'd spent the past couple of days thinking about Kristina and praying for God's guidance, and he couldn't wait to see her any longer. He showered, put on fresh clothes, and hurried downstairs, ready to make his way over to Kristina's house to try to work things out between them. He longed to tell her how Rosetta had destroyed their plans all those years ago. His heartbeat surged at the idea of finally planning a future with Kristina—a real future that he wanted to start as soon as possible.

"Please tell Kristina we said hello," *Mamm* said with a grin.

"I will." Aidan waved. "I'll see you later." Then he climbed into his buggy and guided his horse toward the road.

Please, Lord, help me find the right words to tell Kristina how I feel about her.

ELEVEN

Kristina put the girls down for a nap and then pulled her cell phone out of her pocket to check it for what felt like the hundredth time. When she found no calls or messages, she headed out to the barn, only to find there were no messages waiting for her there either. She'd spent the last few hours silently praying while she played with her nieces.

She felt as if she was coming apart at the seams with worry for her sister. Guilt and frustration were her constant companions while she tried to figure out what she'd done wrong during the birth. What had she missed?

She stepped out into the warm May air and stared up at the gray clouds that seemed to mirror her mood. She breathed in the scent of rain and then started to pray.

"Please, Lord, protect Marlena. And please send me someone to talk to before I go mad."

She walked back up toward the porch and stopped

when she heard the *clip-clop* of hooves and the whir of buggy wheels. She spun and rushed back down the steps to see Aidan climbing out of his buggy.

"Is everything okay?" he asked as he stalked toward her.

"No!"

His face clouded with a frown. "*Was iss letz?*"

"It's Marlena." Her voice broke. "The ambulance had to come for her." Then with tears streaming down her face, she explained how Marlena bled too much and passed out after her son was born. "I completely botched this delivery. Aidan, what if I killed my own *schweschder?*"

She sniffed and wiped at her eyes. "I'm a terrible midwife. I have no business being involved with delivering *bopplin.* What if I killed the only person I have left?"

"Come here." He pulled her into his arms, and she buried her face in his shoulder as her tears continued to fall. "I have faith in God and in you. You were right to call the ambulance right away. At the first sign of trouble, you called for help—and I'm sure the doctors are taking *gut* care of her." He rubbed her back, and she felt herself relax against him. "Everything will be fine, Krissy. I'm sure of it."

She stepped back from him and pulled a tissue from her apron pocket to wipe her eyes and nose. "*Danki.*"

He started to say something, but his words were interrupted by the ringing of her phone.

She yanked it from her pocket and found a number she didn't recognize on the screen. "Hello?"

"She's going to be okay," Richard said, sounding drained.

"Oh, praise God!" Kristina looked up at Aidan. "She's going to be okay."

Aidan took her free hand in his.

"The doctors managed to stop the bleeding, and now they're giving her a blood transfusion," Richard explained. "They're going to keep her and the *boppli* overnight for observation, but we should be home soon."

"Oh, I'm so glad." When happy tears began to fall, Kristina wiped her eyes again. "And the *boppli* is okay too?"

"*Ya*, he's great." He gave a little laugh. "He's healthy as a horse. Marlena wants to name him Jacob after your *dat*."

Kristina felt her eyes sting at the mention of her father. She sniffed. "*Gut*. I love that name."

"Kristina, you saved her life by telling me to call the ambulance when you did. If we had waited, the outcome could have been terrible."

Kristina closed her eyes. "I'm so sorry."

"Did you hear me? You saved her life." Richard spoke slowly as if to make sure she understood. She heard voices in the background and then he said, "I need to go. I'll call soon."

Kristina disconnected the phone and then took a deep breath. "Oh, I'm so relieved." She slipped the phone into her apron pocket and then launched herself into Aidan's arms. "And I'm so *froh* you're here."

"I am too."

She pulled away from him, and then he leaned down and brushed his lips over hers. The contact sent her stomach fluttering with the wings of a thousand butterflies.

When he broke the kiss, she gasped and stepped away from him, her head spinning with disorientation as her body continued to tingle.

"I came to tell you I still love you, Krissy."

Her mouth dropped open. Was she dreaming?

Panic welled in Aidan's chest the longer it took her to answer him. He'd just confessed his love, yet Kristina stood staring at him, mouth agape. Had he completely misread her feelings?

"What about Rosetta?" she finally asked.

Aidan ran his fingertip down her cheek. "We were only *freinden*."

Kristina seemed to study him with suspicion. "But you gave her a ride home after church again two days ago."

"That's right, and I told her the truth about how I felt about her. Then she told me the truth about the past."

Kristina cocked her head. "What do you mean?"

"You'll never believe this, but she broke us up, Krissy. She planted that letter from Louise." His nostrils flared as renewed anger flashed through him. "She found the real letter from Louise and then wrote a new one making it sound like I was going to break up with you. Then she left the fake letter on your porch for you to find."

Kristina gasped. "She did?"

"*Ya*. She admitted everything, and now I understand why you thought I chose Louise over you." He lifted his hat and pushed his hand through his hair. "If I had only known, I could have tried to fix things back then."

"I'm so sorry for not having faith in you or in us." She cupped her hand to his cheek, and he leaned into her touch.

"The past is the past. We can only look toward the future." He took her hands in his. "Krissy, I love you. I feel a connection to you that I've never felt with anyone. The truth is I've always cared for you."

Her lips trembled as she stared up at him. "I never forgot you. I love you, Aidan, and I'm sorry I hurt you too. I suppose we've both made mistakes. But Lester was there to comfort me, and I let him take care of me. I didn't plan it, and I don't regret marrying him, but maybe our moment is now. Maybe this is what God intended for us."

He pulled her into his arms and kissed her head. "*Ich liebe dich*. I want to marry you and have a family with you."

She sniffed and looked up at him. "I'd be honored to marry you. As long as you don't mind being married to a midwife who works crazy hours."

"I would be honored to be the husband of such a talented and hardworking woman."

"Then what are we waiting for?"

Leaning down, he brushed his lips against hers, and as she deepened the kiss, he felt liquid heat crash through his veins. He closed his eyes and lost himself in the feeling of kissing the love of his life.

EPILOGUE

Kristina sat on the porch swing and held Aidan's hand more than a year later. She breathed in the warm, humid July air and the sweet smell of the flowers in her nearby garden. Then she rested her free hand on her protruding belly, and a smile turned up her lips.

The past year had rushed by in a joyous blur. After Aidan proposed, they were married in a small, intimate ceremony the following month. Since this was Kristina's second marriage, they only invited their immediate families. That night, Kristina moved in with Aidan at his farm, and his parents relocated into the *daadihaus*.

Kristina started her happy new life, enjoying each day with her new husband. She continued to work as a midwife while also helping with chores on the farm. And soon they were ecstatic to realize that she was pregnant.

Aidan gave her hand a gentle squeeze. "We only have a couple of months left before the *boppli* is here and we find out if it's a *maedel* or a *bu*."

She looked down at her belly and then up at him. "*Danki* for making all of my dreams come true."

"*Gern gschehne.*" His smile was warm. "I'm so grateful God led me back to Gordonville and to you."

He leaned over and kissed her, sending happiness buzzing through her.

Kristina leaned her head on his shoulder as she smiled up at the cloudless, azure sky and silently thanked God for bringing Aidan back to her and giving her a second chance at having love in her life.

All of her dreams had come true, and thanks to God's perfect timing, she and Aidan finally had their moment together. She couldn't wait to see what else God had in store for their love, their family, and the rest of their lives.

ACKNOWLEDGMENTS

As always, I'm grateful for my loving family, including my mother, Lola Goebelbecker; my husband, Joe; and my sons, Zac and Matt.

I'm also grateful for my special Amish friend who patiently answers my endless stream of questions. You're a blessing in my life.

Thank you to my wonderful church family at Morning Star Lutheran in Matthews, North Carolina, for your encouragement, prayers, love, and friendship. You all mean so much to my family and me.

Thank you to Zac Weikal and the fabulous members of my Bakery Bunch! I'm so grateful for your friendship and your excitement about my books. You all are awesome!

To my agent, Natasha Kern—I can't thank you enough for your guidance, advice, and friendship. You are a tremendous blessing in my life.

Thank you to my amazing editor, Jocelyn Bailey, for your friendship and guidance. I'm grateful to each and every person at HarperCollins Christian Publishing who helped make this book a reality.

Thank you to editor Karli Jackson for polishing the story and connecting the dots. I appreciate your expertise!

Thank you most of all to God—for giving me the inspiration and the words to glorify you. I'm grateful and humbled you've chosen this path for me.

DISCUSSION QUESTIONS

1. At the beginning of the story, Kristina is convinced she's missed her chance at having a family. What do you think caused her to change her mind during the course of the story?

2. Aidan is convinced Kristina broke up with him unjustly ten years ago. Do you agree with his point of view?

3. Marlena tries to get Kristina and Aidan back together by arranging for them to sit on the porch together. Do you think Marlena's intentions were out of line?

4. Rosetta broke up Kristina and Aidan ten years ago by forging a letter from Louise to Aidan. She believes Aidan's return to the community is her chance to win him once and for all. Have you ever known anyone as devious as she is? If so, how did you handle that person?

5. Which character can you identify with the most?
   Which character seemed to carry the most
   emotional stake in the story? Was it Kristina,
   Aidan, or someone else?

6. Kristina decided to become a midwife after
   losing her husband. Have you ever encountered a
   difficult season in your life? If so, where did you
   find your strength? What helped you through
   your difficulties?

A MIDWIFE
FOR SUSIE

SHELLEY SHEPARD GRAY

Only God gives inward peace,
and I depend on him.

Psalm 62:5 cev

Reach up as far as you can. God will
reach the rest of the way.

Amish proverb

ONE

The stars were out, the July evening held a touch of welcome breeze, and the faint scent of honeysuckle mixed companionably with the aroma of burning wood in Dwight Eicher's firepit. All told, Joanna Zimmerman couldn't have imagined a finer place to be.

Except for the fact that her best friend and next-door neighbor could not seem to let the current thread of conversation go.

His stubbornness was starting to get rather annoying. "I don't know why you're acting so put out with me, Dwight," she said. "My job doesn't exactly concern you." After all, he was a single man and she was a midwife. Well, she used to be a midwife. She wasn't sure if she was ever going to help deliver a baby again.

"Since my sister Susie is involved, it does."

Although Susie was happily married, Dwight still acted as protective as ever. "I'll speak to Susie. Now, may we talk about something else?"

Even in the firelight, she could tell he was not about to switch gears so easily. He looked as obstinate as a mule next to a loaded wagon.

"Jo, all I'm trying to say is I thought you'd be much more excited about Susie's wish."

"I'm excited she's going to have a baby. For sure and for certain."

Dwight sprawled out on the red Adirondack chair. "That ain't the same, and you know it. She wants you to deliver it. But here you are, not even giving it a moment's consideration." His voice lowered. "Actually, I don't know if I'm more disappointed or confused by your attitude."

Sitting across from him in a matching blue chair, Joanna attempted to keep her silence. But it was hard because she'd started getting frustrated with him a good twenty minutes ago.

When Dwight had asked her over to roast hotdogs and catch up, she'd been excited. They hadn't spent much time together in weeks. But now that she understood there'd been an ulterior motive for his invitation, she felt both betrayed and annoyed.

Especially now that he was heaping an additional helping of guilt onto her lap. "You took me off guard, Dwight. Give me a minute, wouldja?"

"Give you a minute to do what? You're a midwife, and Susie is gonna need one."

"It's not as easy as that."

Even in the dim light, she could see his eyebrows lift practically into his hairline. "What is so hard?"

Oh, a lot of things. The fact that she was usually asked by the expectant mother and not the mother's brother. The fact that she'd known Susie for most of her life, so they might be too close for her to be the best midwife. Or . . . that Joanna had secretly sworn never to assist another mother through her labor and delivery ever again.

But of course Dwight didn't know that.

Abruptly, she stood up. "You know, I think it would be best if I left right now. Thank you for the hotdog."

"Oh, no, you don't." He stood as well, so abruptly his chair wobbled. "You cannot get up in a huff and walk out of here."

"'Cannot' means 'not able.' Yet again you used the wrong word. It should be 'may not.'"

"Whatever." His eyes narrowed. "What's wrong with you, anyway? For weeks you've been acting distant and standoffish."

"I have not." She was kind of lying.

"Oh, yes, you have. You've been in a mood ever since you got back from Sugarcreek. How come? Did something happen up there?"

Sugarcreek was an almost four-hour drive north of their Amish community in the heart of Adams County. If one took a bus instead of private car, it was easily closer to six. So, if one were *Englisch*, it was only an afternoon's drive—or phone call, of course—away. For most in their community, however, it was practically as far as London or Paris. Rarely did anything in Sugarcreek affect anyone in Adams County. She'd been grateful for that.

"*Nee*, Dwight."

He stepped closer. "Are you sure?" He reached out, looking like he was about to run a hand down her arm, but it dropped to his side after the slightest pause. "You know whatever it is, you can tell me."

Dwight was standing so close she could smell the faint scent of Irish Spring soap on his skin. Close enough that she could see there were new, faint lines around his eyes that hadn't been there a year ago. Close enough that if she lifted her chin high enough, and if he lowered his, their lips could meet. Yes, it was very possible . . . if that were something they would ever want to do.

"I don't want to talk about this any longer. I'm tired."

"Really? It's only seven o'clock."

His words made sense, but her emotions were so frayed she lashed out. "Dwight, why do I have to keep explaining myself? What's wrong with me being tired? Why do I have to suddenly start saying all the right things that you want to hear?"

"I don't expect you to say anything, Joanna."

"It sure seems like it. Now, I'm leaving. Good night." She turned and started walking before he could come up with another question for her.

Dwight muttered something under his breath. But other than the sound of a chair scraping against the cement,

Joanna didn't hear anything more as she passed through the opening in the wooden fence that divided their yards.

When she finally walked into her house, she lit a kerosene lantern and pulled down the shade on the kitchen window. Only then did she sit down, cover her face with her hands, and start fiercely praying for peace.

"Lord, I don't know what to do anymore," she whispered into the empty room. "There's a part of me that wants to tell Dwight about what happened in Sugarcreek. I want to confess my mistake and ask him to help me. But how can I reveal something so terrible? If he ever finds out that a mother died while in labor under my care, it's going to change his opinion of me forever. And then what would I do? He's my best friend."

Joanna stopped herself from adding to her prayers. If the Lord was listening, she sure didn't want Him to hear her complain about her nightmares or the guilt on her shoulders or the confusion about the future that seemed to fog her brain. So she stopped and took a deep breath . . . and realized it was a foolish thing to imagine her silence made a difference. Of course the Lord knew everything she was experiencing. He knew it even when she wasn't confessing.

Just as she knew that Dwight was still outside, sitting back in his red chair in front of the firepit and probably watching the windows of her house and wondering what in the world she was doing.

Some things just couldn't stay hidden.

TWO

Dwight had done every little chore he could think of—including taking a long shower and mucking out Henrietta's stall—before pulling out his bicycle and riding the two miles to Susie and Marcus's farm. Honestly, if he could've put off this visit for another week, he would have. He was still irritated by Joanna's behavior. Though they'd been friends for most of their lives, they had recently been flirting a bit more. A couple of months ago, right before Joanna had traveled to Sugarcreek, they'd almost kissed.

But since she'd gotten back, it was as if she'd shut down. She didn't seem to want to see him, confide in him . . . or even flirt. It was like she'd placed him firmly back on the "friend" shelf, and he had no idea how to hop off of it without getting hurt.

And now, to add insult to injury, he was having to tell his sister Joanna's bad news.

"Well, what did she say?" Susie asked the minute Dwight found her in her garden. She knelt in the middle of two rows of tomatoes with her sleeves rolled up to her elbows.

"Susie, what are you doing? It's over eighty degrees out here. You should be resting indoors where it's cooler." He looked around. "Where is Marcus? He should be keeping an eye on you."

His sister sat up straight and glared. "*Mei mann* should be doing what?"

"Don't get on your high horse now."

"'High horse'?"

"Susie, you know what I mean. You're pregnant. Or have you forgotten?"

Susie got another look in her eye as she struggled to her feet. "I haven't forgotten this," she said, patting the rounded curve in her midsection.

"You know what I meant. I'm trying to look out for you. That's all."

After looking like she was about to take exception to that, too, she relaxed and sighed. "I know, Dwight. You are a *gut bruder*. I guess I can be a bit prickly these days."

As prickly as a cactus! "*Danke*."

"If you want to help, you can pick up the pile of weeds and my basket of tomatoes."

"'May,'" he murmured before he could stop himself. Which, by the look in Susie's eyes, was strike three. "Sorry," he said quickly. "I guess I was thinking about Joanna. You know how she is about 'can' and 'may.'"

To his relief, his sister chuckled instead of chewing on

him some more. "I absolutely do know. Our Joanna is a stickler for the right word at the right time, and that's a fact. So . . . don't keep me in suspense any longer. What did she say?"

Luckily, his arms were full of weeds and tomatoes. "Go on inside and I'll tell ya."

"Promise?"

"I promise. Just as soon as I dispose of all this." When she looked at him strangely, he motioned his elbow to the door. "Go on, now. I'll be right there."

The moment she disappeared, he breathed a sigh of relief. Even though he should have guessed that Marcus was over at the livery he ran with his father, Dwight still wished he was home. Then he could get Marcus to help him break the news to Susie gently.

After carefully disposing of the weeds in the compost pile and bringing the tomatoes into the kitchen, he washed his hands. Then he got himself a tall glass of water and drank half of it.

"Dwight, I'm in here!"

Looked like he couldn't procrastinate any longer. "Sorry, I just had to get something to drink. Do you want anything?"

"I have water. Come in here and talk to me."

Pulling up the waistband of his britches, he walked into her living room. It was Susie's pride and joy. The room had gorgeous wood floors stained a dark cherry color, two love seats made of pale-green tweed, an antique white wicker rocking chair that had once been their grand-mother's, and a sewing machine in the corner. All of those things were nice. However, what made it truly eye-catching was the large oval-shaped rag rug Susie had spent over a year making and the primitive-looking quilt hanging on the wall. Both the rug and the quilt were done in black, cherry red, and lapis blue. The colors popped and drew one's eye to them like a child following an ice cream vendor in July.

"Dwight? Now what has your tongue?"

"Sorry. I was just admiring the quilt. You did a good job on it."

"*Danke.* But now talk to me about Joanna." Susie smiled. "When does she want to meet with me and Marcus?"

"Well, about that . . ."

"Oh no! Does she think I waited too long to reach out to her?" She frowned. "I kept meaning to set up an appointment, but there didn't seem to be any need. Everything's been going well, and my girlfriends have been answering all my questions."

"Not exactly." He took a deep breath. "You see—"

"Really?" she interrupted. "I'm six months along now. Surely she doesn't think I need to wait any longer to visit with her?"

Ack, but this was terrible! He felt like he was about to tell her it was snowing too much to go to school. She used to hate those days. But what had to be done had to be done. "Susie, it's like this. Joanna, well, she isn't sure that she'll be able to be your midwife." No, it wasn't exactly the truth, but it was almost close enough.

As he'd feared, she looked completely crestfallen. "Why? Is she really that busy?"

"I'm not sure."

"How come? She didn't explain?"

It was time to deflect and end this conversation. "Susie, there's only so much conversation I'm willing to have regarding my sister's labor and delivery. Now, isn't there someone else you could ask? I know Joanna isn't the only midwife in the county."

"She might be. Dorothy moved to Florida."

Dorothy was not only Joanna's mentor but also their aunt. He loved her dearly, but right now he wished she'd waited a little while longer to retire to Pinecraft. "Come, now. I know there are others."

"There aren't, Dwight. The only other midwife I know about is Rose Borntreger."

"Oh." Rose was older than their parents and never seemed to smile.

"'Oh' is right." She shuddered dramatically. "I know girls who've had to use her, Dwight. My friend Fern did."

"Fern has a fine baby boy."

"She does, but she also has enough horror stories about Rose to fill a book. Fern said she was impatient, told Fern to quiet down whenever she cried out, and she had cold hands!"

All of that sounded bad. Even imagining his younger

sister crying out in pain made him feel a little woozy. "Cold hands are a problem?"

"Dwight, I know you're squeamish, but surely even you can imagine how unpleasant cold hands would be on the most important day of your life."

"Um, of course." And now he was bright red and officially squirming.

Susie covered her sizable baby belly with her arms. "Now do you see what I mean? Would you want her by your side when you were giving birth?"

"That's not going to happen." *Praise the Lord.*

"How about this: when your wife is giving birth? Would you want to hold your dear wife's hand when she's in extreme pain, all while getting yelled at by a grumpy midwife?"

Susie could certainly paint a picture. "*Nee.* No, I would not." He couldn't imagine a sourpuss midwife yelling at his *frau* to be quiet for her husband.

"Good. Now you can see what Marcus thinks about that option. Honestly, I think Marcus would lose his temper and start yelling at Rose if she started yelling at me."

She wasn't wrong. Marcus adored Susie and was always fussing over her. Even their mother had joked that Marcus didn't like people looking sideways at Susie. Marcus would not be pleased to have a surly midwife barking orders during one of the most precious moments in their lives.

Knowing what he had to do, he stood up. "I'll talk to

Joanna again. I can't promise anything, but I will tell her that she needs to speak with you herself."

"Really? You'll do that?"

"Of course, Susie. You need a midwife, and I do not want to be in the middle of this discussion anymore. How about I ask Joanna to come over after church next Sunday? Church is at the Troyers', *jah*?"

"It is." Her eyes lighting up, Susie added, "That will be perfect. We can all walk back here for dessert after the luncheon there. I'll make a pie."

We? "I don't think I need to be here for that."

"Sure you should. You and Jo are best friends," she said without sparing him a glance. "Besides, we both know Joanna isn't going to come over here to talk to me without you. You're practically her lifeline to the rest of the world."

"Hardly that."

"Lately it seems that way." Getting to her feet, Susie smiled. The faint lines of worry on her face had eased. She looked like her regular self again. "Just tell Jo I'm making a peanut butter pie. She'll come over for that."

Joanna loved that pie. So did he. Susie was nothing if not manipulative. Kissing her on her brow, he murmured, "You, Susie Miller, are a force to be reckoned with."

"Only where *mei bobbli* is concerned, Dwight." Walking him to the door, she hugged him again. "*Danke* for coming over. You're the best *bruder* in the world."

He wasn't, but he didn't argue. Especially because he'd

now promised Susie he was somehow going to convince Joanna to come over after church to discuss midwifing.

He had a feeling even peanut butter pie wasn't going to make Joanna excited about that.

THREE

Joanna's lemon bread wasn't edible. Neither was the butter-milk chocolate cake, the zucchini bread, or the cinnamon rolls. Just thinking about those cinnamon rolls, which had been both hard as hockey pucks and raw in the center, made Joanna grimace.

It was a fact: no matter how well she tried to follow the recipes, she was a pitifully poor baker.

Looking around her messy kitchen—which now displayed not only empty bags of flour and brown sugar on the countertops but also drops of lemon juice, oil, and the remains of a cracked egg—Joanna sighed. The only thing worse than creating a terrible dish was cleaning up the evidence of that failure.

She wasn't even going to think of how much money she'd just wasted on ingredients. That would be enough to keep her up at night.

Turning on the hot water, she squirted some dish soap onto the lot of it and started scrubbing.

"Knock-knock!"

Surprised, Joanna turned to the back door, which was country style, divided in two like a horse's stall so one could keep the bottom latched and the top wide open. When she saw who was standing there, she realized that her day had finally gotten better. "Emma!" She turned off the water and wiped her hands.

"You've got this latched. Joey and I canna get in. Let us in!"

"You have Joey?" Joanna ran over to unlatch the door as she smiled at her sister and her three-year-old nephew, who stood next to his *mamm*. "I didn't know you two were going to stop by."

As soon as she got the door open, she looked down and feigned surprise. "My word. Who can this be?"

"Jo!" her nephew sang out.

She got down on one knee and played her favorite game with him. "Joey, my stars! We have the same name."

"*Jah*!" With a giggle, he tackled her.

Joanna pulled him close in a tight hug. "Oh, you smell so warm and good. This is the best part of my day."

"I would imagine so," Emma said as she peered into the cluttered sink. "Joanna, what is all this?"

"It's exactly what it looks like. A pile of dirty dishes."

"*Jah*, but why?"

"Why are there so many? Or why have I not cleaned them up yet?" she joked.

"Neither." Her sister wrinkled her nose. "Why have

you been cooking? I swear, sometimes I'm tempted to remove all of your pots and pans just to save you from yourself." She wrapped a white dishcloth around her waist and turned on the faucet.

"Emma, stop. I can do my own dishes."

"I think we both know that these would take you two days."

"You're exaggerating."

"I am, but only slightly." Emma waved one hand at Joanna in an impatient, get-to-the-point way. "Stop arguing with me and let me help you."

"Fine."

"*Gut.* Now, give Joey some pots and pans and a wooden spoon to play with and come help me dry."

This was classic Emma. Bossy and practical. She'd always been that way too. Even back when Emma was five and Joanna was six, her sister would tell her what to do all the time. The worst of it was that Joanna could never argue too much with her. Simply put, Emma got things done.

After placing a plastic mixing bowl, a tin pie plate, four plastic measuring cups, and a new wooden spoon on the rug, Joanna guided her nephew to the collection. "Would you like to *kocha* for a little bit?"

"*Jah.* I want to cook." He giggled. "Cookies!"

She laughed as he plopped down on his bottom and started stirring his make-believe food in the bowl. "I think you're a better cook than I am, Joey!"

Emma handed her a towel. "He might be. Oh, Jo. I don't know how you got everything so caked on in this muffin tin."

She did. Yesterday, when she'd been attempting to crochet, she'd forgotten all about the blueberry muffins in the oven. By the time she remembered, they'd been practically charred. "How about, at the very least, I scrub and you dry?"

Emma ignored her as she got out a knife and scraped the inside of one of the cups. "What were these supposed to be, anyway?"

"Blueberry muffins."

"Why didn't you simply go to the Brown Cow and get some like you usually do?"

The Brown Cow was her favorite coffee shop and bakery. Joanna was practically a regular there. "I don't know. I just thought it would be good to be a bit more domestic."

"Why?"

"Because I'm the only woman I know who burns toast. I need to get better."

"No, you need to stop worrying about cooking. Like, ever."

Almost hurt that she was such a failure in the kitchen, Joanna blurted, "What's wrong with me learning to be a better cook?"

"You know. You are a great many things, Joanna, but *domestic* you are not. If our parents and Caleb were here, the four of us would be laughing hysterically right now."

Of course Emma had to include their firefighting brother in that group. "I'm not laughing. You know, one day I'm going to be married, and my husband is going to expect me to make a simple meal."

"You should be laughing. The Lord gave you the ability to help bring babies into the world, Jo. That's a gift most of us will never have. I figure if He can give you that, He can also give you a spouse who knows how to cook." She paused. "You need to take crochet out of your life too."

"You saw that?" Joanna asked as she took the now spotless muffin pan from her sister and carefully dried it.

"It's bright yellow. Yes, I did."

"Oh, just hand me that bowl."

Emma gave her the bowl she'd just washed and started on the loaf pan that had held the unfortunate lemon bread.

Twenty minutes later, Joey was eating, Emma was sipping peppermint tea, and Joanna was getting grilled.

"What's going on with you, Joanna? You haven't been yourself for several months. All of us are starting to worry."

"Who is 'all'?"

"Everyone who counts. *Mamm* and *Daed*, for one."

"Or two."

Emma rolled her eyes. "All I'm saying is that they're starting to worry about you as much as the rest of us are."

"No one should be worrying about me."

"Joanna, you've hardly left this *haus* the past month. And I haven't heard you mention delivering a baby in weeks. All you're doing is cooking terrible things and ruining your pots and pans."

Ignoring the last comment, Joanna asked, "*Mamm* and *Daed* truly spoke to you about me?"

"Yes! They've mentioned their concerns both to me and to Matthew in letters and when they've called and left messages."

Joanna knew her sister was referring to the phone shanty they shared with her neighbors on the street. "Hmm."

After another sip, Emma added, "They've spoken to Caleb as well—which is why he brought up his concerns when he stopped by the house last week."

"Caleb is worried about me? Emma, you should have reassured him that I was fine." Caleb had become a Mennonite when he was eighteen and gone right to firefighting school. It had been an adjustment, but now they were all proud of him and his good works.

Joanna was also fiercely protective of their little brother, who wasn't "little" at all. He actually towered over the lot of them. "He shouldn't have to think about anything other than keeping safe."

"I'm not going to tell Caleb that you're fine when you aren't. He feels the same way." Emma crossed her legs. "Actually, Caleb told me that if I didn't figure out what was going on with you, then he was going to drive over here and ask you himself."

There were two ways of going about this. She could keep holding everything inside and unsuccessfully trying to divert attention away from herself . . . or she could come clean and maybe even find some peace. Put that way, there was no choice.

"Fine. I'll tell you. But you've got to promise not to share everything with Caleb and our parents."

"You know I canna promise you that."

Ugh. Her sister was such a stickler for honesty. "Fine. But at least promise me you'll take my wishes into consideration." When her sister looked mutinous, Joanna pressed. "I mean that, Emma. Which also means that if Caleb shows up here spouting a lot of nonsense, I'm going to know exactly who is at fault. You."

"It's not nonsense if it's true."

"That's my rule if you want me to tell you anything. Now, do you promise or not?"

Emma sighed. "Fine. I promise. Now, what is going on?"

"I lost a mother up in Sugarcreek."

Emma blinked as she obviously filled in the gaps of Joanna's story. "Was it in childbirth?" she asked quietly.

The truth hurt so much she could hardly look at her sister. "*Jah.* I saved the baby, but the mother was bleeding and in distress." Realizing her hands were shaking, she folded them together. "She died before she could even see her babe. Her husband was devastated. I . . . I felt so bad, Emma. I still do."

Emma reached for both of her hands. "Joanna."

"I've been dreaming about it. Having nightmares, really." That was putting it lightly too. Over and over she'd dream of the delivery, the panic, the blood . . . and the terrible look in Mr. Fisher's eyes as he gazed down at his son. He'd looked devastated. No, he'd looked like he was never going to be the same, and she couldn't blame him either.

He and his wife had trusted her, and she'd let them down.

"I wish I'd known you lost a mother, Jo. You care so much and are so conscientious. That must have been so hard."

"It was. I mean, it has been."

Emma sipped her tea and set down her cup again. "I feel terrible for ya, I do. What did Dorothy say?"

Dorothy was Joanna's mentor. She was kind, proficient, and an amazing midwife. Joanna had helped her during dozens of labors and deliveries, and never had Dorothy acted rattled or unsure. She had also never lost either a babe or a mother. "I haven't told her."

Her sister looked incredulous. "Why not? If anyone would understand what you're feeling, it would be her."

"I don't know if she would understand, Emma. I don't think she's ever lost a mother."

"You don't know that for certain."

"Anyway, you know the other reason. She's Dwight's aunt." Dorothy also now lived in Pinecraft, which meant Joanna would either have to deliver the news in a letter or over the phone. She hadn't been able to stomach either idea.

"Are you worried about her being disappointed in you or telling Dwight?"

"Both."

"Oh, Joanna. You are always so hard on yourself."

Emma had a point—she was her own worst critic. But this time she really was justified. "Can we not talk about it anymore?"

"Fine. But I don't understand why you're baking so much."

"No reason. It's just been helping to fill my days. I have a lot of time now."

"Why? I've seen plenty of expectant mothers waddling around town. Surely they're keeping you busy. I know I did!" she joked.

"I have decided to stop being a midwife."

Emma stared at her. "You're going to end a whole career because a mother died in delivery?"

"That's enough of a reason, Emma." Joanna knew her voice was hard, but she resented her sister making light of it.

"Tell me what happened. Did you make a mistake? Could you have done something different?"

"*Nee*. She had placenta previa. I wouldn't have known unless I did a sonogram."

"Which you don't do."

"I know."

Emma's voice softened. "I feel sorry for the woman and her husband and the babe who is going to grow up without a mother. But you can't take all the responsibility, Joanna."

"Emma, *halt*."

"*Nee*, I will not. Listen to what I'm saying, please? You are not God. I'm sure the mother knew the risks about childbirth, especially having a baby at home. You canna take it all on your slim shoulders."

"You may be right, but that doesn't stop how I'm feeling."

"You're right about that, Jo. There's only one person who can stop heaping on the guilt, and that's you. You're going to have to decide if you are ready to move on or not."

"But that woman . . ." Joanna paused, hating how after all this time she could still barely say the woman's name. But she deserved more. Taking a deep breath, she said, "Cheryl was so young."

"I'm sure she was. And I'm sure you'll always feel regret whenever you think of her. But feeling guilty and quitting your job won't honor her memory. For some reason, the Lord decided he needed Cheryl sooner rather than later. For the life of me, I canna think that all He wanted for your life was for you to live in guilt. I think God intends for you to do something more."

Joanna leaned back. She was faithful, but did that mean He was always in charge and she didn't have to take any responsibility? "I don't know, Emma."

"I hope one day soon you'll know, then."

The words hung in the air like a hint of jasmine in the springtime. A promise of what could be, if she chose to hope. "*Danke.*"

"I don't know if I helped."

"You did. I don't know what I'm going to do, but I do know that sharing some of my burden has made me feel better."

"I'm glad of that, then." Looking down at Joey, Emma brightened. "So, want to hear what Joey did yesterday? It was so smart!"

Getting down on the floor next to her favorite nephew, Joanna grinned. "Of course. Tell me everything about this dear boy."

Kneeling down as well, Emma began talking a mile a minute. As she listened, Joanna felt all her worries drift away as Joey moved into her arms.

She held on tight.

FOUR

Dwight had dreaded the visit all day, so much so that he'd almost volunteered to take on another shift at the lumberyard when the boss asked if anyone could help out. However, he'd never been one to put off what had to be done. And he had to talk to Joanna about Susie. He'd promised, and he liked to keep his promises.

After washing up and putting on a fresh shirt, he walked the short distance to her house and knocked on the door.

She answered immediately. "Hiya, Dwight."

"Hey." Just as he was about to explain his visit, he noticed she had a smudge of flour on her cheek, her *kapp* was askew, and she was sporting a dark stain on her purple dress. "You look a fright."

"Hmm? Oh, I suppose I do. Want to see what I've been working on?"

"Of course." But he didn't get much farther than a couple of steps into the kitchen before he stopped in his

155

tracks. He wasn't one for fanciful thoughts, but it looked rather like an ax murderer had been set loose in her kitchen. "Oh, Jo. What in the world have you been doing in here?"

"Canning."

Gazing at the mess that sat congealing over the countertops, he took an experimental sniff. "Let me guess. You're canning . . . blueberries?"

"Of course it's blueberries." She smiled. "I might be messy, but even you have to admit that it smells like blueberries in here."

"It looks like they exploded over every available surface too." Unable to help himself, he ran a finger over one of the blotches on her cheek.

Meeting his gaze, her cheeks bloomed a bit before she stepped out of his reach. "So, I had a bit of trouble when the berries came to a boil. Next time I need to put a lid on the saucepan, I think."

"Hmm. So . . . you're making jam?"

"Oh, no." She pointed to the four half-filled mason jars nearby. "This is blueberry pie filling."

"I've never heard of that."

"You've truly never heard of a blueberry pie? Dwight, you're missing out."

Joanna was acting so smug, so full of herself, he almost hated to explain how a blueberry pie was made. Almost. "Usually folks just put in fresh blueberries and sugar and bake it. The heat in the oven bursts the berries and turns it into that consistency."

"Oh."

Her look of consternation was adorable. He almost gathered her into his arms while he chuckled at her expression. He would have, except he was worried about hurting her feelings. "Where did you find the recipe?"

"I couldn't find one, so I made it up." Her eyes widened. "Dwight, maybe that's why I couldn't find anything. Because no one boils blueberries before putting them into a pie shell."

No one but his Joanna. Staring at the basket of berries, the large pot of water on the stove, the jars half filled with goopy, soggy blueberries, and the distinctly blue stains on the countertops, he said, "Where did you get all these berries anyway?"

Still looking at the jars, she folded her arms across her chest. "Rhoda Beachy stopped by with her two *kinner* and brought them to me. It was a gift."

There was his opening. "It was a thank-you gift for delivering her babies, wasn't it?"

"*Jah.* Rhoda delivered those twins in under ten hours. She was amazing." Obviously seeing the "I told you so" look on his face, she sighed. "I know what you're thinking."

"Do you?"

"*Jah.* That you still want me to be Susie's midwife."

He nodded. "I visited her the other day. She has her heart set on you, Jo."

"I just don't know if I can."

He reached for her hand and linked his fingers through

hers. "Then you should tell me a reason, because right now I can't understand why you are being so stubborn. Is it because you know Susie so well?"

"*Nee*." She looked down at their joined hands and pursed her lips.

"Is it because she's my *shveshtah*?" he asked softly.

She met his gaze again. "Kind of, but not really."

She was hedging, and it was driving him crazy. He couldn't help her if she kept everything to herself. "Joanna, please, just talk to me."

"Dwight, something terrible happened when I midwifed a woman up in Sugarcreek."

"What could have happened?" He doubted much—everyone said she was a phenomenal midwife.

"The mother died, Dwight!"

He felt like he'd just been hit with a sledgehammer. "What?"

"You heard me."

Before she could move away or bat at him, he pulled her into his arms. For a few seconds she struggled, but then stilled. "I didn't want to tell you."

"Why not? You know I would never judge you."

"But your aunt Dorothy—"

He cut her off. "Is my aunt. Not you. Even though I can't imagine her ever thinking anything but the best about you, it has nothing to do with me."

She sniffed and pulled away far enough to look him in the eye. "You mean that, don't you?"

"Of course, Jo." No one was like her. No one tried so hard, worked so hard, cared so much. Though he might be wrong, it didn't really matter to him anyway. He knew without a doubt that he would always take Joanna's side. Always.

Running a hand in a soft motion along her shoulders, he added, "Tell me what happened."

"I'd rather not."

"Have you shared the whole story with anyone yet?"

"I talked to Emma." She averted her eyes.

She also sounded so defensive, Dwight was fairly sure that she wasn't telling him the whole truth. So he pushed. "Be honest. Did you tell her *everything*?"

"*Nee*, not everything. But a lot of it."

"Tell it all to me now."

"Dwight—"

"I mean it. You've got to share the whole story with someone so you can finally start healing."

Joanna looked like she was about to argue but only said, "The whole story isn't easy to hear. You're going to get queasy."

At any other time, he would have been embarrassed by his flaws. But now he only hoped that by revealing his weaknesses he might be able to help her feel better about sharing hers. "I know. But I still want to hear." Squeezing her hand, he said, "It's important. No, *you're* important, Jo. You're never going to feel better if you don't confide in someone."

"Are you sure? It's not easy . . ."

"I'm sure. I can take it. I promise."

Looking down at their linked hands, she took a deep breath and then started talking.

At last.

FIVE

Joanna supposed some people might say that confiding one's darkest secrets was cathartic. Unfortunately, after relaying Cheryl Fisher's entire labor-and-delivery nightmare, she knew she would only recall it as painful. It wasn't easy to place all of one's faults out front and center, boldly displayed and open to criticism.

Especially since her audience wasn't just anyone. It was Dwight.

He had been incredible, though. While most people would have asked questions, interrupted, or even allowed a myriad of expressions to appear on their face, Dwight had done nothing but sit quietly as she walked him through all seven hours of Cheryl Fisher's labor, delivery, and eventual death. Every time she'd paused for breath and glanced at him worriedly—he really was rather squeamish around blood—Dwight had simply stared at her, every muscle in his face completely composed. His only reaction had been to squeeze her hands gently and nod.

Emboldened by that, she'd continued, sparing no detail, including how upset Cheryl's husband and parents had been. Saying it aloud had felt as if she were ripping open an old wound, except that it was her heart and, yes, pride that was injured. But finally, she was done. Relieved that now someone knew the whole, terrible truth, Joanna collapsed against her chair with a ragged sigh.

She half expected Dwight to get up and leave.

Instead, he only looked perplexed. "Is that all of it?"

She raised an eyebrow. "Wasn't that enough?"

Dwight ran a hand over his face. "*Jah*. It surely was. Joanna, I'm so sorry. It sounds like it was a horrible experience. And that poor man."

"Emmitt."

"*Jah*, Emmitt. I canna imagine his loss. That's a terrible thing."

Remembering the vacant look in Emmitt Fisher's eyes, she swallowed hard. "He looked like his whole life had been taken away from him." Still unwilling to spare herself a thing, she added, "I guess it had."

"Indeed."

After another minute or so passed, Joanna said, "So, um, now I think you can see why I don't want to deliver any more babies."

To her surprise, he stood up and pulled her into his arms. Caught off guard, she rested her palms on his shoulders.

"*Nee*, Joanna, I don't."

She was not only surprised by his embrace, she also felt a little betrayed by his words. She attempted to pull away. "Dwight—"

But he held firm. "*Nee.* Stop arguing and listen for a second."

"I'm not arguing—" Okay, maybe she was. Embarrassed, she looked up at him. "I'm listening now."

He didn't wait long at all. "I'm no *doktah* or midwife, but I canna help but think that one doesn't go into either profession thinking there will never be dark days. Am I right?"

"You are." She relaxed a bit in his arms.

He pulled her an inch or two closer, near enough that she had to loop her hands around his neck. "Now, I haven't ever talked to my aunt about this, but I have a feeling Dorothy might tell you childbirth isn't without its dangers. Even in today's day and age."

"That is true."

"If it is true, then I hope you will also remember with me who is in charge."

She swallowed. "You are speaking of God."

"I am." He rubbed her back, one of his hands tracing the length of her spine. "He is in charge of all our lives. And sometimes He has a plan for each of us that we don't necessarily find easy. I know that to be true for myself."

Thinking about the many decisions she'd had to make, Joanna couldn't deny Dwight's words. "It's true for me too," she said softly.

"That's why I think there has to be a reason that our Lord gave you the gifts one needs to be a midwife. I don't think He would have given you so much just to take it away."

Suddenly, all the hours she'd spent at Dorothy's side rushed back to her. She remembered the years she'd helped the woman, all the time listening to her explanations and, little by little, becoming braver and more proficient. None of it had been easy; there'd been many, many nights when she'd gone to bed exhausted and some mornings when she'd been so afraid she'd do something wrong that she'd been almost paralyzed by her doubts.

But still she had continued.

"I . . . I think I needed to remember that, Dwight."

"I hope you'll remember the many other moments in your career that were far happier. I hope you'll take the time to recall the many times you delivered healthy babies to grateful mothers." He smiled down at her. "I can't count the number of days in which you came home all aglow."

"There were many of those." Too many to count, but somehow she hadn't bothered to think of them in weeks.

"You've spoken to me often about the miracle of birth. You've given the glory to God. I'm not saying Cheryl's death was His fault alone, but maybe it was her time. Or, at the very least, maybe the fault wasn't yours alone."

He was right.

His voice softened. "Joanna, I canna force you to do

something you don't want to do. I know Susie doesn't want to do that either. But . . . I can't help but think it would be wrong to only dwell on one instance instead of looking for all the blessings that have happened—and that can happen."

"You're right."

"You really think so?" he teased.

"Like I told you, *mei shveshtah* came over, and she gave me a talking-to as well. I listened."

"*Gut.*" He kissed her brow. "So, will you speak to Susie?" he asked as he released her.

She knew she had to. But it was still going to be hard. "Dwight, I'm not the only midwife in the county."

"She's afraid she's going to have to hire Rose."

"Rose?" Belatedly, Joanna realized that she sounded horrified.

"Aha." With a look of triumph, Dwight pointed a finger at her. "You feel the same way about Rose as Susie does."

"Rose Borntreger is a very knowledgeable midwife." That wasn't a lie either. But what couldn't be denied was that Rose was also a rather unpleasant person. Joanna knew more than one woman who'd refused to have Rose deliver their second babies. It was generally thought that Rose didn't always make one of the most joyous occasions in a couple's life all that joyous.

"Please, Joanna? Just go talk to Susie."

"Fine. On one condition."

"Name it."

"Help me clean up this mess?"

"I will. And because I like you, I'll even bake you a pie."

"You're serious, aren't you?"

"Of course I am. I'm not going to allow you to ruin three pounds of blueberries, Joanna. That's criminal. Now, go get out the shortening. I'm going to make a crust."

She did as he asked, but she grumbled. "You're the only man I know who can bake better than me. It's not—"

"Natural?"

"Fair."

He laughed. "Blame my mother and grandmother. They taught me to cook so I'd stop following them around asking for food. My culinary skills have served me well too."

"You are the best-fed bachelor I know."

"Lucky for you, I live right next door to ya. Now give me a bowl and a pie plate."

She picked up one of the mason jars from the row on the countertop. "What should I do about all this jam?"

"No offense, Joanna, but I canna imagine who would want to eat that." He for one didn't exactly trust her canning. And who even knew how sweet or sour the berries would be. Joanna seemed to be missing some essential taste buds.

"I suppose you're right." Walking to the sink, she said, "I'll get started cleaning all this up."

"You clean, and I'll cook."

"We're a good team, aren't we?"

They really were. Actually, he was beginning to think they were a good pair for a lot of things. They evened each other out.

Glancing at her, noticing the way her eyes sparkled in a way they hadn't in weeks, his heart warmed. "There's no one I'd rather be with, Jo. Now, go turn on the oven."

She did as he asked without another word.

SIX

Within twenty minutes of her arrival at the Millers' on Sunday afternoon, Joanna realized that even if she had intended to refuse the mother-to-be's wishes, she was no match for Susie Miller. It wasn't a surprise. Not really. But still, it was a bit disheartening to realize that she couldn't stand her ground against a giddy mother-to-be.

To his credit, Dwight hadn't encouraged Susie at all. If anything, he'd seemed more worried about Joanna than his sister's wants. Once, he'd even given Marcus a look when Susie acted impatient with the way Joanna hesitated.

But in the end, Joanna did what she'd feared she would do from the moment she'd agreed to visit Susie in the first place. She was seriously contemplating being Susie's midwife. Oh, she still hadn't said yes, but she had agreed to give it more careful thought than before.

Susie looked mighty pleased about that.

Later, the four of them went out onto the Millers' back

patio and pulled up chairs around the firepit. Susie looked like a cat who'd just gotten a bowl of cream. Marcus appeared relieved. And Dwight? Well, Dwight kept casting concerned looks her way. Joanna shrugged them off as best she could. There was no doubt that later tonight she'd most likely be pacing and wondering if she could actually go through with it.

But for now?

Now she was just happy to feel almost like her regular self for the first time in months.

"Joanna, I guess you have a lot of stories about women in labor," Marcus said. "But I'm curious as to how all the husbands act during labor and delivery. Has any man been particularly memorable?"

As stressful as the mothers-to-be could be, the fathers-to-be were always a source of amusement for Joanna. "The husbands can be a handful, I'm afraid," she said with a laugh. "I've had expectant fathers gain as much weight as the women, complain about swollen knees and feet . . . And some even seem to go through almost as many labor pains as their wives."

Marcus grinned. "Surely not."

"Oh, yes." Remembering one of the funniest instances, she added, "But my favorite father-to-be was the man who fainted the moment I told his wife to start pushing."

"What?"

"There I was, coaching the mother, trying my best to be encouraging and all business, when the next thing I knew, the woman's husband fell in a heap to the floor. Of course, he had to go ahead and hit the side of his head, so he was bleeding too."

"What did you do?"

"Honestly, I didn't know what to do. Sometimes a woman will have a sister or her mother in the room, as well, but not this time. It was just the three of us."

"And two of you were occupied!" Susie said with a laugh.

"Indeed we were. I was in a bit of a pickle, for sure and for certain."

"Well, don't leave us wondering about what happened. What did you do?"

"It was the baby who cooperated the most. A minute or two later, the little girl was born. In no time, I got the babe settled in her mother's arms and then knelt down to help the father . . . who had just awakened."

"He missed his daughter's birth." Marcus shook his head. "That poor fella. I bet he felt terrible."

"He was embarrassed, but I don't think his wife minded too much. I surely didn't."

"Truly?" Susie reached for Marcus's hand.

"For sure." Remembering how flustered the poor man had been, she added, "He hadn't been a lot of help, if you want to know the truth."

Susie, Dwight, and Marcus all burst into laughter, and Joanna joined in. It felt good to remember that day. She'd been so consumed by bad memories lately that she'd

forgotten just how many humorous episodes she'd experienced over the years.

Susie smiled at her husband. "Marcus, that's something you're going to have to keep in mind."

"Got it. Don't faint. But if I do decide to lose consciousness, I'll do my best to stay out of the way—or at
least fall without incurring an injury."

"You better not faint on me. I'm going to need you."

"I don't plan on it." He held up Susie's hand and pressed
a kiss on her knuckles before looking back at Joanna.
"However, I'm hoping that Susie and I won't be having a
baby by ourselves . . ."

This was it. She couldn't put off the truth any longer.
"Susie, Marcus, I'm happy for you both. We've all known
one another for so long, and nothing will make me happier than to see your newborn babe. I'm sure you will be
wonderful parents."

Susie leaned forward. "Does that mean you've made
your final decision? Joanna, will you be my midwife?"

"I want to, Susie, but I'm not sure if I can."

"Why not?" Susie looked like she was struggling not
to cry.

Hating to disappoint a good friend so much, Johanna
closed her eyes, then plunged forward. "Something happened to my last mother-to-be . . ." Oh, but she didn't
want to do this.

"Go on, Jo," Dwight said quietly. "It will be all
right."

"You're starting to make me nervous," Marcus joked. "Just spit it out."

He was right. Hemming and hedging wasn't helping. Not one bit. "The mother had a condition I wasn't aware of and started bleeding while she was in labor. She . . . Well, she didn't make it."

Looking stricken, Susie inhaled sharply. "She died?"

"*Jah.*" Of course Joanna could add more explanations, but what did they help?

"What about the baby?"

"He survived. He is a healthy babe." He was perfect in every way. He just didn't have a mother.

Well, at last she had done what she'd needed to do. Shaking, she looked down at her feet. Even though she felt miserable, it was over. She'd given Susie and Marcus the truth. As hard as it would be to see them now, at least they wouldn't have any more secrets between them.

After several uncomfortable seconds passed, Dwight cleared his throat. "So, that is what we came over to tell you."

Lifting her head, Joanna cast a smile at Dwight. She was so very grateful for his friendship. He hadn't needed to take on any responsibility, yet here he was, helping her bear this burden.

"I'm sorry, but I'm still not sure what you are saying," Marcus said.

"Beg pardon?"

Susie shrugged. "Me either. Forgive me, but does that

mean that you will still be my midwife, or would you rather not?"

"You still want me to be? Even after everything that happened?"

"I think I now want you to be my midwife even more than I did before I heard your story," Susie said. "Joanna, you were able to save the baby even after the mother went into distress and died. I want a midwife who will be that dedicated."

"But—"

"I hear what you're saying, Joanna. And *jah*, to be sure, I am mighty sad for the woman. My heart breaks for her and her family. But I want a midwife I can trust to care for my baby no matter what happens. I want you, Joanna."

A giant lump had formed in her throat. Susie's words meant so much. "Marcus, do you feel the same way?"

"I want what Susie wants. And, if I'm being totally honest, I think you're giving yourself too much credit, Jo."

"Pardon me?"

"Don't get upset. Listen. I mean, you always say when a baby is born that the mother and the Lord allowed the miracle to take place and you were simply helping it happen. So I'm not real sure why you're so intent on taking on all the responsibility for this one situation."

Dwight raised his eyebrows at her. "What do you think about that?"

"I think maybe I should have talked to Marcus and Susie weeks ago."

"Do you have an answer?"

"May I tell you tomorrow morning?"

"Of course. But please, don't make me be with Rose."

She winked. "I will promise you that."

SEVEN

Realizing Joanna was both exhausted and rattled from the conversation that had just taken place, Dwight did his best to shuttle her out of the house after her announcement. Susie and Marcus had looked taken aback by the way Dwight stood up and blurted a flimsy excuse, but they hadn't argued. Instead, each had hugged Dwight and Joanna before sending them both on their way. Dwight knew he'd made the right decision when he saw Joanna breathe in the warm July air and visibly relax. Jo had never been one to particularly enjoy hot summer days.

They'd elected to walk to Susie's house and were now ambling home together through a field that was owned by one of Marcus's cousins. The field had fresh grass and a smattering of wildflowers. It was a pretty sight. That, combined with the lingering sun overhead, lent Dwight a feeling of calm he hadn't even realized he'd been missing.

"Every time I walk through this field, I get such a feeling of satisfaction, it always makes me wonder if I should've been a farmer."

Joanna sputtered. "You? Dwight, you love working in the lumberyard."

"It's true, I do. But that said, there's something about an open field in the summer that makes me feel as if everything is right and good in the world. Don't you think?"

Looking skeptical, she scanned the area carefully. At last she grinned. "*Jah*, I can see it feeling all right and good here . . . if one doesn't mind getting stung by bees." She waved a hand toward a patch of wayward clover. "They're everywhere, Dwight."

"Oh, they won't harm ya. They're just buzzing around the clover and dandelions."

"And wildflowers. And, uh, myself."

"If you ignore them, they'll ignore you. See, they're just looking for pollen."

"I suppose." She still looked wary, though.

Glad to see her not stewing about Susie, he continued to tease. "I never realized you were so frightened of bumblebees."

Joanna didn't disappoint. She lifted her chin and popped a hand on her hip. "I'm not afraid of them. I just don't want to get stung."

"Have you ever gotten stung before?" Maybe she'd had an allergic reaction he had forgotten about.

"*Nee*. I guess I've just always been afraid of the unknown." She wrinkled her nose. "At least where, um, bees are concerned."

Thinking about the two of them and how he'd been a little reluctant to tell her his feelings in case it ruined their friendship, Dwight said, "Uncharted territory can be scary, I suppose." When she looked at him in confusion, he added, "Well, you know . . . bee stings, relationships . . . life. Every day gives us something new to tackle. Ain't so?"

"That's true. I suppose I do need to stop worrying so much about new things. And maybe stop taking too much for granted too."

"Like what?"

"Like now." As they started walking again, she smiled at him. "It's a lovely day, the sun is out, and I'm walking with you. I mean . . . a longtime friend. That's a lot to be grateful for."

"You're exactly right. We do have a lot to be grateful for right now."

"Do you think it's silly that I have to remind myself about that?"

"*Nee.* I'm guilty of doing the same thing. My *dawdi* would have said that's my second nature, though."

"Oh?"

"Oh, *jah. Dawdi* was always telling me to stop over-thinking things and just enjoy them. Then, of course, he'd probably top it off with some trite phrase like 'Rain is just warm snow.'"

"Which means?"

"I couldn't tell ya. But I sure never would've told him that."

Her expression softened. "I'd forgotten about your grandfather. Boy, he was a *gut mann*."

"He was, but he was tough too." Rubbing his fingers, he said, "He was gifted in rapping my knuckles with a spoon every time I complained at the supper table, I'll tell you that."

"At least you have those memories of sitting down at the table with him. Both of my grandparents passed away when I was still a little girl."

Dwight smiled. "I am grateful, though he got a little crotchety in his old age. My mother would sometimes look like she was biting her tongue when he ordered her about." A memory flashed forward. "But I also remember finding her in the *dawdi haus*, sitting on his favorite chair and crying."

"Just because someone isn't perfect doesn't mean they won't be missed."

He laughed. "Listen to you. Spouting off good advice like him—or as if you were in a card shop."

"Oh, stop. I didn't say anything that we both haven't heard a hundred times."

"I haven't. What other bits of wisdom do you have for me?"

"None, now. And it's your loss too." Her lips twitched. It was obvious she was having a difficult time even pretending to look annoyed.

He nudged her shoulder. "I'm sorry for being so cheeky."

She looked up at him. Something new flickered in her eyes, echoing the very same thing he was feeling in his heart. It also made him wonder how so much time had passed without them seeing what had been there all along.

At least for him it had been.

"Joanna?"

"Hmm?"

"Do you ever wonder how we came to be so old?"

"'Old'? Speak for yourself."

"You know what I mean. I mean, here we are, both thirty years old. Thirty sounded ancient when we were seven."

Her teasing expression sobered, and a hint of despair slid in beside it. "Dwight, if we're going to discuss the state of our lives, you might as well finish that thought. We're thirty years old and never been married. We have no *kinner* either. Some might find that very sad."

"Hey, now. I didn't mean to make it sound so dire. It just occurred to me that the years went by fast."

"They did." She gazed toward the horizon. "I don't know what happened. One day all of us were walking to school together and the next we were graduating eighth grade."

"And starting our jobs."

"*Jah.* Before I knew it, I was following Dorothy around and helping her midwife as much as I could."

"And I worked at the lumberyard, trying to get promoted." Those years had passed in a blur.

"Then there were all those weddings."

"And we attended every single one of them." Though he would never admit it, many of them had felt bittersweet, especially since they'd gone to most of them together.

"Then, next thing we knew, we were waving our parents off as they moved on too. I've never blamed them," she added quickly. "I understood why mine wanted to live near my sister Marie."

"I didn't blame mine either. But now here we are. Both living alone in the very houses that we grew up in."

She stopped again, looking stricken. "Oh, my word, Dwight! You're making us sound so, so pathetic!"

"I am not. I'm only speaking the truth."

"*Nee*, it's more than that. You're practically making us sound like old folks tottering around our properties. We're barely thirty, you know."

"I haven't forgotten our ages. I'm merely pointing out that it's time to stop waiting until 'the right time' to do something with our lives."

"I haven't been waiting for anything," she retorted. Then, looking chagrined, she added, "I mean, I have a good career." Before he could do so much as raise his eyebrows, she added, "I mean, I did."

Dwight almost felt like apologizing. Like reassuring her that she was correct. That they had lots of time to figure out their lives. Lots of time to figure out *them*.

But in his heart, he didn't think that was the case. More important—at least to him—he didn't want to wait anymore. "All I'm saying is that maybe we shouldn't let too much more time pass before we get started doing all the other things we've planned. After all, one never knows what the future has in store for us."

She slowed. "You know, at first I thought you were just talking about things in general terms. But maybe you aren't? Is there something specific you have in mind?"

"*Jah.*" He couldn't lie about that.

"What is it?" Her pretty hazel eyes sharpened. "What, specifically, are you referring to, Dwight?"

They were almost at their houses now. It was time to share more, but he didn't want to blurt out something so important without doing some planning. After all, there would only be one first time for him to share just how much she meant to him.

And so—much to his shame—he chickened out. "Oh, nothing much. I'm just talking."

"You're just talking?" She looked frustrated. "Are you sure about that?"

"Of course. Oh, look. Here we are."

"Yes, here we are. Home again." She took a step toward her house but didn't go any farther. "So, I guess I should thank you for taking me over to see Susie and Marcus."

"You don't have to thank me for anything."

"Still, *danke.*"

Even that small bit of thanks made him uncomfortable. "I'll see you later, Joanna. I've, ah, got some chores around the house that I really need to get to."

"Oh. Well, I do too. I'll see ya."

"There's no doubt about that. I will be seeing ya soon." He gave her a small wave before walking back to his house.

But as he opened his door, his mind was already making plans. And none of it had anything to do with household chores.

EIGHT

Well, that had been strange. Joanna wasn't quite sure what had just happened, but she was pretty convinced she and Dwight had circled around their relationship. Even more, for a moment there she'd been sure Dwight was about to reveal his feelings for her.

Worse, she'd been eager to hear those words. Not only because she was eager to actually hear what Dwight would say, but also because she wanted to tell him the same things.

She might be brave in a lot of ways, but she was afraid to be the first one to say she didn't feel just friendship for him. But, yet again, it seemed they'd both been too afraid to reveal what was hidden in their hearts.

Gazing around her living room and kitchen, noticing that as usual everything was in its place and scrupulously clean—since she'd stopped cooking—Joanna walked out her back door to the patio. At first glance, the space was nothing special. It was simply a large rectangle made of older mismatched brick, big enough to hold a good amount of furniture, a grill, and a firepit.

It was so much more than that.

Years and years ago, her father had found a big supply of bricks on sale and bought the lot of them. Then, for weeks, he and Caleb had discussed how to arrange them. Herringbone? Long strips? In a log-cabin pattern?

It had driven her mother mad. Practically every Saturday morning, she'd said, "John, you fix this and now." Oh, but Joanna and Emma had giggled about that in the privacy of their room.

Then, one day, just when Joanna was sure her mother was going to start laying bricks herself, *Daed* and Caleb had begun. And the outcome had indeed been an intricate log-cabin design. Somehow they'd even managed to make use of the darker and lighter hues. It was a beautiful thing. So beautiful their mother pretended she'd never complained about the project even once.

Even now, ten or twelve years later, it was still perfect.

Sitting down on the couch rocker, Joanna looked at the patterned brick and thought about how so many things had had to come together in order for the patio to become a reality—from the many workers making and firing the bricks to the company sorting them and putting them on sale to her father's purchase to even her brother's knack for design. If any of those things hadn't happened, she wouldn't now have this wonderful work of art to enjoy day after day.

That's when she realized it was a good metaphor for her and Dwight. Just like the bricks, the two of them had had other goals in mind. But now it was time to appreciate their differences and the fact that they weren't fresh and new . . . but they could combine to make something perfectly lovely together. If they had the patience to see it through.

Though she had so many worries on her shoulders right now, there was one thing she couldn't deny: she and Dwight were meant to be together, so much so that they were worth the trouble too.

She knew the end result would be so right.

She also knew there was someone she needed to talk to, and that was Dorothy. Craning her neck, she looked at the phone shanty she shared with her neighbors in the distance. If she wasn't mistaken, it was empty.

It was time to call her mentor.

Now that Dorothy lived in Pinecraft in Florida, she had changed a bit. She was still Amish, but she had elected to become part of a New Order Amish community there. They worshipped in an actual church building and often signed up for community and worldwide mission work. And Dorothy now had a phone in the small cottage that she shared with an old friend of hers who was also a widow. About half the time Joanna called, either Dorothy or her roommate answered the phone. The other half? It seemed Dorothy was either doing volunteer work or at the beach, and Joanna had to leave a message.

Walking into the phone shanty, Joanna dialed her mentor's number from memory and was delighted that Dorothy herself picked up the phone on the second ring.

"Joanna, what a nice surprise," she said after Joanna said hello. "How are things going?"

"Well . . ." she began, then stopped abruptly. Dorothy sounded too chatty, almost like she'd been warned that Joanna might be calling her. "Wait a minute. Have my parents said anything to you about me?"

"I'm afraid they have."

Her stomach sank. This was just what she'd feared would happen. Her parents had confided Joanna's faults, and now Dorothy was going to lose faith in her. "What did they say? I mean, if you don't mind sharing."

"They didn't tell me all that much, Jo. Only that they thought you had been experiencing some difficulties of late." Sympathy colored her words.

Sympathy, not judgment. Closing her eyes, Joanna knew she should have known better. Dorothy wasn't one to invent problems. She liked facts. "I have had some difficulties lately," she said. "The truth is that one of my mothers . . . Well, she died, Dorothy."

A full second passed before the other woman responded. "Oh, Jo. That must have been mighty hard. You'd best tell me what happened."

Bolstered by the previous conversations, Joanna relayed everything as quickly and as matter-of-factly as possible. She ended by sharing the latest news—that she had just agreed to be Susie's midwife. "Do you think I'm making a mistake?"

This time Dorothy didn't hesitate. "No, I do not."

Joanna raised her eyebrows. "You sound so sure."

"I'm sure because I believe in you, Jo. Plus, it sounds as if Susie believes in you too."

That startled a laugh. Honestly, it was as if Dorothy was a mind reader. "I think she does."

"Then don't betray that faith by concentrating only on doubts."

"I won't."

"*Gut*. Now tell me what else you've been doing."

That was Dorothy. Caring and kind but also a little brusque. She also didn't dwell on the negative. Joanna needed to stop doing that as well. "I've been attempting to cook."

"Oh, *nee*."

"You aren't the only one who's reacted that way," Joanna said with a laugh. "And, just in case you were wondering, I'm as awful a cook now as I've ever been."

"Are you surprised?"

"Kind of. I thought maybe I just needed practice. But I seem to have been mistaken. No matter how many times I try to make a cake that rises or soup that doesn't taste like dishwater, I still fail."

"I guess it's not wrong to want to try. Um, why, exactly, have you been cooking? You've never enjoyed it."

"I was looking for something to fill my time."

"Maybe you should do something else. I like walking on the beach now."

"I'd like that, too, if I had Siesta Key nearby." Just thinking about Siesta Key's wide beaches with sugary-soft white sand made her sigh.

"You should come down here to visit one day soon, Jo. We would have a grand time. I know all sorts of places to take you now."

"Really? Tell me what you've been doing."

"I will . . . as soon as you tell me about Dwight."

Honestly, Dorothy really was a mind reader! "Dwight? Oh, he's *gut*."

"I know that. I want to know what is happening with the two of you. Is there something new?"

"Maybe." Thinking about the silly conversation that had taken place just an hour ago made her smile.

"Come, now, Joanna. You know that's not all I want to hear. And?"

Even in the confines of the phone shanty, she could feel her cheeks heat. "And . . . we've started to become closer."

"Thank heaven for that."

This was getting a little too personal. As much as she admired and liked Dorothy, these feelings Joanna was experiencing with Dwight were too fresh to share. "Now, may we please talk about you for a moment?"

"Of course. Let me tell you about the alligators Mary and I saw on our walk last week."

"Alligators?"

"To be sure. They were sunning in someone's front yard."

As Dorothy talked, Joanna giggled and felt her heart lifting. She also felt a new sense of peace. Yet again, she wished she hadn't shut everyone out and attempted to sort through all of her problems on her own.

It seemed that she might be thirty years old, but she also had much to learn, both in romance and in life.

NINE

Joanna would've been lying if she said her life had gotten easier since word spread that she was accepting patients again. Now, three weeks after she'd agreed to be Susie's midwife, everything felt much harder. At least every couple of days a woman would stop by her house, her cheeks all flushed with happiness, and ask Joanna to be the midwife.

With the exception of one woman who had a wealth of complications and needed to be in a hospital for delivery, Joanna had agreed. Feeling a bit overwhelmed, she wrote down appointments on her calendar, listened to babies' heartbeats, tried to alleviate expectant mothers' concerns, patted hands, gave hugs of reassurance, and did her best to always be positive. These were all things she'd done dozens and dozens of times. However, now she felt as if she were merely going through the motions.

She still experienced a lot of dark moments. During those times, all her fears would tumble down and get the best of her. Her hands would literally start shaking as she contemplated everything that might possibly go wrong during delivery. Only falling on her knees and praying for strength and God's will helped.

Well, only prayer and Dwight's now constant presence in her life. It turned out Dwight could be a rather exuberant suitor—much to her surprise and happiness. He constantly stopped by with flowers or a card or some little trinket he'd "just happened to see" that made him think of her.

Here she was, thirty years old, something of an expert when it came to pregnancy and delivery. However, she was hopelessly naïve when it came to falling in love. Honestly, she'd probably blushed more in the last two weeks than she had in the last thirty years.

"Knock-knock," Susie called out from the half-open doorway. "Are you ready for me, Joanna?"

Realizing she'd been sitting at her kitchen table mooning over a giant heart shaped cookie Dwight had presented to her the night before, Joanna sprang to her feet. "Of course, Susie. Come on in out of the heat. Would you like something to drink? Some lemonade, perhaps?"

"I've heard you're mighty busy now. Do you have time for that?"

"Of course I do." She winked. "I schedule extra time for longtime friends."

"In that case, I'd love a glass of lemonade." Susie sank down onto a chair and kicked her legs out in front of her. "It's so warm, I couldn't bear the thought of wearing tennis shoes, but these little rubber flip-flops don't offer much support on my walks."

Setting the icy-cold drink in front of her, Joanna gazed at her worriedly. "Did you walk over here by yourself?"

"Oh, *nee*. Marcus came with me. He's over seeing Dwight right now."

"Does he want to be here for your appointment?" Most husbands did.

"*Nee*. He said he'd come in next time. I told him I wanted to be alone with you for this first visit."

"Any special reason you didn't want him here?"

"Only that I was afraid he'd get worried by my questions."

"Do you have some concerns?"

Susie nodded. "I'm tired all the time, and my feet and ankles are swollen, but all my friends and *mei mamm* said that didn't happen until they were almost due." Before Joanna could say a word, she added, "Plus, I'm huge! Do you think I'm too big for being six months along?"

"Susie, I think it's time we checked you out a bit, *jah*?"

"Maybe so." Susie wrinkled her nose. "Tell me the truth. Do you think I'm being silly?"

"Not at all." Resting a hand on the back of the chair, Joanna said, "Come now, let's get you in the examining room."

As Susie followed her, still asking question after question, Joanna felt all the worries she'd been harboring slowly fade away. Susie, with her nervousness and excitement, was exactly what Joanna had needed to feel better. She was open and friendly, and of course they also had a long friendship.

But it was more than that. Susie was exactly the type of patient Joanna had dreamt of working with one day. Though of course every pregnancy was different, Joanna knew she was at her best with women who, beyond the normal medical care, really just needed some hand-holding and reassurance.

Moments later, after she'd measured Susie's belly, taken her weight and blood pressure, and listened to the baby's heartbeat on the monitor, Joanna helped her back to a sitting position.

Susie didn't wait even a minute to blurt out her question. "So, am I too big?"

"*Nee*. You are just right."

"Just right, how?" Her eyes widened. "Could I be having twins?"

"I'm afraid not. I only heard one strong heartbeat."

"What does that mean?"

It was hard not to start laughing. "It means that you are pregnant with one healthy babe, not two."

"Okay, one babe is *gut*."

"I think so too."

Susie held out her right leg. "But my feet are enormous. Shouldn't we be worried?"

"*Nee*. Your feet are a bit swollen, but you were just out walking in the heat, *jah*?"

"*Jah* . . ."

"When you get home, put your feet up, drink lots of water, and rest some. The swelling should subside."

"That's it?"

"That's it. I promise, you're going to be just fine."

With some surprise, Joanna realized that she truly felt that way too. She wasn't worried about losing Susie or the babe or about making a mistake. It was abundantly evident that Susie was much different than Cheryl Fisher. Her friend was healthy, at a good weight, and was getting a lot of rest. Cheryl, on the other hand, had had multiple health problems that she'd neglected to tell Joanna. If Cheryl had shared any of her issues, Joanna would have told her she needed to deliver her baby in the hospital.

Only now did Joanna realize she'd been so consumed by guilt that she'd forgotten all the extenuating circumstances surrounding Cheryl's death.

Susie exhaled like the weight of the world had just been lifted off her shoulders. "*Danke*, Joanna. This is why I couldn't bear to have Rose as my midwife. She probably would have gotten irritated about me asking so many foolish questions."

"I don't know if she would have, but I'm glad I'll be with you through this journey, Susie. It's a blessing for me." Walking to the examining room's door, Joanna said, "Come back to the kitchen when you're ready. I'm going to get you a cool glass of water and a little snack."

"You have food?"

"It's just cookies and pretzels from the store. I promise I didn't make any of it."

"Pretzels sound *wunderbaar*."

Joanna found herself chuckling as she walked back to the kitchen. Susie was a delight, for sure and for certain. And her husband . . . Well, he was standing in the kitchen with Dwight. Both of them looked like fish out of water.

"I'm sorry, did you knock on the door and I didn't hear you?"

Looking embarrassed, Dwight answered. "Sorry, Jo. Marcus started worrying about Susie, so we came over here right away. But then we didn't know where to go. I didn't think you'd mind us letting ourselves in."

"I don't."

"Where's Susie?" Marcus asked.

"She's getting dressed. She'll be here soon." Joanna snapped her fingers. "Which reminds me. I told her I'd get her some cold water and a snack. Would you men like an oatmeal cookie?" Reaching into a cabinet, she pulled out a bakery box. "I promise that I didn't bake them."

"A cookie sounds great, Jo. *Danke*," Dwight said.

Marcus was still looking down the hall. "Is she all right? Do I need to go find her?"

Marcus was a good friend, but no way did she want him wandering around her house. "*Nee*. I think Susie will find her way back here soon enough. Now, how about a cookie?"

"*Danke.*" Marcus sat down, but he looked a little at loose ends.

Glancing Dwight's way, she saw that he was just as amused as she was. She decided to simply get glasses of water for all of them as well as a dish of pretzels and a plate of cookies.

"Joanna, I feel so much better now. I'm— Marcus?"

Her husband had jumped up. He strode to her side and walked her back to the table. "I was worried. I should've come over here too. Are you all right?"

"I'm fine. Stop worrying so much! Goodness. Sometimes I think you forget that women have been having babies for years and years."

Susie's confident tone was such an about-face, Joanna almost burst into giggles. She was starting to think maybe it was best that Susie had wanted to be seen on her own. Marcus was going to need a lot of hand-holding as well.

"What do you think, Joanna?" Marcus asked.

"I think that you both are going to be wonderful-*gut* parents," Joanna said. "Now, sit down, sip some water, and eat a cookie."

When they both sat down immediately, Dwight winked at her. She winked back and smiled. Things were better now. They really were.

TEN

"What was all that about?" Dwight asked moments after his sister and her husband left. "Though it was amusing, I've never seen you practically force-feed people cookies before."

"I canna share too much, but it seems both your sister and her husband had a lot of questions saved up." She shrugged. "Sometimes all a Nervous Nellie needs is something specific to do. Even if it's just eating a cookie."

Her comment took him by surprise, but he supposed it did have some merits. "They did seem a bit calmer when they left. I guess you've encountered jittery parents-to-be before?"

"Once or twice." She smiled. "It works every time. But, ah, don't tell either Marcus or Susie that's what I was doing. I don't want to hurt their feelings or make them feel like I'm not taking their worries seriously."

"Of course not." Picking up another cookie, he leaned back. "I didn't see you eat any, however."

A new, sweeter expression filled her gaze. "Well, I bought those cookies for my patients. And I just happened to have a very big cookie of my own to eat."

Looking over at the pie-sized cookie on the counter, satisfaction filled him. Two days ago, on a whim, he'd stopped by Miller's Bakery and ordered the cookie for Joanna. He'd thought it might make her smile. Now, seeing just how much his gesture had meant to her, he was even more certain it had been a good idea. "I guess you do," he said lightly.

"You've been spoiling me, Dwight."

He knew Joanna well. He knew her moods, knew when she was upset about something . . . or especially pleased. He was even familiar with the times her temper flared. But he had to admit that her current behavior was a bit confusing. If he didn't know her better, he would say that she was suddenly bashful and shy.

Hmm. Maybe his Joanna, who was so independent and strong and could handle any number of problems, was needing him to lead her now. "Jo, as far as I'm concerned, you've been needing to be spoiled."

She looked taken aback. "What does that mean?"

"It means exactly what you think it does. It means that although we are good friends, I think we should be more than that. Furthermore, I want to be the person who spoils you." He stood up and walked to her side and reached for her hand. "I want to be the man who makes sure that you're taken care of."

Tentative hope filled her eyes, though she clasped his fingers tightly. "Dwight, everything you're saying is sweet, but . . . are you sure about this? I mean, I'm not easy. I have doubts and worries. And even though I've been anxious about my call to be a midwife, I don't want to give it up."

"I don't want you to."

"It means that I'll be gone sometimes in the middle of the night. Sometimes I'll even miss things that we've planned." She worried her bottom lip. "Suppers might not get made."

"I've been making my own supper for a while, Joanna. Believe it or not, I could even make yours, which would probably be a good thing."

"It would certainly be more edible!"

Remembering her last attempt at lasagna, which had ended up a runny, undercooked mess, he said, "I can assure you that it would."

"Goodness. You seem to have an answer for everything."

"I don't. You know as well as I do that I've had a lot of missteps and made mistakes. I've been hesitant and overthinking us. I think what I've actually been doing is trying to pigeonhole the two of us into a neat arrangement. Into something just like everyone else's relationship. But maybe I don't want 'easy.' Maybe I just want 'us.'" He stood over her and squeezed her hand. "What do you think about that?"

Joanna got to her feet as well. "That has to be the nicest thing I've ever heard."

He felt like grimacing. "If that's the nicest thing, then I need to remedy that. You deserve sweeter words and more of them." Pleased that nothing separated them now, Dwight wrapped his arms around her waist. Held her close enough that she had to lift her chin to look into his eyes.

When her lips parted slightly, there was only one thing to do, and that was to kiss her. Afraid to startle her—or to be reading all the signals wrong—he simply brushed his lips against hers, then paused, half afraid she was going to turn skittish and pull away. Instead, she pressed her palms to his chest and kissed him back.

And then?

Well, then he didn't need another sign for him to follow his heart. Dwight held Joanna more securely in his arms and kissed her the way he'd always wanted to. And when they parted at last, her cheeks were flushed, her expression languid, and she still had her palms resting against his chest. He liked the weight of them there.

Covering one of her hands with his own, he said gently, "Are you okay?"

"Oh, yes."

He grinned. His Joanna seemed so dreamy. It looked good on her. "*Gut*. Well, I'm going to be on my way now."

"Truly? So soon?"

"I need to get back to the farm. And . . . didn't you say you have another patient coming today?"

Still appearing bemused, she glanced at the clock.

Then abruptly stiffened. "Oh! Oh, my word! I've gotta go, Dwight! My next patient will be here in twenty minutes. I need to get the examining room set up for my next mom-to-be."

"Don't worry. I bet she can cool her heels for a moment."

"Maybe."

Realizing he needed to leave right then and there, he pressed his lips to her forehead, right above her eyebrows. "Come by my *haus* when you're done for the day."

"All right. I will," she said as she disappeared down the hall.

When Dwight walked out her door again, he realized everything had changed between them. Now all he had to do was figure out how to make sure she didn't even consider hesitating when he eventually got up the nerve to propose.

ELEVEN

~⌒⌒~

Joanna wasn't one to be outwardly rude, but enough was enough! Ever since she'd sat down in Emma's lovely living room, her sister had looked like she was very amused by a secret joke. It was getting irritating.

"Emma, you need to stop smirking at me," she said at last.

"No way. All my life, you've been so organized, thoughtful, and serious. Whenever I've been confused about something, you've always had the perfect answer. I always felt like I should've been smarter and wiser. Until today."

"I haven't always had the perfect answer." Surely she hadn't been that smug?

"*Nee*, it was pretty much always," Emma countered, her expression gleeful. "It doesn't matter now, though. At long last, I have the upper hand! No way am I going to give that up."

"I think you're making quite a fuss out of nothing."

"Oh, no, I'm not. Jo, from the moment you came over,

you've been distracted. You keep looking out the window too. Honestly, I don't think you've heard a single word I've said."

It sounded like she'd been awfully rude. "I'm sorry. I haven't meant to act so distracted. I guess I'm just tired. I've had a lot of patients lately." Plus, she hadn't been sleeping all that well.

"I can believe that. But I don't think that's the only thing that's going on."

"Oh?"

"Oh, yes! Joanna, you're in love."

Though she was tempted to argue with her sister the way they used to back when they were in their teens, she didn't dare. Joanna might have been smarter in school, but Emma was always better at getting her way. She could be fairly devious too. So devious and wily, she'd won every board game they'd ever played.

Then there was the other reason Joanna didn't want to argue. It was because Emma might just be right. Shifting uncomfortably, she bit her lip.

Emma noticed. Triumph gleamed in her eyes. "Ha! You're not saying a word!"

Joanna rolled her eyes. "You always were a sore winner."

"Does that mean what I think it does? Joanna Zimmerman, are you finally in love?"

"*Jah*. I mean . . . I think so?" She knew she'd spouted off a question, but honestly, she was rather stunned over Dwight's sudden courtship. And then there was that kiss.

Of course she'd been kissed before. But it had never been like that.

Because it had never been Dwight. That was the difference.

"I'm not exactly sure."

Emma scooted so she was completely facing her. Looking less smug and far more concerned, she murmured, "What's going on?"

"Dwight is courting me, and it's been lovely."

"Why, that's wonderful."

"*Jah*. It is."

"If it's so wonderful-*gut*, why do you look so upset? What's wrong?"

"Oh, I don't know. I guess this change feels rather unexpected." Realizing that she wasn't explaining it very well, she added, "I kind of feel like we're venturing into new territory, and I don't know how to act."

Emma sighed. "Joanna, your big brain is getting the best of you."

Well now. That was rather blunt. "Pardon me?"

"You are overthinking everything. Dwight is a good man. You are smart, kind, and caring. A perfect match for him! I have no doubt that the two of you will be happy together."

Her sister was probably right. But just because she was, that didn't make her feel any better. "I canna turn off my head just because I should, you know."

"I know." Emma leaned back, seeming to consider

Joanna's words for a few more minutes. Then, looking more determined than ever, she leaned forward. "Jo, do you remember what you told me when I got pregnant on my honeymoon?"

"Not really. All I remember is being happy for you and Marcus."

Emma smiled. "*Shveshtah*, you told me that just because something is unexpected, it doesn't mean that it's not a blessing. You've given me a lot of good advice, but I canna think of any other words of wisdom that resonated more with me." Folding her hands over her midsection, she added, "I happen to think it's something that you need to heed as well."

"I guess that statement does ring true for a lot of things. Maybe even for me and Dwight."

"*Nee*, I *know* it does, and especially for you and Dwight. Although, I'm sorry, but if you polled the rest of our family and friends, they'd all tell you that you and Dwight falling in love isn't unexpected at all." Crossing her legs, she added, "As a matter of fact, you might be the only one who is surprised."

Joanna's retort froze on her lips. Because the only other person she could think of who might have been surprised was Dwight.

Huh. Maybe they were perfect for each other after all.

TWELVE

TWO MONTHS LATER

Joanna jolted awake the moment two sharp raps hit her door, even though it was the middle of the night. She reckoned her ability to awaken in an instant was a side effect of her chosen occupation. Babies never seemed to want to be born in the light of day.

Figuring it was either Sarah's or Anna's time—the two women had started to see her well into their third trimester—Joanna shuffled to the door, already anticipating any problems she might need to be mentally prepared for.

She was, however, stunned to see Dwight.

"Praise God that you're such a light sleeper. I feared I was going to have to knock on your bedroom window."

"You would've scared me half to death if you'd done that," she replied.

Looking at him more closely in the dim light, she noticed that he had on dark pants, an untucked shirt, a straw hat, and bare feet. The blond hair that she could see was standing up this way and that. She'd never seen him so unkempt. "What has happened?" she asked, pulling the collar of her robe closer together.

"It's Susie. Marcus's *bruder* just knocked on my door and told me that she's in labor."

"Really? She isn't due for another few weeks."

"I guess the baby doesn't know that. Joanna, she needs you now."

"All right, then," she said, amazed at how calm she now felt. It happened every time. No matter how worried she might be about her general life or her past decisions, when babies were involved, a sense of calm always filled her. "I'll go get dressed, get my medical bag, and head over to Susie within fifteen minutes. Tell your sister and Marcus that I won't be long."

"Oh, no. You're not going out in the dark night on your own. I'm going to take you."

"Are you sure?"

"Positive. I'll meet you back here in ten minutes."

Arguing over that would only waste precious time. "*Danke*, Dwight."

As soon as they parted, she slipped on her most comfortable dress—a dark-gray one of the softest cotton. It was a little big; one of the mothers-to-be she'd delivered had made it for her three years ago when she'd been a little heavier than she was now. But because of that, it was her favorite midwife gown. The dark color hid any number of stains, and its roominess made the hours helping a mother through labor that much easier.

After slipping on her *kapp* and a pair of her most comfortable tennis shoes, she reached for her bag that she'd placed on a bench near the kitchen and hurried to the door. If she'd had more time, Joanna would have made herself a piece of toast and brewed a pot of coffee. Now she would just have to hope and pray that Marcus or one of their neighbors would bring her a cup sometime in the next couple of hours.

Dwight was striding up her walkway when she stepped outside. His shirt was tucked in, boots were on his feet, and it was obvious he'd washed his face and smoothed back his hair. She was slightly disappointed. She'd rather liked seeing him unkempt—it felt as if she was seeing a private part of him that he never shared with other people.

Only then did she realize he was also holding two large paper cups in his hands.

"Is that *kaffi*?"

He chuckled. "Of course. Would I be bringing you anything else at three in the morning?"

"Is that the time? I didn't even look."

"I'm grateful you heard my knock," he said as he handed her a steaming cup of plain black coffee, just the way she liked it. "I was afraid you'd be sleeping too hard."

She paused to take a sip, enjoying the feel of the hot liquid gliding down her throat. "I think my subconscious must stay awake while the rest of me sleeps. For some reason, I rarely ever hear the door when I'm in the kitchen, but I always jolt wide-awake whenever someone knocks on the door in the middle of the night."

He took her medical bag from her as they started walking. "Thank the good Lord. But you need a cell phone, Jo. At least then your patients could call you from a phone shanty. Or, if they were New Order, from their house."

"I've been doing all right so far."

"Not me. I was a nervous wreck, wondering what I was gonna do if you didn't come to the door."

She squeezed his arm. "You shouldn't have worried so much. I don't need a cell phone. I haven't slept through a babe's birth yet."

"I'll talk to the bishop for you, if you'd like."

"There's no need for that. And, just for your information, if I thought it was necessary, I would visit Bishop Schlabach myself. Now, take a deep breath, Dwight, and try to relax. Susie will be all right." To her surprise, she truly felt that way. No longer did she have a hundred doubts about her abilities as a midwife. Dorothy's reminder all those weeks ago that the Lord was in charge had been mighty helpful. It had relieved so many of her selfish fears.

After they'd walked in a comfortable silence for a spell, Joanna pointed to the sky. "Look at the moon! It's a lovely one tonight. Ain't so?"

"Hmm?" He lifted his head. "*Jah*, it is a *gut* one."

"It's almost full, and it's so big. I feel like the Lord lassoed it toward us so it could light our way."

Dwight, who'd been sipping his drink, started coughing. After he caught his breath, a burst of laughter rushed out. "Lassoing a moon? Where did you come up with such a thing?"

"I don't know. I guess it was a fanciful thought." However, she didn't care if she sounded ridiculous or not. All that mattered was that Dwight didn't look quite so upset and worried.

"I know it was."

She shrugged. "I don't think it matters, anyway. You've stopped frowning at long last."

"It's not my fault that I'm a mess. Susie is my little sister."

"Susie is twenty-six years old and in perfect health. She'll be fine." When he still frowned, she squeezed his arm again. "If you are like this with your sister, Lord help us all when your wife goes into labor. We're going to have to sedate you or something."

After taking another sip of his coffee, Dwight shook his head. "*Nee*, I'm going to be far better when it's my wife."

"And why is that?" She'd kept her tone light, though in truth her insides were tingling nervously. Had he meant what she thought he did?

He smiled softly. "Why do you think, Jo? Could it be that perhaps *mei frau* will already have so much experience with childbirth that nothing will take her off guard?"

Her heart melted. Just melted. But since it wasn't the

time or the place to dissolve into a mess of happy tears, she did her best to sound pert. "Is this your poor excuse of a marriage proposal, Dwight Eicher?"

"*Nee.*" His lips twitched as he visibly attempted not to laugh. "But if it was . . . what would you say?"

She stilled, so ready to announce that she would say yes. Of course she would say yes! However, sharing that felt like too much. Especially now.

But she had to say something, didn't she? After all, Dwight had just been brave enough to put his feelings out in the open.

Joanna took a deep breath, attempting to give herself a moment . . . then spied the perfect opportunity to postpone the inevitable.

"My word. There's Marcus!" She waved at him when he opened the door farther and stepped outside.

"Joanna. Praise God! Come in here quick. We need you."

After hastily grabbing her medical bag from Dwight and passing her empty cup into his hands, she rushed forward.

Dwight called out, "Jo, hold on. You didn't answer me."

Pausing only long enough to smile at him, she said, "It seems you're going to have to wait a bit, Dwight. I'm a little busy right now." Then she hurried to Marcus's side and followed him into the house.

But she had a feeling she wasn't going to forget Dwight's sweet words anytime soon.

THIRTEEN

"I'm so glad you're here at last, Joanna," Marcus said as he ushered her down the hall. "It's been mighty hard, waiting on you."

The comment stung a bit. A full hour hadn't passed since Dwight had first knocked on her door. "I got here as soon as I could."

He turned to her. "I'm sorry. I didn't mean that waiting on you was hard. It was everything else."

Marcus looked so tense, Joanna knew she needed more information before walking to Susie's side. Placing her hand over his on the knob, she stopped him from opening the door. "Marcus, what is going on?"

Obviously aggrieved, he said, "See, Susie started having contractions two hours ago, but she wouldn't let me send for you. She thought they were Braxton-Hicks pains. It's been mighty frustrating."

"I imagine so. How is she doing? Is Susie alone right now?"

"*Jah*. When I offered to have Ruth from next door come sit with her, she said she wanted a few minutes to herself." Looking hurt, he added, "I'm at a loss on how to help her, Jo. Susie even snapped at me when I tried to tell her to breathe more deeply."

Though Susie sounded like practically every other mother-to-be that she'd assisted, Joanna did her best to sound surprised and sympathetic. "Oh, my! Well, let me go in and check on her." She smiled reassuringly. "Try not to worry so much."

"What should I do?"

Knowing that busy hands helped anxious husbands, she said, "I'm going to need some towels and sheets and a clean bowl of hot water and a few washcloths."

"Anything else?"

"Oh, yes. I'd like a cup of crushed ice for Susie. And a cup of coffee for me, if you could."

"You want *kaffi* right now?"

"*Jah*, Marcus. A big cup, if you please. Get Dwight to help you. He knows how I like it." She slipped into their bedroom before he could say another word.

She found Susie wearing a pink loose-fitting linen gown. She was sitting in her rocking chair and staring out the window.

When she didn't move an inch when Joanna entered the room, Joanna got a little worried. "Susie?"

"You're here!" Susie turned to face her.

Joanna noticed that Susie's eyes looked swollen and

that she had tear tracks running down her cheeks. Hurrying to her side, she said, "Are you crying? What's wrong, dear?"

Susie swiped an eye. "Nothing. Other than I'm uncomfortable, scared that the babe is too early, and these contractions hurt a lot more than I thought they would."

"Let's not worry about the baby coming too early just yet. As far as the contractions? Well, I'm sure they do hurt. Honestly, some women have told me that they can take one's breath away. But you're tough, Susie. I know you can do this."

Susie swiped at the stray tear that meandered down her cheek. "I hope so."

As much as her heart went out to her, Joanna knew that what Susie needed was a bit of tough love. "No, no, no," she said firmly. "Susie Miller, you stop that right now."

Eyes wide, her patient hiccupped. "Excuse me?"

"You heard me," Joanna said as she picked up Susie's wrist and took her pulse. "Sounding weak and worried is no way to talk. You need to be positive!"

"I'll try."

"You must do better than that. Come now," she encouraged, no doubt sounding like a cheerleader. "You can do this, Susie. I know you can."

Looking a tad fiercer, Susie nodded. "You're right. I can."

Joanna smiled. "There you go."

"Oh, Jo. I'm so glad you're here."

Joanna hugged her friend before guiding her to the bed. "I'm glad I'm here too," she said as she arranged the pillows behind Susie.

"I'm sorry it's the middle of the night."

"It's a baby's prerogative to choose when he or she wants to be born, I fear." Joanna winked. "More than one mother has told me that it's good practice for living with a newborn."

Susie smiled just as a contraction hit her hard. "Oh, here's another one."

Joanna placed her hand on Susie's belly and felt that it was a strong and even contraction. She glanced at the time and made a mental note of it as well. "How long have you been having these?"

"A couple of hours."

"And how far apart are they now?"

Susie looked at the clock next to the bed. "Seven minutes or so?"

Glad for the kerosene light on the bedside table and the flashlight in her bag, Joanna stood up. "I think it's time I checked to see how things are coming along. Let me go wash my hands and get some towels and such from Marcus."

"Can . . . can you ask him to come back?"

"Indeed I can, dear. I'm sure he'll be here in a moment."

Retrieving her flashlight and a better watch, she slipped out of the room and walked to the kitchen. There,

Marcus stood next to Dwight watching the percolator on the stove brew coffee. His hands were full of towels and sheets.

He looked a bit pale too.

"Marcus, Susie's asking for you."

"At last."

Noticing that he was about to toss the linens onto the kitchen counter, she shook her head. "Oh, no, you don't. Bring those things to the bedroom and place two towels on the bed, if you please. I'm going to wash my hands, and then I'll be right in."

After the door closed, she realized she might as well have saved her breath. It was obvious Marcus was aware of no one but his wife.

FOURTEEN

Joanna had come out, drunk a glass of water, and washed her hands before returning to Susie's side. Dwight had asked her if she needed anything, but after getting another cup of coffee, she'd shaken her head.

After twenty minutes, then thirty minutes, passed, Dwight came to the conclusion he was not going to be able to merely sit in his sister's living room and watch the clock. He needed to do something besides worry about his sister and Joanna.

He decided to make some soup.

He knew it was late summer—not the usual season for hot soup—but he didn't let that bother him. He could cook, although it wasn't like he had a wealth of recipes in his head. But any man could chop vegetables and boil a chicken.

So, after investigating a bit in Susie's refrigerator, freezer, and cabinets, he pulled out a bag of frozen chopped chicken, some onions, celery, and carrots, and began. He diced the vegetables, shoveled them and the chicken into a pot of water, then discovered some frozen cubes of chicken bouillon and tossed that in too. When all that was boiling, he cleaned up the worst of the mess.

Then he heard Susie cry out, followed by the low murmur of Marcus and Joanna.

Realizing his hands were shaking, Dwight decided to make some bread too. Pulling out a sack of flour and a package of yeast, he started reading the recipe he found on the back of the flour sack. He didn't know much about bread rising, but it looked easy enough. Even if it was a failure, at least he wouldn't have to just sit, listen, and fret.

Just as he'd finished kneading the dough and put the covered bowl in a warm place to rise, the bedroom door opened and Joanna walked out, holding an empty glass and her coffee mug. She looked tired but not upset.

Torn between his worry for Susie and her, he said, "How is it going?"

Stretching her arms above her head, she smiled. "It's going well. Susie likely has another hour or two, but things are progressing just fine. I decided to give her and Marcus a tiny break and maybe relax a bit myself." Just then she noticed the pot on the stove and the flour on his hands. "Ah, what are you doing?"

"Cooking."

"I can see that." She smiled. "That's nice of you to do."

"I couldn't very well just sit here and worry."

"I know. The waiting and worrying part is hard, for

sure." Walking over to the stove, she lifted the lid and peered inside. "Soup?"

"Chicken soup and rice."

"It smells like heaven. You are full of surprises these days, Dwight."

"I don't like sitting and waiting and doing nothing."

"I guess not." Motioning to the glass bowl in the corner with a towel laying over the top of it, she said, "Are you making bread too?"

Maybe he had been a bit too industrious. "I am. I figured fresh bread would go well with the soup."

Joanna looked like she was at a loss for words. "*Jah*. I'm sure it will."

Picking up the coffee cup that she'd placed on the table, he asked, "What would you like me to get you? Are you hungry? I could make you a sandwich if you'd like."

"*Danke*, but *nee*. I never eat much during labor. But I would like another cup of coffee."

He walked over to the percolator on the stove and poured her a fresh cup. "I never knew you drank so much."

"I don't . . . unless I'm midwifing in the middle of the night." She sipped the cup and sighed. "Boy, I'm stiff. I don't remember feeling so achy back when I first started with Dorothy." She smiled at him. "I guess I'm getting old."

They had gotten older, but they weren't that old. "Hush, Jo. I know what you need. Come on over here."

"And what would that be?"

"A break. Come on." Grabbing a soft blanket that was thrown on the back of one of the chairs in their living room, Dwight wrapped it around Joanna's shoulders and guided her outside.

She tried to stop. "Dwight, I don't want to go for a walk."

"We aren't walking. Look."

"Hmm? Oh!"

And "Oh!" was exactly right. The horizon to the east was a colorful mixture of pinks and oranges, roses and grays. It was glorious and perfect.

"Look at that, Jo. It seems it's the middle of the night no more."

She smiled. "You're right. It's morning now. And what a beautiful start to the day this is."

Throwing an arm over her shoulders, he said, "I might be partial to this morning, but I happen to think that this is the prettiest sunrise I've seen in years. Maybe ever."

"It does seem better than most, doesn't it?" Her voice was soft as she leaned against him. "I'm so glad you brought me outside, Dwight."

He was too. "I canna help but think that this is a good sign for Susie and Marcus and their babe. Nothing bad can happen after such a glorious sunrise."

"She is going to be okay, Dwight. I would have never left the room if I was worried."

"I know that." He pressed a kiss on her temple as the sky cleared. "I have faith in you."

"*Danke*, but I think it's best if we simply rely on our faith in the Lord," she said with a smile. "And now, I think I'd better go back to Susie."

"I'll make a fresh pot of coffee in case you need it. Does Marcus need anything?"

"I don't think so. I don't think I could pry him from her side even if I wanted to." She chuckled. "One day soon, you'll have to take him out for a long hike, just so he can let off a bit of steam. No offense, but your sister has a bit of a temper."

"She always has. She's as calm and pleasant as can be—and then *bam*! She erupts."

Joanna chuckled as he handed her the cup and then walked down the hall.

When he was alone again, Dwight found himself clutching the afghan that had been around Joanna's shoulders and remembering the sunrise.

He had a feeling that many months from now he would realize it had been a turning point in their relationship. Surely a moment to treasure.

FIFTEEN

Susie had done it. Twelve hours after her first labor pains, she'd delivered a beautiful, healthy baby girl. It was a blessing. Just as wonderful was the fact that Susie didn't seem to be suffering any problems beyond the usual aches and pains.

It was such a relief. Joanna had had to turn away for a few seconds after she'd handed Susie her sweet babe. She was so glad the delivery had gone all right that she hadn't been able to stop tears from filling her eyes. She was not just happy for and proud of Susie but also of herself. She'd overcome so many doubts and fears. There had been many, many days when she didn't think she'd be strong enough to midwife again.

"She is so beautiful!" Susie said for at least the fifth time since Joanna had gently cleaned the babe with a warm washcloth and wrapped her in a soft blanket. "Oh, look at her, Marcus," she whispered. "Isn't she perfect?"

"She is at that," Marcus said, carefully running a finger along Margaret Mary Miller's tiny hand. "You did a good job, Susie," he murmured. "You made us a family."

Chuckling, Susie pressed a kiss to little Meg's brow. "*Danke*, but I think you might have had something to do with it." Glancing over at Joanna, who was now gathering towels and sheets to wash, Susie added, "We are incredibly grateful for your help, Jo. I couldn't have done it without you."

"I was glad to be here. Little Meg is a miracle indeed." Gazing at Meg, who was staring up at her parents in wonder, Joanna felt another lump form in her throat.

Meg's birth had been as easy and uneventful as a midwife could ever hope for. Susie had experienced minimal pain, the labor had gone like clockwork, and adorable Margaret Mary had arrived with a loud, grumpy wail. Joanna had felt like laughing, she'd been so pleased at the baby's first moments of life—and Susie's condition as well. Susie was going to experience all the minor aches and pains that accompanied delivering a child, but other than what was to be expected, Joanna didn't think she'd suffer any other lasting effects.

"I'm going to take these linens to your washing machine and have a cup of hot tea, then I'll come back in and check on you," she said.

"*Danke*, Joanna," Marcus said without looking up. "Take your time."

Joanna smiled to herself as she quietly let herself out of the room and shut the bedroom door behind her.

Dwight, who had been hovering just outside the door, strode to her side. "Here, let me help you." He took the heavy load of sheets and linens from her and headed down the hall. He had gotten a quick look at Margaret Mary soon after she was born, then had retreated back into the kitchen. "Is she still doing all right?"

"*Jah.*" She wasn't sure if he was referring to his sister or the babe. No matter. The answer was still the same.

He tossed the laundry through the open door of the machine and added soap. "Is this all?"

"All for now."

He closed the lid and turned on the washing machine. As always, Joanna was grateful for the gas line some of the large appliances like this and the refrigerator were attached to.

"Now, how are you?" he asked as they walked into the kitchen.

"I'm tired." She grinned. "And so very happy."

He pulled her in for a hug. "I'm in awe of you, Jo. I thought I knew what you did, but to be here and get the chance to observe your hard work and patience? It was an amazing thing to see."

She leaned in to him, appreciating his support. She was grateful for his words, too, but she didn't necessarily believe she deserved so much credit. "All I did was coach Susie. She did the hard work."

"Susie's amazing, but so are you."

"Thank you, Dwight. Thank you for staying all night. I felt better knowing you were nearby."

He kissed her temple before motioning her to sit down. "I wouldn't have wanted to be anywhere else. Now, how about some tea and maybe some cinnamon toast?"

"How did you know exactly what I wanted?"

"How could I not?" he threw over his shoulder as he buttered two pieces of bread and put them in the oven to broil before pouring hot water from the kettle into a large mug.

She was happy to watch him make her snack—and watch him make himself a peanut butter and jelly sandwich too. When everything was at the table, they both bowed their heads and silently gave thanks. Joanna made sure to offer up another prayer of thanks for His strength during the last twelve hours.

"What happens next?" Dwight asked when she started eating.

"I'm going to give Susie and Marcus a little bit of time alone with Meg, then I'll send Marcus and Meg out to you and help Susie clean up and put on a fresh gown. Then it will be time to let all of them get some rest."

"When will you finally rest?"

"Soon." Because he looked tempted to argue, she added, "This is my job, Dwight."

"*Jah.* It is, isn't it?"

She smiled, knowing what he was saying without the

words. It did feel awfully good to feel competent and assured again. She had missed feeling this way. She felt stronger too. She wasn't naïve enough to imagine she would never lose another patient or that nothing would ever go wrong in a labor and delivery. However, she felt that she would always look back upon these last few months as a turning point in her life. It was so easy to be confident and faithful when everything was going well. It was a much different story when it didn't. Though she wished that Cheryl had survived, Joanna felt that she, personally, had needed the loss to become the midwife she wanted to be.

And maybe even the person she felt God wanted her to be too.

"You're awfully quiet all of a sudden," Dwight murmured. "Is everything all right?"

"*Jah*. I was just taking some time to count my blessings."

"I like that. I hope I'm one of them?"

"Of course. Dwight, you've been my constant through all of this. I hope one day I'll be able to help you as much."

"Oh, Jo. You already have."

Three hours later, Dwight walked Joanna into her house and carefully put her medical bag on the bench near the front door. "Now, it's time for you to rest."

"I will."

She smiled up at him, which was all the encouragement he needed to take her into his arms and hold her close. She felt perfect; he loved how she always relaxed against him and pressed her cheek against his chest. It always made him feel like he was taking care of her.

Realizing that she was practically asleep on her feet, he murmured, "It's time I left you."

"I know." But she didn't move an inch.

She didn't want their time together to end either. It was probably the wrong time, but his heart was telling him there wasn't a better opportunity to finish the conversation they'd started so many hours ago. "Joanna?"

"Hmm?"

"I don't want to leave you. I don't want to say goodbye and go back to my *haus*. I mean, not for much longer."

She lifted her head. "What are you saying?"

"I'm saying that I love you. I'm saying that I want you to marry me. Soon." Like yesterday.

"Soon? How soon?"

He ran a hand along her spine. "Is that a yes?"

Even in the dim light of the entryway, he could see her blush. "It is. I love you too."

"Will you marry me soon? As soon as we can arrange it?"

She laughed. "I'm beginning to think you would marry me tomorrow if I said that was fine."

"I'd marry you this minute if I could." Dwight knew he wasn't exaggerating either. After a lifetime of wondering and hoping and finally yearning, he didn't want to wait any longer to make Joanna his.

She pressed a hand to his chest, right over his heart. "How about in one month?"

"I suppose I can wait that long." Even though his words sounded casual, there was no way he could stop himself from grinning from ear to ear. "Tomorrow we'll call our parents, and I'll walk over to meet with the bishop."

"*Jah.* Tomorrow I'll speak with Emma and Caleb and see if they can help me put together a small wedding and luncheon."

"And Susie."

"*Jah*, and I'll speak to Susie too." She laughed. "It's really happening!"

"*Jah.* All we have to do is seal the moment with a kiss."

And so he did just that.

Ten minutes later, as he walked home fighting exhaustion, Dwight knew he was so thankful to the Lord. He'd gotten him and Joanna together at long last—and maybe in the only way possible.

By encouraging Joanna to be a midwife for Susie.

EPILOGUE

It turned out Joanna had a lot to learn, much to all of her former patients' delight. By the time she'd reached the ninth week of her pregnancy, morning sickness had hit her hard. Everything her husband offered to make her sounded bad, most of what she did manage to choke down turned her stomach, and tears came to her eyes without warning.

She'd never felt more miserable.

One particularly bad day, Joanna had ended up sitting on the cold tile floor of her bathroom for almost an hour. Only Dwight bringing her Triscuit crackers and lemon-lime soda had helped.

She'd begun to wish she'd been a mite more sympathetic toward some of her ladies when they'd complained to her about their queasy tummies, sore backs, and exhaustion.

Now that Joanna was nine months along and wad-dling everywhere, she'd never felt more like a whale. And a very unattractive whale at that. To make matters worse, she was a whale with a persistent backache.

Yes. She was now a lumbering, rather plain-looking whale with a dull, persistent backache. And indigestion too.

Sitting on her bed, staring at her swollen ankles over the huge expanse of her belly, Joanna groaned. Had nine months ever felt so long? To make matters worse, her stomach was acting up a bit. And maybe it was cramping too?

Surely all that had to be why she'd burst into tears when she'd asked Dwight to help her pin her dress together—and he'd had to leave two of the pins out because there wasn't enough fabric.

When was it going to end?

Glad that she'd somehow gotten her feet into her tennis shoes, she scooted to the edge of the bed. Somehow, she was going to need to find the energy to stand up.

Dwight appeared in the doorway. His smile turned to worry. "Joanna, are you sure you want to take a walk right now?"

"I'm sure." But she still didn't move.

He walked closer. "Don't get mad, but you seem a little tired. Don't you think it might be a good idea to rest?"

"*Nee.*"

"Joanna, are you sure?"

"I just said I was sure, Dwight," she snapped. "Honestly, you'd think I wasn't a midwife. I know what I'm doing."

A muscle jumped in his jaw. "*Jah*, but you've never been pregnant before."

Even though what he said made perfect sense, her temper erupted. "If you don't wish to go with me, just say so."

With a long-suffering sigh, he walked to the front door. "Let's go, Mrs. Eicher."

"*Danke.*"

The fresh air did feel good on her skin. It filled her senses, too, making her more optimistic. And, if she was honest, embarrassed about how she'd been talking to him. "I'm sorry for being so grumpy. You didn't deserve that."

His gaze warmed. "I know you're uncomfortable. No need for apologies."

He was too good for her. "Want to walk to the end of the street?"

"Wherever you'd like to go is fine."

Pleased that he wasn't mad, she picked up her pace. Started pointing out some of the daffodils and crocuses that had started to bloom. "One day I'd like to plant a whole field of daffodils, Dwight. Wouldn't that be a sight?"

"It would indeed. I'll plant a mess of them in November so we'll have something to look forward to next spring."

She smiled at the idea of that. "Indeed we will." She ignored a twinge of pain.

"What just happened? I saw you wince."

"Hmm? Oh, it's nothing. I've just been having a little bit of an upset stomach or something."

"You're nauseous?"

"*Jah*. I mean, *nee*. It feels different." Trying to find the words even though she was suffering terribly from pregnancy brain, she continued. "Actually, the pains I'm feeling are more like cramping. They start in my back and kind of roll toward my—" She froze. Suddenly everything that she'd been experiencing fit together. The backache. Mood swing. Cramping. Yesterday's sudden unexplained burst of energy . . .

Oh, for goodness' sake!

She was the most foolish midwife ever. "Dwight, I think I'm in labor."

He grinned, showing he had known that all along. "Truly?"

All of a sudden, a real pain rolled through her middle. Pressing her hands on her tummy, she felt the tightening that she had felt on dozens of other women. "Absolutely. We need to get home right now."

Some of Dwight's humor faded. "You're serious."

"So serious. We need to contact the midwife."

Wrapping an arm around her middle, he encouraged her to walk a bit faster. "Where does Miriam live?"

As she felt another contraction, she realized Miriam was too far away for Dwight to be able to get to. "We're not going to be able to have Miriam."

"So, Rose?"

"*Jah*." Rose wasn't the woman she had chosen, but Joanna knew she was a fine midwife and would take care of her. "Dwight, go ask one of the neighbors if they could fetch her, okay?"

"Whatever you want."

The next two hours passed in a blur. When they got to the house, Dwight did go ask his brother, who rushed out on his bike to Rose's house. While they were waiting, Joanna prepared her bed between contractions. She was already exhausted, and she had hours to go.

Then Rose burst in and took control. It turned out the woman's bossy nature was exactly what Joanna needed. Instead of giving her own opinions, Joanna became the patient instead of the midwife.

Dwight hovered and held her hand and offered words of encouragement. And then, with his sweet words ringing in her ears, she delivered a beautiful baby boy.

After inspecting him for a few seconds, Rose gently washed him, wrapped him in a blanket, and then deposited Andrew Dwight Eicher into his mother's arms. "You did *gut*, Joanna, especially for a first-time *mamm*," Rose said with a gruff smile.

Even though she was exhausted and only had eyes for her son, Joanna had to laugh. Rose's compliment had been accurate indeed. She had done a good job delivering her baby—even though she'd been as nervous and awkward as any other new mother she'd coached.

Before stepping away, Rose ran the back of one finger along Andrew's cheek. "He is a mighty fine babe, Mrs. Eicher," she said before leaving the room.

When they were alone, Dwight kissed her brow. "I love Andrew already . . . almost as much as I love you."

Staring down at her son, feeling Dwight's arm around her shoulders, Joanna felt the same way—blessed and happy and secure.

She already loved Andrew so much. She adored Dwight and her life with him. Everything was exactly how it should be. She was a midwife and Dwight's wife too. And now, she was a mother.

She was so very grateful for it all.

ACKNOWLEDGMENTS

I'm so grateful to editor Kimberly Carlton for extending the invitation to contribute a story for this collection. I'm also very appreciative of editor Leslie Peterson, as well as the entire HCCP team, for their guidance during the publication process. Many thanks also go to author buddies Amy Clipston and Kelly Long. I'm delighted and honored to share a cover with y'all!

DISCUSSION QUESTIONS

1. I used one of my favorite Amish proverbs for this novella, *"Reach up as far as you can. God will reach the rest of the way."* Do you find this proverb to be true? Can you think of a time when the Lord helped as soon as you reached out to Him?

2. I thought the scripture verse from Psalm 62, *"Only God gives inward peace, and I depend on him"* was fitting for my story. Only when Joanna gave her problems up to God was she able to find happiness in her professional and personal life. What have you experienced when you've handed your problems to the Lord?

3. Do you have a favorite character in the novella? What was it about her or him that you enjoyed?

CHRISTMAS CRADLES

KELLY LONG

ONE

The fading light played with the reflection of the kerosene lamp against the window of the old Amish farmhouse and illuminated the stray snowflakes just beginning to fall. Inside the warm and simple room, Asa Mast bent his broad back over his father's bed and lifted the older man into a more comfortable position against the pillows.

"*Danki*, Asa." Samuel coughed, giving his son a bleary-eyed look. "The flu is bad this year and it moves fast, or else I'm growing old."

Asa sat on the edge of the bed and poured a fresh glass of water from the pitcher his sister-in-law had just brought.

"You seem as young to me, *Daed*, as the day you took me out behind the barn and tanned my hide for driving the colt through *Mamm*'s kitchen garden."

Samuel smiled as Asa knew he would, his fever-bright eyes, so dark and so like his son's, growing warmer for a moment. "*Jah*, to think that you were ever that young . . ."

They sat in silence for a moment, remembering. Then Asa lifted the cloth napkin from the tray on the bedside table and saw untouched thin slices of ham, mashed potatoes, pickled beets, and a wedge of apple pie.

"Can't you bring yourself to eat anything, *Daed*? Would you like something lighter, maybe broth?"

"I'm not an invalid; I asked for all of that. I guess my eyes were just bigger than my stomach."

Asa recovered the plate. "I hate to leave you alone tonight, *Daed*."

Samuel waved the words away. "Your *bruder* and sister-in-law are here; they will care well for me."

"I know, but I guess I'd feel more comfortable if you'd let me take you to the hospital to get checked out. I don't like the sound of your cough."

"Ha! Going to the hospital for the flu, and on First Christmas too. I don't think so. And I made a promise to *Frau* Ruth; you must keep it for me."

Asa sighed. "I know, but . . ."

Samuel tapped his son's large hand. "You're making excuses. Perhaps you don't want to go because it's a woman you'll be helping. Hmm?"

Asa's dark eyelashes drifted downward.

"So that's the truth of it?" Samuel smiled as he settled back once more against the pillows.

"*Nee* . . . it doesn't matter."

Samuel snorted. "Women always matter."

"I'm going to point that out to *Grossmuder* the next time she visits."

"Bah, and I'll point out to her that you've yet to get over something that happened more than a decade ago."

"I didn't think you'd kept track."

"Your *mamm* did," Samuel rasped. "She worried for you. Now that she's gone, it's my job."

"I'm over it, *Daed*. There's nothing for you to worry about." Asa touched his father's arm.

His father sighed. "We celebrate Christmas, my son. A season of expectancy, of hope. But you, I don't think that you expect anything wonderful to happen to you in your life. You don't look at your days, or your nights, with the hope of *Derr Herr*."

"I know *Derr Herr* has a plan for my life."

"Then look for it. Watch for it, like a candle in the snow. This is what your *mamm* would want for you. It's what I want for you."

"*Daed*." Asa smiled. "I'll think about it. And I know you miss *Mamm*—I do too."

"Now you're changing the subject . . ."

Asa got to his feet and adjusted the quilts, tucking them around his father's shoulders but leaving room for his long, gray beard to stick out. "*Nee*, now I'm going to keep your favor—woman or not. Happy Christmas, *Daed*."

The old man sighed. "Happy Christmas, *sohn*."

Anna Stolis breathed a prayer of gratitude when the large white van took the last corner around Lincoln Street and came to a ragged halt in front of Dienner's Country Restaurant. She'd endured the *Englisch* teenager's reckless driving for two and a half hours. At the last minute her transportation from Pine Creek had canceled, but she had needed to get to her *aenti* Ruth, who was due to leave town for a brief but much needed vacation.

The *Englisch* boy grinned at her. "You're a pretty good sport. A couple of those turns were icy coming down the mountain."

"Thanks." She adjusted her *kapp* and reached into the side pocket of her large midwifery bag and paid him the agreed-upon amount plus a tip. "Drive back safely."

"No worries. Merry Christmas. Hey, and I'll pick you up the same time tomorrow evening." He grinned, cranking up the radio, and she could only nod to him through the deafening sound. The van sped away, and she stepped back in relief.

She entered Dienner's Country Restaurant, glad that it was open for a few hours on Christmas Day to cater to those who had to work or just wanted time out. She took a deep breath of the fragrant air, happy for the opportunity to warm up. She caught sight of her *aenti*, Ruth Stolis, seated at a table near the window, and she hurried to shake out her cape as she crossed the room to greet her.

Ruth Stolis was a comfortably round, keen-eyed, middle-aged widow. And at twenty-six, it seemed as though Anna might follow in her *aenti*'s footsteps, as she already had an intelligent mind, generous curves, and lack of suitors on the horizon. Still, she possessed the proper training to practice midwifery in the state of Pennsylvania, and she told herself with stout reassurance that was worth ten men. Though the wishful thought did pass through her mind that if the good Lord saw fit to send her a husband, she'd be more than grateful.

Ruth rose to enfold her in a warm hug. "I was getting worried, Anna, but I should have known better."

"Midwives always deliver." Anna grinned and they shared a smile of camaraderie as they sat down.

"How was your First Christmas? And my favorite *bruder*?"

"*Daed* and *Mamm* are doing well, but I had a delivery call just after I'd helped *Mamm* serve the noon meal. And it was twins, no less. I didn't see that coming, as I'd only had two prenatal visits with the mother. I'm still not comfortable delivering twins outside the hospital, but our women would much rather stay at home. What about you?"

"Only one delivery. My quietest Christmas ever. I relaxed by the fire, then stopped in to visit with my friend Rachel Fisher for a few minutes. You remember I wrote you a few years back to pray for her *sohn*, Seth, who was in that accident? Anyway, she would have liked me to stay longer, but I wanted to get home and curl up with Bottle."

Anna grinned at the image of her *aenti*'s cat. "You're lulling me to sleep right here."

"Well, it'll be the first Second Christmas I've spent with my daughter since she married. I'm excited, but I wouldn't be able to do it without you. Even with the other midwives in the area and the local hospital, it's hard to get away, even for a day."

"My pleasure, and I know what you mean. Although, there is a new *Englisch* physician in the area who is a great help; he's an older man and he's got an intern with him for a time. They're covering for me tonight and tomorrow."

Anna ordered a roast beef sandwich from the *Englisch* waitress, then took a sip from the thick mug of coffee. "*Ach*, I almost forgot . . . I brought a gift for my favorite *aenti* . . ." Anna reached into her oversized midwifery bag, which looked more like a folded piece of flowered carpet with wooden handles. She withdrew a small package with festive wrapping and a flattened bow.

"*Danki*, Anna . . . you didn't have to. Just coming is enough." But *Aenti* Ruth's fingers moved with happiness as she opened the gift. She laughed aloud when she saw what it was.

"A retractable tape measure—in pink and blue. Do you know how many tape measures I go through?"

"Me too." Anna smiled.

Ruth reached across the table to squeeze Anna's hand. "*Danki*, Anna. This is one I will not lose." She bundled her gift back up, then folded her hands, obviously preparing for a more serious discussion. "Now, I'll be back by seven o'clock tomorrow evening, providing everything goes well. And I want you to know that anytime you want to have a partner or just get away, I'd love to share my practice with you here in Paradise."

Anna's gray eyes shone with gratitude. "*Danki, Aenti* Ruth. *Derr Herr* has blessed me with your love and your friendship."

"All right." Ruth patted Anna's hand. "Here's my list of potential deliveries. Three possibilities. Two are further than remote."

Anna rolled her eyes at the suggestion that any possibility was remote in the realm of pregnancy and delivery. Her *aenti* laughed.

"Sarah Raber, age thirty-two, fifth child. No previous problems. Probably could deliver without you if she had to.

"Mary Stolis, some vague cousin, I bet, age thirty, three children. She had a miscarriage late term last time, but she would not allow an autopsy, naturally. She's healthy as a horse, as she likes to say, on this go-around. I don't foresee any difficulties, but if she does put in a call, you'll want to keep a sharp eye."

Anna nodded.

"And Deborah Loftus. Twenty-three. First baby. Still two weeks out. Just in case."

"Just in case, hmm? Isn't it always the 'just in case' ones that deliver early?"

"Yep." Ruth's eyes twinkled. "And Samuel Mast will spend the night in the barn and drive you out if any calls come through. His kids are all grown and pretty much gone from home, and his wife passed last year. It'll make him feel good to have something to do at the holidays besides visiting. Here's the key, and the supply room is well stocked. Just make yourself at home after dinner. Folks are saying it'll snow, but Samuel knows every inch of this area. Hopefully there'll be no calls."

They both had a hearty laugh at the idea, then Anna bid her *aenti* goodbye, promising to pray she would have a safe trip. Anna sat down and finished her sandwich, savored a last cup of coffee, and made her way to the yellow house and small, attached barn that her aunt rented on one of the back streets of the town. The weather looked grim, but lights burned with good cheer in storefronts and upstairs apartments.

She removed her glove to fit the key into the icy lock and entered to Bottle's purr and caress. She bent to stroke the animal and glanced with pleasure at the banked fire burning in the grate. She laid her bag on a chair and had just stretched her hands out to the warmth when a heavy banging on the front door interrupted her.

"Well, that was all of two free minutes," she muttered, going to open the door.

A tall Amish man stood in the shadows of the street-lamp, and she searched his handsome face to assess the possible status of any pregnant wife. She saw nothing but calm, deep-brown eyes, which made her think of dipped chocolate, and a thick fringe of lashes like icing on the cake, so to speak. She blinked. He looked rock steady, so his wife was probably just experiencing Braxton-Hicks or practice labor. Anna assumed a professional manner.

"Please, come in, Mr. . . . ah?"

"Mast. I'm Asa Mast, Samuel's son. *Daed*'s down with the flu. He sent me out to drive you tonight if need be." His voice was husky, inviting, making her think of the steady creak of well-worn rockers moving in unison. Anna decided the ride in the cold van had done more than rattle her nerves. She had never reacted like this to a man's voice; the truth was she usually saw men as vague nuisances, always underfoot when she had work to do.

"I'm, uh . . . Anna, Anna Stolis. You must know my aunt Ruth well. Please come in out of the cold." She held the door open wider, but his tall form didn't budge.

"*Daed* said I was to sleep in the barn."

"*Ach*, right—I forgot. I mean, of course. If you'll wait, I'll get some blankets—"

He held up a large gloved hand. "No need. I'm warm."

His words caused her to inadvertently trail her gaze down his high, ruddy cheekbones to his sculpted chin and on to his broad, bundled chest. He did radiate a certain warmth; she fancied she could feel it from where she stood. And he smelled as clean as Christmas, like pine and snow.

Anna decided she was truly addled.

247

"Well, all right then, Mr. Mast—"

"Just Asa. Mr. Mast's my father." He gave her a warm smile.

"Right. Asa . . . I . . . call me Anna. I'll, um . . . I'll wake you if the need arises."

"Afraid I'll have to wake you most likely, ma'am— Anna. The phone's in the barn. Your *aenti* has a keen ear . . . or a sixth sense, they say." He smiled, a flash of white teeth, and a stray dimple appeared in his chiseled jaw. "She left my *daed* an extra key. I'll just holler up the steps, if that's okay?"

"Fine . . . fine." She watched him tip his black hat, then step off the porch; he was probably married, she thought, and the idea depressed her. Still, she decided she'd sleep in her clothes. She told herself that she had no desire to have Asa Mast "hollering" to her while she was in her nightgown.

A candle in the snow . . . Asa shook his head as his *daed*'s words echoed in his mind. He tried to relax against a pile of hay in the small barn, but the image of the nicely curved midwife danced before him like shadows thrown from a lantern. He couldn't remember being so struck by a woman, not for years, not for a decade. It made him feel like a teenager again, and that, in itself, was something to pray about.

Anna was dreaming. It was summer, incredibly hot, and she was debating the merits of removing her shoes and socks to dip her toes in Pine Creek. It would only make her want to swim, she decided, something that adult women were forbidden to do in her particular community, and yet she felt herself searching the bushes with a furtive glance. She was far enough away from any of the farms for anyone to see her, and her dark skirt was dreadfully warm. She fumbled with the waist, frustrated by the weight of something more than the skirt, when she heard her name being called in a low tone. She jumped, snapping her eyes open. She realized that she'd been in a deep sleep, buried under clothes, quilts, and her aunt's cat, and that Asa Mast stood near the bed, holding up a kerosene lamp.

"What's the matter? Is it a case?" She flung back the covers and the cat and made to rise.

"You sleep in your clothes?"

"All midwives do," she quipped fuzzily.

"I never knew."

"Trade secret."

"Interesting."

Anna sank back down on the bed, trying to get her bearings.

"Here . . . I brought you some hot chocolate." He offered the mug and she took it with grateful hands. She loved chocolate.

"Danki."

"You sleep like the dead. I tried hollering, but it didn't work. I'm sorry to have startled you."

"No problem."

He smiled down at her. "Were you dreaming?"

She burned her tongue on the chocolate. "Hmm? What?"

"You seemed all ruffled, like . . . I don't know."

Ruffled? She put a hand to the mousy brown hair escaping her *kapp* and looked down at his mammoth boots. Honestly, the man would be hard to dress in proper clothes at his size. She found a knot in the back of her hair and pulled.

"Here, don't do that." He put the lamp on the bureau and moved so fast she didn't realize what he was doing. He pulled her hands down and quickly worked the knot loose with his long fingers, then stepped away. He cleared his throat, and Anna thought he seemed as surprised as she was by his actions.

"Your hair's as fine as corn silk," he said, seeming to try to explain his impulsive movement. "Pulling on it won't do any good."

She was mesmerized. *Corn silk*. No one had ever said anything as direct and complimentary about her before. And the way he touched her—as if she were a porcelain doll, not the hearty and capable woman she knew herself to be. There had to be a sin involved in this thinking, she considered, her thoughts muddled.

"*Danki* . . . for helping me . . . my hair . . ."

He nodded as a brief look of sadness crossed his face, but then he changed the subject. "The call's out at the Loftuses'."

She racked her brain. Deborah. Two weeks out from delivery. First baby. Probably lots of time, but you never could tell. She pulled on her cape and her bonnet and picked up her bag, which she'd prudently filled with supplies before she lay down. Asa went ahead of her down the narrow staircase, holding the light high. She glanced out a window, and in the faint moonlight she saw that the snow had picked up.

"What time is it?" she asked, peering at her brooch-pin clock.

"Nearly ten."

She nodded and yawned, then glanced around, trying to think if she'd forgotten anything. "We'd better go then."

"I've got the buggy pulled up. My horse, Dandy, doesn't fuss much, no matter the weather."

A gust of wind nearly snapped the door out of his hand, and Anna had to catch her breath at the biting cold. She recognized more ice than snow in the air.

"He must be a *gut* friend then," she shouted. He nodded and flashed her a fast grin, and then the giant of a man swept her up and into the warm buggy.

"How far to the Loftuses'?" she asked, attempting to break the intimate quiet of the buggy as they started off.

She felt as though she and he were the only two alive in the world at that moment, insulated by the press of the weather.

"Five miles, give or take."

She nodded, understanding "give or take" to mean anything from nearly another whole mile to less than a quarter of a mile farther. She watched him handle the reins with ease.

"You cold, Doc?"

She turned, surprised, when he addressed her so. No one back home could get past her being Anna Stolis, the eldest of three sisters, even though she had her training and had delivered babies as regular as rain for the past two years.

"I'm not a doctor," she said, feeling obliged to make this known.

"Close enough for Miss Ruth to leave—that's saying something. What's your husband think about you being gone?"

She started at his question. "I'm not married."

He grinned. "Me neither."

She gave a tentative smile back and then looked out the small side window. It occurred to her that she'd never once thought of herself as a pretty woman. Passable, yes, but too curvy in the bosom and hips to be of interest when other women were as slender as reeds. But here she was, sitting in a snowstorm with an unmarried man and a dependable horse, thinking for the first time in the twenty-six years of her life that she actually might be pretty.

"Are you cold?" he asked again.

"I'm okay."

He pulled a neatly folded Jacob's Ladder patterned quilt from beneath the seat and began to spread it across her lap with one hand.

"*Ach*, it's beautiful." She loved quilts as much as she loved hot chocolate, and she ran her gloved hands over the fine workmanship, apparent even in the half-light. The color-play of the triangles somehow made Anna feel comforted, soothed.

"My *grossmuder*'s. She gave it to me last year before she died."

"Really?" Anna asked, knowing that quilts were usually left to female relatives.

"Yep. Said I should carry it with me to—" He broke off, almost in confusion.

"To what?" Anna couldn't contain her curiosity.

"Well, she said I should carry it with me in my buggy to warm the girls up. She was afraid I'd never . . . marry." He stumbled over the last word.

"*Ach*."

"I'm sorry—I've never told anyone that. I didn't mean to be forward."

Anna's heart warmed to him even as she blushed. "Please don't mind. People tell me lots of things in my role as a midwife . . ."

In actuality, her mind was alternating between the images of girls snuggling with Asa beneath the quilt and her curiosity as to why he hadn't married yet. He was probably her age at least . . .

"Twenty-eight." He smiled.

"Girls under the quilt?"

He laughed, a sound that managed to tickle her spine.

"*Nee*, I'm twenty-eight, and you're the first girl to have ever used the quilt."

"I'm twenty-six," she confessed.

He nodded.

She stared at his perfect profile, the dark edges of his hair standing out only a bit lighter than his hat. He'd called her a girl . . . *a girl* . . . who was long past marrying. She'd even taken to sitting with the married women during church meetings, and nobody seemed surprised. Girls got married at twenty or twenty-one, or sometimes twenty-two—but not twenty-six. And, if he was telling the truth, that she was the first female under this warming quilt . . . Her mind spun with stars and dreams and things long forgotten.

"Why haven't you married?" she asked, deciding she had nothing to lose by being so bold. She'd be going home tomorrow and would never see him again.

At first she thought she'd offended him because he didn't answer right away. But then he smiled and gave her a warm look and a sidelong glance that made her clutch her hands beneath his grandmother's quilt.

"I'm just picky, I guess."

She shook her head, feeling sleepy and spellbound. Surely he couldn't be implying that he was being preferential in showing attention toward her.

"Is that your only reason?" she asked, refusing to allow herself to give in to the pull of his words.

A tightness seemed to come over his strong features, but then she decided she'd just imagined it when he gave an amiable shrug.

"That and the fact that I'm not very good at being anything but myself. You don't get to practice charm when you're just a farmer and the hind ends of horses are all you see for half the year."

"What?"

"Guess that didn't come out right." He chuckled, and she shifted on the seat, clapping a hand over her mouth to suppress a giggle. A giggle . . . she, Anna Stolis, Anna the serious, the studious, the stern even, was giggling.

"I'm sorry, I'm not laughing at you." She took a breath. "I—I've just never met anyone like you."

He swallowed, his throat working. "Well, like I said— you're the first one under that quilt."

She savored her surprise at his response, not even caring when the snow picked up. A dim light shining in the distance alerted them to the turn, and he swung the horse with ease. He drove down the short lane, stopped the buggy, then jumped out to come around and help her. He lifted her down as though she were weightless, then grabbed her arm and her bag, steering her to the porch in the thickening snowfall.

"Step!" he hollered when they'd reached the porch, and she did.

They piled in through the front door as an anxious Amish man opened it, his light hair and fine blond beard betraying his youth and concern.

"Miss Stolis? Your aunt told us before that it might be you. I'm John." His voice quivered a bit.

He shook her hand, then Asa's. "Asa? Your father is ill, I heard today?"

"*Jah*, making tough weather of it, but he'll pull through. *Danki*. How is Deborah?"

Anna glimpsed the anxiety in John's face as he took her wet cape and hung it on a hook behind the door. "I'm not sure . . . We hosted the family here, but then everyone left early because of the storm. Deborah seemed fine, but then she started feeling sick and her contractions started."

"It will be all right, John. You'll see. I'll just go and put the horse up." Asa excused himself and went back out into the swirl of snow.

"First pregnancies are always difficult to gauge. Has she been having regular contractions?" Anna slipped off her boots and gathered up her bag.

"*Jah* . . . they were six minutes apart . . . but . . . that's not all. She's in here." He led the way to the master bedroom as Anna registered his vague comment. Concerns were already swirling through her mind when she heard the cough followed by a faint groan from the woman in the bed.

"Hi, Deborah, I'm Anna, Ruth Stolis's niece. I've delivered a lot of babies, so you're in good hands." She entered the bedroom with deliberate cheerfulness, talking as she walked, and glanced around at the variety of inhalers and prescription wrappers on the carved wooden bureau. "Do you have asthma?"

Deborah was pale and obviously between hard contractions. "*Jah*." She coughed.

Anna got out her stethoscope and approached the comfortably piled bed, a fixed expression of encouragement on her lips.

TWO

Asa led his horse into the Loftuses' warm barn and turned up another kerosene lamp. He stared at the small, glowing flame for a moment and thought about Anna Stolis's generous red lips and the flash of her smile. She'd appeared from behind Ruth Stolis's door like some sparkling thing, the catch of sunlight on a white splash of creek water, or the freshly washed windows of home in the springtime. But in the few minutes of knowing her, she'd also managed to bring back all the hurt and pain he thought he was good at hiding—even what he thought he was over. But it was there, raw and open and aching until he had to bend his head against the warmth of Dandy's side to regain control. And even then the memory of his intoxicating *rumschpringe*—deceptive in power and poignancy, like dandelion wine on a hot day—forced images of Jennifer back into his head and heart.

Jennifer and her incomparable beauty, her way of smiling and making others serve her, her whispered words and his desperate desire to do anything she wanted, no matter the cost. His horse shifted and he lifted his head, wiping the damp sleeve of his coat across his face as he realized he'd wasted precious moments when the midwife might need help inside.

He made his way back out into the storm and considered what everyone else had told him over the last few years—that he was going to end up an old bachelor. He'd come to rather believe it, he supposed, and viewed the girls at meetings or hymn sings with a detached interest. Truth was, he'd rather go fishing than spend time with any of the ladies of his community, but maybe that was because *Derr Herr* had never allowed anyone like Anna Stolis to cause him to think beyond his own hidden self.

He stomped his snowy feet on the porch and opened the door. It was quiet inside the house except for the sound of the wood burner popping. He slipped off his boots and placed them on the mat by the door, then hung up his heavy coat and took off his hat. He felt like he was intruding somehow and wasn't quite sure what to do with himself. He padded over to a rocking chair near the stove and eased his large frame into the carved wooden seat. He jumped up a moment later, though, when a door opened and Anna walked briskly from a room off the kitchen.

"What's wrong?" he asked in a low voice, searching the tense lines of her face.

She walked toward him, and he was surprised that he had to resist the urge to look at the sweetly curving swells and sway of her body. He concentrated instead on her expression. She reached his side, and he had to bend from his much greater height to hear her whisper. Her breath smelled like summer, and her gray eyes, with their tangle of lashes, held his steadily.

"She has asthma, but I think it's gotten worse because she's caught the flu too. Her regular medication isn't getting her breath where it needs to be. I have a small portable tank of oxygen in my bag; I think that should help. Once the baby comes, I'll give Deborah a steroid shot, which should also help, but I don't want to worry John about it now. I told him to sit with her. The baby should come anytime. John suggested a few poultices might work to clear her chest, so I wondered if you'd help him brew up some things. They can't hurt and might help; that way I can focus on Deborah and the baby."

Asa nodded, then caught her arm gently when she turned away. "You're a good doc."

She flushed. "*Danki.*"

He watched the fabric of her skirt swish against the end table as she walked back to the bedroom, then pulled himself up to start on his task. John emerged a few moments later from the bedroom, his blond hair rather on end and his eyes dazed.

Asa approached him the way he would a riled-up horse and laid a hand on the younger man's shoulder.

"Doc says we should make up those poultices for Deborah's breathing. I know a few remedies from taking care of *Daed* in the past. Can you show me where things are?"

"*Jah.*" John nodded. "I'll be glad of something to do. We've got a cabinet of herbal medicines stocked, but maybe we should have gone to the hospital . . . I should have suggested that."

"*Should haves* are worthless in life, I've always believed," Asa said. "You just keep moving forward into what the Lord gives you." The words convicted him even as he spoke, as he realized he had spent years doing the exact opposite.

"You are right, Asa. *Danki.*"

The two men soon had multiple kettles on the boil full of wild cherry bark, honey, and melted horehound candy. Ground mustard, cinnamon, cloves, ginger, allspice, and lard were also brewing, and John was beginning to look more relaxed. Asa glanced now and then at the closed door of the master bedroom and prayed that all was going well for the Doc and her patients.

Anna ignored the abrupt sound of a branch scratching the window and concentrated on the pale face of the woman in the bed. Deborah's reddish-brown curls had all but escaped her *kapp*, and her traditional long-sleeved white nightdress was damp with perspiration. Anna slid a long plastic drape beneath her and arranged it to fall over the bottom edge of the bed. Then she opened packages of large, flat, absorbent pads and arranged those as well. As she expected, Deborah's water broke after the next few contractions.

The young woman instinctively gasped at the rush of fluid.

"It's all right, Deborah. Your water's broken, and I have a feeling that things are going to move fast now. You're doing great! Do you want me to get John?"

Deborah shook her head as she inhaled from the oxygen cannulas. "*Nee*, not yet—he gets sick to his stomach, even at calvings." Her faint smile melted into a grimace as she arched against another pain.

Anna strained with her. "Hold my hands. Let me carry the pain with you, just like *Derr Herr* does, *jah*?"

Deborah gasped. "*Jah*, you are right." She regained some composure after a moment. "Do you have children of your own?"

Anna shook her head. "*Nee*, so I don't know quite how you feel, but I can imagine."

It was a question that she was asked often. Each time she answered, she had to remind herself that the Lord had blessed her with the chance to serve others and to see new life come into his world. But there was one part of her that longed for a husband and children of her own. Sometimes the most elated moments in her practice were also the loneliest, when the new baby came and she watched the mother take it to her breast. It was like there were two

Annas—the professional and the woman . . . or the girl, as Asa Mast had called her.

Deborah's sharp cry brought her back to the moment. Realizing that the contractions were becoming more intense, she glanced around the cozy bedroom, with its simple, carved cradle, seeking a distraction for Deborah's mind, when she noticed the Turkey Tracks patterned quilt hanging on a display frame near the bureau. The wide, feathered patterns in each square did indeed resemble turkey tracks, but Anna knew another story about the quilt.

"You have a beautiful Turkey Tracks quilt, Deborah."

The woman glanced in the direction of the bright red pattern and nodded, the tension in her brow easing a bit.

"*Jah*, John's mother gave it to us . . . a wedding gift. I forget now what she said about it . . ."

Anna breathed with her through another contraction and then began to speak. "Actually, one of the first names of that pattern wasn't Turkey Tracks—it was Wandering Foot. The story goes that any boy who slept beneath the quilt was destined to lead a life of endless wandering, never having a home or family. So mothers renamed the pattern."

Deborah smiled. "That's right . . . and my John would never wander. *Danki* for reminding me." She grimaced again, and Anna adjusted the pile of quilts that covered her patient's chest. She bundled up the plastic sheet and put it in a trash bag she pulled from her midwifery case. Then she put down sterile towels and pulled on a pair of sterile gloves. She began laying out supplies from her bag, including the antibacterial wash.

"Deborah, I'm just going to check you again because I think you're very close, okay?"

"*Jah*, I think—I have to push."

"Okay, just hold on." Anna was quick. "You're right—it's time to push. Do you want John?"

Deborah nodded with visible concentration.

Anna opened the door and peered out into the kitchen where Asa and John were talking to each other by the stove.

"John, it's time now."

Anna took in the blanched face of the father-to-be and ushered him to the door. Then she saw Asa's encouraging smile, as if he held her responsible for the whole moment to come. She quickly checked her vanity and reminded herself she'd be returning the next day to Pine Creek. The thought sobered her as she eased the door closed on the man she'd just met but who had made a surprising impact on her. She refocused and followed John to the bed.

She turned up the oxygen to three liters and concentrated on encouraging Deborah. Anna always made it a habit to allow the couple to feel comfortable and in control of the moment while she was there to provide reassurance and spiritual, mental, and physical support. When John looked rather lost as to what to say as his wife squeezed his hand, Anna suggested that he climb behind Deborah in the bed and be a support for her to lean against. John latched on to this idea, and soon both husband and wife were working together as Deborah delivered a healthy firstborn son to the Loftus house. Anna laid the baby on Deborah's belly and then clamped the umbilical cord and worked on her own chores with the afterbirth as the new parents murmured thanks to *Derr Herr* over their child in soft Pennsylvania Dutch.

"Would you like to cut the cord, John?" she asked after a few minutes and was surprised when he nodded and snipped the area between the two clamps with calm precision. Anna smiled as she made a brief examination of the child. She lifted the baby onto the portable sling scale. "Seven pounds, five ounces," she announced as she laid the baby on the end of the bed to clean and dress him in the traditional tiny undergarments, gown, and head covering that had lain waiting in the cradle. Then she swaddled him in a yellow patchwork baby quilt and handed him to John, who'd moved to stand by the bed, while she finished her cleaning and eased Deborah into a fresh nightdress. John laid the infant in his wife's arms, and Anna smiled in satisfaction.

"You both did great! Now I'm going to check Deborah's lungs and give her a little shot to help her breathing and we'll see if we can't get the oxygen turned down. But"— she eyed John—"I want them both to be seen tomorrow at the hospital in Paradise, just to make extra sure that everything's all right."

John gave a solemn nod, seeming to have grown older in just a few minutes. "We'll be there, Doc."

"Great. Now, what are you going to name this handsome little man? I've got to fill out the paperwork."

They spoke in unison. "John Matthew."

"After his father," Deborah murmured.

Anna nodded. It was common to have three or four people with the same name in an Amish community, and it made it all the more confusing when a midwife got a nervous phone call and someone forgot to leave an address. "All right. I'll give you three some alone time." She walked toward the door, then turned back around with a smile. "By the way, I have to make it a habit to check my watch at each delivery. Your son was born on Second Christmas, 12:05 a.m." She closed the door on the happy family and walked out to the kitchen table, which was laden with covered trays of Christmas cookies that Deborah must have prepared before her labor began. She saw Asa folding white tea towels and dipping them with tongs into the steaming kettles, which filled the room with rich, spicy scents. He must have taken her instructions about herbal remedies to heart. He turned and laid the tongs aside when she sat down.

"How did it go, Doc?"

She smiled up at him. "A healthy baby boy. John Matthew Loftus."

Asa leaned back against a counter and half closed his eyes in consideration. "The babe will be the sixth John Matthew Loftus to bless the community."

Anna laughed. "I wondered how many there might be."

She drew the necessary paperwork and forms from her bag and began to write in her copperplate handwriting.

Asa came forward and put a cup of coffee in front of her. "Here. Now, tell me—how are you?"

She paused in her writing as his question penetrated. She couldn't recall a time that anyone had ever asked her that after a delivery . . . not even her mother when she returned home. The simple question brought a rush of emotion and longing with it, sharp and piercing in its intensity. How was she? She bit her lip as the birth certificate blurred before her eyes.

He sat down at the table next to her. "Did I say something wrong?"

She shook her head, then realized he was waiting for a response.

"It's just that . . . you'll think it's silly, but it's just that no one's ever asked me that before and I've never realized how lonely a job it can be . . . I mean, people say thank you and are so grateful, but right after a birth no one's ever asked me how I was. Thank you." She looked away, hoping he wouldn't notice the tears that she barely held in check.

He repeated his question in a soft whisper. "So, how are you?"

She laughed, feeling jubilant in her spirit with a realization from the Lord that tomorrow didn't matter, nor the rest of the night; this moment was enough. She met his gaze, drowning in the dark depths of his eyes. "I'm fine—tired but so happy that everything went well."

"*Gut*," he murmured. "That's good. I'm glad." She caught her breath as he leaned closer to her, and for a wild moment she thought he might actually kiss her, but then the bedroom door opened and John emerged.

"They're both asleep. Thank you again, Doc. Deborah wanted me to offer you some cookies, or would you like a sandwich?"

Anna penned out the remainder of the paperwork with haste. "Cookies would be good . . . to go." She glanced at Asa. "Actually, I'd like to check on another patient my aunt told me about, depending on where she lives. I just feel a responsibility to *Aenti* Ruth to make sure all of her possible deliveries are okay."

John shook his head at the darkened window where the snow beat without mercy. "It might be better for you to stay until morning, Doc. The storm's bad." He looked at Asa over the top of her head, and Anna turned to Asa.

"*Nee,* if the Doc says we go, we go. I trust her instincts. Who is it?"

Anna thought. "Sarah Raber."

John looked relieved. "*Ach*, that's only a mile away then."

"*Gut*." Asa rose. "I'll bring the horse and buggy out of the barn while you get ready."

"And I'll have one last look at Deborah and the baby." Anna bustled into the bedroom, much more pleased with Deborah's eased respirations. She reminded John about the hospital, then stuffed the side pockets of her bag with the cookies he pressed on her. He opened the door and held a lantern high as she stepped out onto the porch, rocked by the combination of wind and snow. Asa moved like a huge shadow in the blur of white, coming to the steps and leading her into the buggy while his horse stood still. She waved toward the light of John's lantern, then refocused on the bleak road before them, but Asa was energetic and cheerful.

"That was great," he announced as he tucked the Jacob's Ladder quilt across her lap once more. She tried to focus on his words instead of his gloved hand and nodded in agreement.

"It's always something wonderful when it's a first baby, but each one is special."

He was navigating the buggy through the blowing snow with apparent calm.

"I think it's a *gut* plan to stop by the Rabers' tonight. The weather's not going to give any. I can't believe there are so many women due to labor tonight."

She decided not to tell him about the third possibility at that moment. "Babies don't wait on the weather or holidays," she pointed out instead.

He grinned at her and once more she had to resist the myriad of sensations that danced across her usual reason. Her gaze dropped to his mouth, and she imagined what it might be like to steal a kiss from him. She'd only been kissed by two boys during her young adulthood, and both were memorable for their sloppy lack of prowess. One had been from a boy who'd called her stuck up and who'd kissed her out of taunting more than desire, and the other had been from a youth one year her senior who'd been on his *rumschpringe* and smelled of sweat and alcohol. After that, Anna had focused all of her mental energies on her studies once she'd gained her parents' approval to proceed. She'd had no time for men, but now she discovered that she had a great potential for fantasizing. She could imagine Asa sleeping somewhere, maybe in a grassy field, and her leaning over his firm mouth to . . .

"*Ach*! We can get through!"

She jumped in her seat and he regarded her with a quizzical smile.

"Dreaming again, Doc?"

She blushed and was grateful for the dim interior of the buggy.

"No . . . I, ah . . . was thinking about . . . ah, what we might find at the Rabers'." Her voice ended on a squeak and she swallowed hard.

He eased on the reins and pushed his hat back a bit, exposing more of his dark mane of hair and strong brow. "Hmm . . . well, *Derr Herr* has his plans for what we'll meet at the Rabers', but I know that I do a fair bit of daydreaming myself, especially when I'm plowing."

"What do you daydream about?" she ventured with a guilty conscience, considering the train of her own thoughts.

His laugh was husky, causing a knot of feeling to tighten

in her stomach. "Weird things, I guess, like picturing the sky a different color, or the way dew bounces on a spider-web, or just remembering climbing trees when I was a kid . . ."

She was silent, drinking in the unconscious poetry of his words.

"Think I'm *narrisch*?"

She shook her head. "I think you're—real." *Real as honey on hot bread*, her mind whispered.

"Thanks." He smiled. "If I ever told any of my brothers what I just told you, they'd take me down to the creek and give me a good dunking to fix my addled brain."

"How many brothers?"

"Four. I'm the second oldest. What about you?"

"Two younger sisters . . . both married." She felt she should add their marital status for some reason.

"Does that make them more 'real' than you somehow—that they're married?"

She looked at him in surprise, amazed at his intuitiveness. "*Jah*, but why would you ask me that? How could you know?"

"My own brothers are married and neither they nor their wives ever stop pointing out to me that I'm missing out on real life because I'm not married."

She laughed aloud. "And are you?"

He looked at her and again she thought she saw a shadow pass over his face, but he just shook his head. "Maybe I've never considered it fully until now."

She found that she couldn't proceed with her line of questions without blushing and felt relieved when he turned the buggy into a drift-deepened lane. Anna marveled at how well the horse responded to the control of its master as it navigated through the snow. "You're a *gut* driver."

"Thanks, but a buggy's the best way to travel in snow this deep. After that, you need something from the *Englisch*." She felt him study her profile and tried to sit up a little straighter.

"Is this your first winter delivering babies?"

"*Ach*, no . . . my second, but I didn't expect Paradise to be having a storm like we do up in the mountains at Pine Creek."

"It's a doozy, all right. You drive yourself at night?" he asked.

"*Jah*, it's safe."

He grunted but didn't respond.

"*Ach*, that must be the house, and from the looks of things, we might be just in time," Anna said as she peered through the haze of snow at the farmhouse and saw that all the downstairs windows blazed with kerosene lamps. Even the barn door, farther on, revealed a thin line of welcoming light.

"I'll get you in there first and then wipe down Dandy." Asa leaped out of the buggy as she folded the quilt back. She waited only seconds before she felt him grasp her around the waist. Somehow, even through the bulk of her clothes, she could feel the warm press of his hands and the length of his leg as he hugged her to his side and swept her onto the porch.

She glanced over her shoulder to watch him stride against the wind and back to the buggy before she knocked at the front door. She decided that no one could hear her over the subdued din of the storm, so she pulled off a glove with her teeth and tried the knob. It gave with no problem and opened to a typical Amish kitchen: neat, well ordered, warm with light, but silent. She tiptoed inside, recalling her aunt's primer that Sarah Raber already had four children, and hoped she wouldn't wake anyone. Considering the hour, perhaps everyone was asleep and they'd just left lights burning because of the storm.

She was debating whether to knock on the master bedroom door or head back out to the barn when the door burst open behind her with a gust of swirling air.

"Anna," Asa gasped, his cheeks flushed, light snow dusting his face. "Sarah and Ezekiel are in the barn. They were trying to make it to the hospital or her *mamm*'s, but she's in their buggy . . . I think the baby's coming now!"

Anna pulled the edges of her cloak together. "Let's go."

The wind was piercing in its intensity. Even a few moments of respite from the cold hadn't prepared Anna for heading back outside. She caught her breath when Asa lifted her with ease off her feet, bag and all. "I'll carry you; you'll stay drier," he yelled.

Anna forgot about the cold and wished the few feet

of being held against his chest could go on forever. His damp wool coat rubbed against her tender cheek like a hushed secret. And his purposeful steps made her wonder what it would be like to have someone to help carry her through life's burdens, or at least through clover fields in high summer. She smiled and knew she'd remember this Second Christmas for as long as she lived.

He bumped open the barn door with his hip, then slid her to the ground, twisting to shut out as much cold as possible. She was surprised at the overall warmth of the barn, its walls insulated by the hay, the feed bags, and the animals' bodies themselves. She noticed Asa had withdrawn his quilt from beneath his coat and laid it on a clean hay bale. Lamps burned, highlighting the hay and the shadowy movements of the animals' bodies, as cows chewed from their mangers and horses shifted with gentleness. Asa had stabled his horse in a stall to her right and must have left the buggy outside, though she'd been in no frame of mind to notice it.

But now, Anna couldn't help but compare the comforting warmth of the scene to the one so long ago, on that first Christmas. Only the starkness of a woman's cry brought her back to reality and reminded her that her Lord and Savior had few of the comforts that lay before her. The Rabers' buggy was hitched and ready to go with one door still wide open. Mr. Raber, a middle-aged Amish man with a blue shirt and black suspenders, was running his hands through his hair and speaking in earnest, soft

Pennsylvania Dutch to the occupant of the buggy while Asa stood tense with his back turned.

Mr. Raber caught sight of Anna and hurried over, his hand extended. "You are Anna, *Frau* Ruth's niece, *jah*? Thank *Derr Herr* you've come. How did you ever know?"

He wrung Anna's hand with goodwill, and she caught a firmer grip on the handle of her bag. She smiled with reassurance. "The Lord is in control. So this is your fifth child, Mr. Raber? May I examine your wife? I take it that things have moved rather fast?"

He led her to the buggy. "*Jah*, so we thought, but something is wrong now." He kept his voice low, then stepped away to unhitch the horse, who was beginning to dance restlessly.

Anna peered inside at the laboring woman. She met the anguished green eyes of Sarah Raber and recognized worry mixed with pain in equal amounts. Her first job was to calm her drained patient.

"I'm Anna Stolis, Sarah. Have you had problems or delays with your other deliveries?"

"*Nee.*" The woman shook her head and put a hand up to push her *kapp* back on her head. "And we thought this one . . . would be as easy, but . . . we got into the buggy and I felt like pushing, but nothing's happened. I'm afraid it's been too long . . ." Tears dripped from her eyes as she clutched the sides of the buggy seat with white-tipped fingers.

"*Aenti* Ruth said that you could probably deliver

without me," Anna told her with a heartfelt smile. "Now, let's just see what's going on, shall we?"

Anna disinfected and pulled on her gloves, praying as she went through her comforting preparation rituals. She had a sick feeling of what might actually be wrong.

Lifting her head a few moments later, Anna kept a reassuring smile plastered on her face. The baby was Frank breech, and Sarah was right: time was growing short. She thought for a moment, knowing there was no way to get the mother and baby to the hospital in time.

Just then the barn door slid open, letting in a blast of snow. A wide-eyed girl of about ten stood in her nightgown, oversized boots, and a shawl.

"*Was en der welt*, Esther?" Mr. Raber exclaimed. "You will freeze, child!"

"I had a nightmare, *Daed*. I called for you and *Mamm* . . . what's wrong?"

Sarah spoke to her husband in quick Pennsylvania Dutch from inside the buggy, and Mr. Raber went to gather up his daughter. "I will take her back and tuck her in."

Anna spoke in soothing tones to the laboring woman when he'd gone. "Sarah, your baby is breech. Do you understand what that means?"

Sarah choked on a sob. "*Jah*, we will lose the child. My best friend's baby was breech—she couldn't make it to the hospital in time."

"Well, as the Lord wills, you are not going to lose this child." Anna spoke with confidence. She rummaged in her bag and opened a sterilized kit containing a gown, mask, pads, and another pair of gloves. "I've delivered three breech babies in the last two years. It will be okay—you just listen and do what I tell you to, all right?"

"All right," Sarah gasped.

Anna smiled, then called for Asa to come nearer the buggy.

He came reluctantly, clearly feeling it was not his place.

"Sarah, Asa Mast is here," Anna said from behind her mask. "He drove me tonight. I may need his help if Mr. Raber doesn't come back right away. We have to move fast."

"It's—okay—just please help my baby."

"Asa," Anna said in a low tone. "Sarah's baby is breech. Put on a pair of gloves from my bag and find something warm . . . your coat . . . and get ready to take the baby when I hand it to you."

"Breech . . ." he said, meeting her eyes, and she couldn't look long at the fear she saw there.

"*Derr Herr* will not abandon us. Hurry."

"*Jah,*" he murmured, turning to do as she asked.

Anna prayed as she began the delicate delivery, closing her eyes and visualizing the anatomy of mother and baby.

"Everything's fine, Sarah. Don't push, not yet. Just breathe." *Please, Lord, help this baby's head to not be too large. Please let it pass easily . . . help me, Lord, please . . .*

Sarah drew deep, wrenching breaths as Anna manipulated the small bottom and limbs, wishing she could give

Sarah something for the pain. But she'd probably refuse it, and there was no time.

Then everything began to move at once, and Anna took a deep breath when she felt the size of the baby's head. "Okay, Sarah, just a little push . . ."

Sarah pushed and Anna strained to put subtle pressure on the head. Within seconds, the squalls of a newborn baby girl echoed in the vastness of the barn, mixing with her mother's sobs. Anna cut the cord, suctioned the breathing passages, wrapped the baby in sterilized pads, then turned to transfer the bloody, squalling scrap of humanity into Asa's outstretched hands, which were covered by his *grossmuder*'s quilt.

Anna met his brown eyes, finding them welled with tears. "To keep the girl warm," he murmured, wrapping and cradling the baby in his strong arms.

Anna swallowed hard and turned back to Sarah. "It's a girl, Sarah. She looks great; I'll check her over. Let me just see to you for a moment."

Sarah rested her head back against the buggy door, breathing soft prayers of thanksgiving as the barn door opened and Mr. Raber hurried to the buggy. Anna watched Asa hold out the bundle in his arms from the corner of her eye.

"A girl," Asa told him. "Congratulations, *Daed*."

"And Sarah?" Mr. Raber moved to look inside the buggy.

"She did a wonderful job," Anna said.

"*Gut*," Mr. Raber choked. "That's good."

"She was breech, Ezekiel." Sarah sniffed. "We could have lost her . . . but *Derr Herr* . . . he was with us."

"He is always with us, Sarah," Ezekiel Raber whispered as he stared down at his new daughter. "He gives and takes away, but praise him for giving this night."

Sarah nodded, then stretched to pat Anna's hand. "And you, and Asa Mast—we could not have done this without you both."

Anna smiled and finished with the usual post-delivery chores, pleased that Sarah did not bleed too much with the delivery of the placenta. She covered the new mother with her cloak, which had dried somewhat, then cleaned everything in sight. She turned to see Mr. Raber's eyes filled with tears as he rocked from side to side with his new daughter.

"*Dunki*, Anna, and Asa too."

"What will you name her?" Anna asked after examining the baby again. She had drawn the birth certificate forms from her bag and watched from where she leaned against the top of a bale of hay.

Mr. Raber rested against the buggy and stared with love at his wife. "What will it be?"

Sarah Raber spoke. "That quilt she's wrapped in— where did it come from?"

Asa had turned his back to the buggy once more but

279

came forward to answer. "It was my *grossmuder*'s. Please, I want you to keep it—for her hope chest maybe." He nodded at the cherubic face, half revealed. Anna smiled.

"What was your *grossmuder*'s name, Asa—I can't seem to think straight." Sarah laughed.

"Rachel."

Sarah and her husband smiled, and Anna began to letter the birth certificate even before they spoke.

"Then Rachel it shall be," Sarah announced. "Rachel Anna Raber."

Anna looked up in surprise and felt a thrill of delight. She'd never had a namesake, and now she felt the page in front of her blur with the onset of tears and weariness, which she swiped away before they could smear the ink. "Time of birth . . . 2:20 a.m., Second Christmas. Congratulations."

"Thank you."

Asa humbly bent his head at the couple, and Anna nodded. "*Jah*, thank you so much."

THREE

Asa helped Ezekiel Raber harness the horse to the buggy again as Anna made Sarah and the baby as warm and shielded as possible inside. The trip from the barn to the house was only twenty-five feet or so, but Anna wanted there to be no opportunity for either patient to take a chill. She also made Sarah lie on a makeshift stretcher, created from a wide, thin roll of plastic window insulation that Ezekiel had found and made more secure with two blankets he'd tramped back to the house to get. Ezekiel got up on the buggy seat to drive as Asa went to open the barn doors.

Asa paused a moment, wanting there to be no mistakes now that everything had gone so well. "I'll hold the horse's head, Ezekiel, if you like. Just in case he balks."

"*Gut* idea. The storm is more than anything I've seen in years."

Asa caught the bridle with a soothing sound, glanced back for Anna's nod to proceed, and opened the barn door. The wind whipped inside with wild abandon and the horse attempted to rear. Asa held firm, though he felt like his arms were going to be wrenched out of their sockets, and the horse seemed to relax when it realized that neither man panicked. Asa pushed through the thick, wet snow as tiny pieces of ice, like shards of glass, drove against his face and down the neck of his coat. He felt as if he were wading through freezing maple syrup when they finally got to the steps, and that was the easy part. They still had to get mother and daughter safely and painlessly inside.

It hadn't been easy, Asa reflected as he walked to the whistling kettle at the stove. He decided he never wanted to be responsible for transporting a new mother again, unless—his mind drifted with sleepy lassitude—it happened to be Anna. The thought jerked him wide-awake, and he moved the kettle with more force than he'd intended, sloshing the boiling water over the side of the cup. He put the back of his hand to his mouth and gave it an instinctive suck.

"Here . . . don't do that." Anna sounded worried, and he felt himself flush as though she could read his thoughts. She rose to go to the Rabers' icebox and brought him a clean towel with ice.

"Let me see your hand."

"It's fine."

"Now, please." She smiled sweetly but wearily at him.

He sighed and extended his burned hand. She wrapped it in the ice-cold towel, and he watched her delicate fingers press here and there against his work-roughened hand as she secured the fabric. It made him feel hot behind his collar, and he could only nod when she told him to be still while she hurried to get antibiotic ointment from her bag. It was a blessing that Ezekiel, Sarah, and the baby were in the master bedroom, resting after the precarious trip out of the buggy and up the steps. The wind had almost tipped the stretcher, and Asa's heart had ached at the involuntary moan of pain Sarah had emitted against the wind. They'd finally gotten her inside and into bed, and Anna continued to check between mother and daughter. Ezekiel had hastily shown Anna and Asa where to find the coffee and cookies and then had gone to be with his wife.

Asa held the wet towel in place until Anna crossed back to him with her bag.

"Seems like you must have everything but a church meeting going on in there," he joked, trying to regain his equilibrium of thought.

She nodded with an absent *mmm-hmm*. She was clearly in Doc mode. But he didn't feel dismissed when she gently peeled back the towel and began to massage the clear ointment over his hand. In truth, more than the sudden sparks of sensation her touch sent down his spine, an expanding, ridiculous urge to cry rose up in his chest.

He bent his head and wet his lips as a wash of images invaded his mind. He remembered how he'd wrenched his hand fixing the axle of the car he'd bought and hidden from his family when he was seventeen. It had been one of the first times he'd gone driving with Jennifer. He'd asked her for help as the blood had rushed from the deep laceration, but she'd glanced away, looking disgusted. So he'd wrapped his own hand, using his teeth and a rag, and had decided that such common things were beneath anyone so wonderful as Jennifer. He grimaced now at the irony of it all and forced himself back to the moment as he realized Anna had just spoken.

"Uh, I'm sorry—what?"

She'd turned his hand over, exposing his palm and the long, jagged scar. "I asked how you got this. It looks like you never got proper first aid."

He pulled away a bit and fisted his hand from her gaze. "I was young. It was something stupid."

"Well." She gathered up her supplies. "The burn should heal well."

It will. Because of you.

Ezekiel Raber had just carried the polished cradle into the master bedroom, then returned a few minutes later to refill their mugs. A sudden grinding sound and a flash of lights passed by the dark kitchen windows, illuminating the still-falling snow.

"That'll be Joe Grossinger, a *gut Englisch* friend of

mine. He runs a plow for extra money during the winters and always does our drive for free. He'll only accept a cup of coffee to warm him up," Ezekiel explained.

Anna rose to her feet in obvious excitement. "Is that a dump truck he's driving?"

Ezekiel nodded. "*Jah*, with a plow on front, and he drops cinders or gravel from the back. Why?"

"*Jah*, why?" Asa asked Anna, who swallowed under his alert gaze.

In hindsight, perhaps she should have told him straight off about the three possible labors, but she hadn't thought the storm would be so bad. And in her experience men could usually only handle one labor a night, though Asa had already proved her wrong.

When she didn't respond, Ezekiel lit another lantern and went to the front door. She clasped her hands in front of her and looked at Asa.

"Well, it's just that . . . *Aenti* Ruth told me that there could be one more delivery tonight, and I thought . . ."

He raised his dark brows and half groaned. "Another delivery? Is all of Paradise due to deliver tonight? And when exactly do you sleep, Anna?"

"I . . . don't . . . at least, not a lot. Look, you don't have to go with me. I can ask Mr. Grossinger if he will take me and then I'll—"

He straightened up in his chair. "Do you think I'm letting you go off with some stranger—an *Englischer*—in the middle of the night?"

"Well, you were a stranger too . . ." She trailed off, thinking she felt as if she'd known him so much longer than just a few hours.

He must have caught the look in her eye because he leaned forward and searched her face. "And am I still a stranger, Anna?"

She caught her breath at his words, amazed that they shared the same thought. She shook her head as she returned his gaze. "*Nee*, you are no stranger."

She might have gone on if Ezekiel hadn't led a tall, lanky *Englisch* man into the room.

"Joe, this is Anna and Asa . . . they helped Sarah give birth a couple of hours ago. A little girl this time!" Ezekiel beamed.

"Well, shoot!" Joe exclaimed, whipping off his ball cap to reveal an unruly crop of dark curls. "That makes five, don't it, Zeke? I've got to say that I envy you and the missus." He gave Ezekiel a backslapping hug that was returned enthusiastically, then he stretched big, dirt-stained hands to shake with Anna and Asa. Anna found herself enjoying the open personality of the *Englischer*, who had just plopped himself down at the kitchen table and accepted his mug of coffee as if he'd been there many times.

"How's the storm looking?" Ezekiel asked. "Anna wants me to take both Sarah and the baby into town tomorrow for a checkup at the hospital."

Joe laughed. "I'm about as lonesome out there as Santy Claus, and him a day late. It's bad. But I'll be glad to come back out and get you folks tomorrow morning when it slows down a bit."

Ezekiel smiled. "I think it'll be all right."

Asa cleared his throat. "Well, actually, Ezekiel, Joe . . . uh . . . Anna's got to check on one more woman who could deliver this morning. We were thinking of asking maybe to keep the buggy here and to see if Joe might drive us to—" He glanced at Anna, who had a slight smile on her face.

"The Stolises'," she supplied. "Mary Stolis."

Asa and Ezekiel groaned aloud in perfect unison.

"What?" Anna and Joe asked at the same time.

Asa sighed. "Mary and Luke Stolis are a nice couple. Everyone in the community mourned when she lost the last baby. The Stolises run a big woodworking shop out of their house and outbuildings. A lot of brothers, sisters—"

"So?" Anna queried.

"It's Luke's mother, *Grossmuder* Stolis, who runs the house and kind of makes things difficult for people. She's . . . older, lost her husband, and she's kind of stern."

"Mean," Ezekiel clarified.

"Got a few relatives like that myself," Joe commented with a chuckle.

"Well, I've dealt with plenty of strong-willed older folks up at Pine Creek," Anna said, shrugging her shoulders. "She can't be that bad."

Again, Asa and Ezekiel looked rather like they'd both eaten a bad pickle.

"Well, I'd sure enough be glad to get you there," Joe offered. "I know where that big woodworking outfit is, though I can't promise the lane might not be drifted over."

"Oh, we'd be so grateful." Anna clapped her hands.

Joe drained his cup. "All righty then. Let's get to it. Zeke, tell Sarah congratulations and I'll swing by again to check on you all when it lightens up."

Anna went to examine Sarah and the baby once more, then pulled on her boots and cape and grabbed her bag. She felt a renewed energy, though she could tell that Asa was dragging a bit as he adjusted his hat and gloves.

"Be careful. And *danki* again." Ezekiel shook Asa's and Joe's hands and patted Anna's shoulder, then opened the door to the frigid air once more.

FOUR

Anna had never ridden in a dump truck or any kind of truck for that matter, and she was delighted by the new experience. Joe had left the engine running, and he climbed into the driver's seat while Asa led Anna to the passenger door and then boosted her up to the high seat inside.

She breathed in the heavy scent of the heat that blew from the truck's vents, feeling drowsiness seep into her with the warmth. Then she'd had to crawl over empty plastic water bottles, potato chip wrappers, and an assortment of tools to get to the middle of the seat.

Joe stuffed as many of the oddities as he could behind the seat as Anna got situated. Asa climbed in beside her, and she found herself squashed between the two men with her bag situated on her lap. Joe turned a knob and the blaring sound of Christmas music faded.

"Sorry for the mess."

"No problem." Asa laughed. "You should see the back of my buggy sometimes."

Anna watched as Joe backed the truck down the lane, a loud beeping sound accompanying the movement. She had to press against the seat as he swung the huge steering wheel, his bony elbows protruding here and there. Then he backed onto the lane and began a slow pace across the treacherous piles of icy snow.

"Did you have a good Christmas, Joe?" Anna asked.

"As good as can be. I went to church—I know you folks are big on that. Then I had dinner at my momma's and watched some TV."

How lonely, Anna thought as she considered all the family she had.

"Oh," she murmured.

Joe sighed. "I used to have a wife but she run off. Took the kids with her. It's not been the same since."

"I'm so sorry," Anna said.

"Ah, it's not so bad. I do have a girlfriend now, but I'm kind of takin' it slow like. I don't want to make another mistake like before. You know what I mean?"

Asa cleared his throat. "*Jah*, you are a wise man to be cautious—and a good man, to help Ezekiel and us too."

Anna considered Asa's use of the word *cautious*, but Joe had resumed talking.

"I like your kind, the Amish. You seem—real to me. That matters."

"Thank you," Asa replied with quiet sincerity.

Joe adjusted the plow, then whistled for a few seconds. "So, you folks got kids of your own?"

Anna spluttered at Joe's assumption that they were married.

"Uh . . . no . . . we—"

Joe grinned. "Well, they'll come along, right as rain. Happens that way, you know." He resumed whistling, and Anna couldn't find the voice to correct him. She noticed Asa's silence as well and tried to ignore the warm press of his body against her side.

"Okay," Joe announced after a few long minutes, slowing the vehicle. "I think this is it." He began to turn cautiously into the lane but soon shook his head in frustration.

"Their lane's a lot narrower than Zeke's and the drifts are huge. I wish I could get you a bit closer." Joe tugged on his ball cap and stared out at the blinding white illuminated by the headlights of the vehicle. "I can't take a risk going off the lane; I'd never get her out. I don't know if you should try and walk it."

"We'll get through," Asa said. "Thank you very much."

"I'll keep the lights on high 'til I see that you're near the house, but you'd better move fast. Those drifts look chest deep in some places."

"Thank you." Anna smiled, laying her hand on Joe's arm as Asa lifted the large latch on the door and swung it open, letting in a blast of cold air and a heavy fall of snow onto the vinyl seat. Anna tried to brush it away.

"Aw, leave it," Joe said. "Go on now. I'll keep watch."

Asa swung her down into the snow, and she was amazed that it reached as high as her waist. The cold engulfed her as Asa closed the door and then took her bag and her arm.

"I'd carry you," he called over the wind, "but I don't want to take the chance of dropping you in a drift. Can you make it?"

"*Jah*!" she yelled back as they waded out into the twin beams of the truck's headlights, which reflected a good distance ahead.

Anna gave vague consideration to how quickly she ceased to feel her feet and then noticed that her heartbeat, after a few slogging steps, began to shift from hard pumping to a slow lassitude. She tried to concentrate and took deep breaths of the biting snow, then started reciting anatomy facts as the first insidious thoughts of sleep whispered at the back of her consciousness. She shook herself and almost went down in a drift but felt strong hands hauling her back to her feet.

Asa shook her. "Come on," he called. "We can do this."

She nodded, but it must not have satisfied him because he shook her again, and this time she felt her teeth rattle.

"Anna Stolis!" he yelled. "I am not going in this house, where that wiry old woman lives, to deliver a baby alone! I don't know how—so stay awake!"

"All right," she snapped, and he dragged her on.

Soon they were out of the reach of the truck's lights. Anna felt a moment of fear as the snow swirled with blinding force around them, but she found herself remembering that all was light to *Derr Herr*. He knew the way they were going, and he'd apparently revealed it to Asa as she felt herself yanked along. Soaked to her neck, she staggered, then came to an abrupt halt when she ran into Asa's broad back.

"Are we lost?" she yelled.

"No—clothesline." He reached above his head, and she had to laugh at the thought of Asa getting clotheslined by a diligent housewife in the middle of a blizzard. A few steps more, and Anna saw the reassuring bulk of the house. From a distance, they heard Joe honk his horn as he pulled away, and Asa pounded on the door where only a dim light shone from the inside. Again, Anna hoped she'd not brought them on some fool's errand in the small hours of the night, but the door opened with abruptness.

They staggered into a large, dim living room and Anna tried to steady her breathing. She wiped the wet snow from her face, and it became apparent that, although few lights burned, the room held three women who stared at Anna and Asa as though they were apparitions.

Asa spoke first. "It's Asa Mast and *Frau* Ruth's niece, Anna Stolis. We thought we'd come check on Mary . . ." He trailed off when no one responded. Only Anna's deep intakes of breath could be heard.

Then the oldest woman gave a crack of harsh laughter. "The clock says close to four a.m., and there's a blizzard. Are you drunk or just fools?"

Anna felt Asa stiffen beside her but decided it was a fair, albeit rude, question.

"Neither, ma'am," she said politely, coughing a bit and trying to reach the snow that trailed down her neck with a discreet hand. "I felt a responsibility to *Aenti* Ruth to check on all of her possible deliveries tonight, especially because of the storm, to make sure all was going well."

"Well, all is not well, missy. Luke Stolis is in bed with the flu, as are his brothers, two of the children, and my two sisters. The rest of us, myself and my two daughters, are just sitting here waiting to get it."

"*Grossmuder* Stolis," Asa said with resignation. "I'm sorry you're going through this; my *daed* is down with it too."

"*Humph*—time was nothing could get Samuel Mast down. He's getting old."

Anna heard the small rumble that escaped Asa's lips and ignored the steady drip from her freezing nose.

"Please excuse me, Mrs. Stolis, but you didn't mention your daughter-in-law, Mary. Is she feeling well?"

"Who are you?" The old woman leaned forward with an ominous creak from her rocker.

"Anna Stolis, from Pine Creek. As Asa said, I'm Ruth Stolis's niece and have taken over her midwifery duties for this night."

"Pine Creek, hmm? No relation that I can think of just now."

Anna sneezed, and Asa made an impatient gesture with his arm. "We are soaked and freezing. How is Mary?"

Anna felt his frustration but clung to her diplomacy, not wanting to alienate one of *Aenti* Ruth's patients' family members. But she needed to know how the pregnant woman felt so they could march with good conscience back out into the freezing cold.

"Mrs. Stolis, I've been practicing midwifery successfully for the past two years in Pine Creek, and *Aenti* Ruth briefed me on Mary's last pregnancy. I'm sorry that she lost the child."

"There is nothing to be sorry for in the will of *Derr Herr.*"

Anna did a mental count to ten and tried to wriggle her toes. She knew she had to get past the older woman, but her patience was running out.

"Of course the Lord's will is best, but we've come far tonight. Could you just tell me that Mary is doing well?"

A woman sniffed from the shadows. "As well as can be expected for a body nine months pregnant and in labor."

Dead silence reigned in the room for all of three seconds, and then Anna's patience exploded.

"That's it!" Her voice bounced off the walls, and the two quiet sisters jumped in their chairs. She felt Asa start beside her as well, but she didn't care. She pulled off her icy gloves with her teeth, letting them fall with wet plops onto the hardwood floor. Her cape, scarf, bonnet, and boots followed in quick succession, building an inelegant, dripping pile. She hopped gracelessly from one foot to the other as she peeled off her soaking knee socks, flinging them backward to splat low against the wall. Then she grabbed her snow-covered bag from Asa's hands.

Anna stepped forward into the gloomy room and caught up a lantern from a side table, turning it to its highest flame, then setting it back down with a thump. Her gaze swept the room until it came to rest on the older, black-eyed woman sitting in full Amish church-meeting dress, who was regarding them without emotion. Anna swept toward her, ignoring the two other women, and moved to drop her bag on the floor in front of the matriarch.

Anna caught the arms of the rocking chair and knelt to give an even glare into the dark eyes. "Now let me make myself clear, Mrs. Stolis. I don't care who you are or who you think you are in this family, but—as *Derr Herr* wills—this baby will not die under my watch. So unbend your stiff neck for two minutes and take me to Mary, or I'll search every room myself."

There was an infinitesimal pause.

"You're not married, are you?" Mrs. Stolis asked.

Anna would have given the chair, possibly even the grandmother herself, a good shake had she not heard Asa's sudden choked laughter.

She whirled to shoot him an accusing glance, but he held up a placating hand.

"What," Anna snapped, "is so amusing?"

Asa shook his head. "Ask *Grossmuder* Stolis."

"*Jah*," the older woman said with what could only be described as suppressed mirth. "No one's spoken to me like that in a good long time. Not since Henry died. I— I've missed it, truth be told. He kept me in line, and I've become a shrunken apple without him." She gave a wry glance at her frozen daughters. "There's not much fruit on the trees around here. But you, Anna Stolis from Pine Creek, you just gave me the nicest Christmas gift I've had in nearly fifteen years."

Anna sank to her heels with a shiver and pulled her bag back on her lap. "So, where's Mary?"

"I haven't abandoned her, if that's what you're worried about. I want to keep the flu away from her—her husband has it. So she's comfortable in a bedroom on the third floor. One of us goes up to check on her every few minutes."

Anna was already on her feet. "I'll just have a look."

"You're going to freeze to death, Anna," Asa pointed out. "Your clothes are soaked."

Anna glanced down at her blouse and skirt, which clung stubbornly to every curve she had, and sighed. First, she'd lost her temper in front of the only man who'd ever given her a second glance, and now her generous shape was portioned out in bland revelation by the light she'd turned up herself.

"I'm fine," she said.

Grossmuder Stolis rose to her feet and looked at her daughters. "Esther, Miriam, take Anna Stolis upstairs and get her some dry clothes—though I doubt anything you have will fit. You're both thin as beans."

Anna's eyes widened at the veiled insult and she cleared her throat.

"I'm sorry." Mrs. Stolis laughed. "I've always fancied beans"—she gave Anna's waist a quick pinch—"and fresh bread. Go on now, girls."

Anna grimaced at another stifled laugh from Asa, picked up her bag, and followed the two bewildered sisters out of the room.

The two women, clearly overwhelmed at the abrupt change in events, could do nothing more than lay out clothes for Anna and then they hastily left her alone. She changed quickly, caught up her bag, and went onto the landing to continue up the stairs to the third floor.

She peered down a long, narrow hallway of doors and saw the sliver of light from beneath one at the far end. She went to the door and knocked, not knowing what to expect, and a cheerful woman's voice bade her to come in.

FIVE

~∞~

She opened the door and was amazed to see a lovely, fresh-faced woman, gowned and *kapped*, sitting up in a beautiful bed, reading a magazine.

"Mary?"

"*Jah,* are you *Frau* Ruth's niece? She told me about you on my last visit with her. She's very proud of you."

Anna came into the room and closed the door. "*Jah,* I'm Anna. *Danki.* How are you?" She recalled that Aunt Ruth had said Mary proclaimed herself to be "healthy as a horse."

The woman in the bed cast her an easy smile. "I'm wonderful. Do you want to check my pulse and blood pressure? Ruth always does."

Anna nodded, feeling a little dazed. Perhaps she had dragged Asa on a fool's errand, for no woman in labor had ever looked so serene.

Mary's pulse and pressure were excellent. "Any contractions or pain?" she asked, feeling like she already knew the answer. Mrs. Stolis must have been mistaken about the labor.

Mary laid her magazine, which Anna noted was an *Englisch* publication on labor and delivery, on the full mound of her stomach and nodded. "Every five minutes, regular as can be. I should be ready to push soon."

Anna looked around the bedroom, feeling out of her depth. She noted the elaborately carved cradle that stood ready nearby.

"My husband, Luke, carved that at the shop. After we lost our last baby, he wanted to 'make all things new' for this one's arrival."

"It's beautiful," Anna said as she drew out her stethoscope. She didn't want to have to listen for the heartbeat; it was possible that there were no visible signs of pain because the baby had already been lost in utero. Yet she had no choice. She avoided Mary's gentle smile as she moved aside the quilts and bent her head.

She nearly sagged with relief against the bed when she heard the heartbeat, strong and steady, and saw the now visible contractions that tightened Mary's belly.

"Everything's fine," Mary told her before she could say anything, and Anna nodded.

"Forgive me, Mary, please, but how . . . do you know? You should be in some pain at this point, if not a lot."

Mary smiled again and reached beneath the pile of white pillows at her back and drew out a folded piece of paper. "It's simple, really. For this pregnancy, I saw that there were four of us involved, right from the beginning. Luke agreed with me."

"Four?" Anna wondered if it were possible that her patient carried twins and Ruth had missed it.

"*Jah*, Luke, myself, the baby, and *Derr Herr*." She handed Anna the piece of paper.

Anna bent her head to read. " 'And he that sat upon the throne said, "Behold, I make all things new." ' Revelation 21:5."

Anna lifted her gaze back to Mary's.

"I chose to embrace this verse with Luke and the baby and to make it the theme verse—the quilt pattern, if you will—of this pregnancy. I know that there is newness even in death, of course, but this time I believe that *Derr Herr* has a different plan."

"It's beautiful."

"Our Lord is beautiful. Now it's time to push," Mary said with little ceremony.

Anna drew on her gloves, mask, and gown with haste, but had little time to prepare anything else as Mary urged her to hurry.

Two brief pushes later, a wide-eyed baby boy emerged with perfect breathing and excellent color. Anna had to blink back tears as she laid the baby on his mother's stomach and cut the cord. She'd never felt so humbled by the presence of new life or by the faith of a mother.

She performed her aftercare quietly as she listened to the soft murmurs of love and the prayers of thanksgiving that echoed from mother to child. When both mother and baby were clean and dry, Anna felt enveloped in a peace that would have allowed her to sleep standing upright if she didn't have paperwork to fill out.

She leaned against a bureau and noticed that the sun was beginning to send luminous streaks of light across the window. At some point it had stopped snowing. It was Second Christmas morn.

"What will you call him, Mary?" she asked with pen poised.

"Luke and I decided a long time ago: Christian. Christian Luke Stolis."

Anna nodded and once again felt choked by tears. She wrote down the time of birth, then glanced once more at her watch, amazed that only forty-five minutes had gone by since she'd first come upstairs. She hoped Mrs. Stolis wouldn't visit soon and disrupt the peace. It seemed as though Mary could read her thoughts when she asked brightly if Anna had met her mother-in-law.

"Yes—for just a few minutes."

Mary laughed. "She's got everyone fooled but me; I know she loves me, though I have tried to encourage her to stop terrorizing everyone else."

Anna gave her a weak smile. "Maybe you'll find you've had some success with that."

With the advent of morning and the new baby in the house—in addition to a cheerful, if not tart, elder Mrs. Stolis—the feeling of Second Christmas permeated the air with warmth and goodwill. Several of the flu victims returned from their beds feeling much better and came to eat an abundant breakfast around the large wooden table. Luke Stolis arrived first and couldn't thank Anna and Asa enough, though he'd yet to see his new son; Anna had given orders that he wait at least twenty-four hours after his symptoms had subsided.

Anna accepted a place at the table, refreshed as always by the new day, though she hadn't slept at all. And though she didn't study him directly, she was conscious that someone had given Asa clean clothes, because the aqua-green shirt he now wore so matched his good looks. But it was only when she lifted her head to look at him across her breakfast plate that she noticed the flush on his handsome face. He returned her smile, but his cheeks were red and his dark eyes held the glazed, distant look she'd come to associate with illness in her practice. He coughed once, into his sleeve, then stared with disinterest at his plate of food.

Anna rose from the table. She had no desire to let the household know that there was another case of flu among them until she was quite sure. "Mrs. Stolis, I need to get my midwifery bag back in order, and there are some small chores that Asa might help me with. Do you have an extra room where I can lay all of my supplies out?"

"*Jah,* certainly. Go upstairs to the second floor and turn left. Use any of those rooms; they're all empty. I kept the flu victims on the right wing. If you need to be long, someone can build you a fire."

"I'll do it. *Danki.*"

Anna was sure that only she noticed how abruptly Asa's color changed to pallor when he got to his feet. And by the time they mounted the narrow, darkened back staircase, he leaned on her, and she struggled to get him over the top step and down the hallway.

She chose the first door that she came to and opened it, revealing a large room with a carved bed and pristine patchwork quilt. There was an abundance of pillows, too, she was glad to see. But it was chilly, and she hurried to help Asa to the bed, pulling the quilt and bedclothes down with one hand.

"Asa," she whispered. "Lie down; you'll feel better."

"Just for a minute," he mumbled. "I'll make the fire first."

"But it's already so hot in here." She improvised, knowing his fever would deter him until she could get the blaze going herself.

"Okay."

She pushed him onto his back and he closed his eyes, sinking against the pillows while she tugged and tucked all the bedclothes tightly around him. He opened his eyes to stare up at her.

"You're so beautiful," he said, then choked on a cough.

"And you're so sick," she returned, ignoring the stabbing emotion that threaded across her chest at his words.

"*Narrisch* for you, Doc," he said as he smiled, then closed his eyes until his breathing deepened and leveled off to a nasty rasp in sleep.

Anna swallowed and went to the fireplace, kindling the heat, while his words warmed her mind.

Asa knew that he was sick, very sick. He couldn't remember feeling this awful since he was a kid. He also knew that whether he was dreaming or not, Anna Stolis was taking care of him. He wanted to believe it was real when she softly urged him to swallow from a spoon or stroked his hair back from his forehead with a damp cloth. He wanted to know that it was her who trailed the coolness down his neck to the width of his shoulders. But he couldn't quite make his way through the haze in his brain to know if she was really there, so he let his mind settle for sweetly tangled, tantalizing dreams.

He cast a line into the deep pool of his favorite fishing spot and relaxed against the tall oak that grew broad enough to support his back. The heat of the summer day had yet to relent, and he reached a long arm down to scoop water from the running creek. He drank with eagerness from his cupped palm. When he lifted his head, he was amazed to see a woman wading in the creek toward him. It was the midwife—Anna—and her bare feet shone slender and white through the clear water as she lifted her dark skirt to her ankles and clambered across the damp rocks. He tried to speak, but his voice caught and he had a hard time managing his breathing as she came closer.

He wanted to tell her a thousand things: about the rock candy he used to make with his *mamm*, and learning to chop firewood, and how his coat itched during Meeting. He wanted to share with her what it was like when he'd found a motherless litter of kittens and took care of them in secret for fear he'd be laughed at by his brothers. And what he thought of her—her beauty and intelligence and strength—and her willingness to risk so much for others. It made his throat ache to think of it, but just then she lost her footing on the stones. He dropped his line and scrambled down the bank as she began to fall forward, reaching to catch her.

Anna's frown deepened as the hours lengthened. She listened through her stethoscope as Asa's chest grew tighter. She knew that the flu this season was especially virulent and that it also showed no predilection for age, affecting both young and old. And she'd been the one to have him outside running around for half the night in the freezing cold when he was probably already getting sick.

Asa pushed fitfully against the mound of covers, but

she piled them back on, only to find herself caught against his chest.

"Safe," he slurred, his eyes open and burning with fever and something else. He ran his hands up and down her arms, causing her to shiver through the fabric of her serviceable, borrowed blouse.

"*Jah*, I'm safe. Are you dreaming, Asa?"

"*Mmm-hmm*. About you."

Anna blushed even though she knew he'd probably remember nothing of this.

"Are you dreaming, Doc?" Somehow he'd found her hands and rubbed his hot, callused thumbs over her knuckles in slow, rhythmic circles.

She gazed down at him with renewed wonder. No one had ever touched her hands like this. She felt nurtured and breathless and . . . loved. Her eyes filled with tears. She could never have imagined that *Derr Herr* had such a plan as this waiting for her when she'd arrived yesterday, nor how long and wonderful the night would be. She realized the memory of this man would sustain her through all her earthly life, when suddenly the pressing thought that she might never see him again—like this—intruded.

He lifted his hands to her face and rubbed at the tears, which made slow tracks down the ripe smoothness of her cheeks, and he stared up at her.

"You're crying—are you crying?" he asked, confused.

"No." She shook her head.

"Don't cry," he whispered. "Come here, please."

He tossed restlessly, and she gave in to his pull, laying her head on the quilt that covered his chest. She heard the deep workings of his lungs and bit her lip. She concentrated on praying that he would easily recover from the illness, wanting also to distract herself from being so close to him. "Come here," he said again.

"I'm here."

He lifted her with strong arms despite his fever, until her face hovered inches from his own, and she felt she might drown in the intensity of his dark eyes. His thick lashes lowered as he arched his neck.

"Please—Anna. Please."

She knew instinctively what he wanted and swallowed as she lowered her head to meet his lips, unsure of even what to do. But he knew. He moved his lips tenderly, gently, urging her to kiss him back with a faint lifting of his chin. She forgot to breathe when she finally moved her mouth against his own, and he made a low sound of approval deep in his throat.

A sudden loud knocking at the door bolted her upright as Mrs. Stolis entered without preamble. She raised one eyebrow as Anna made a frantic attempt to adjust her *kapp* and adopt a casual stance by the bed.

"That's a *gut* way to get the flu," the older woman observed dryly.

"I—uh—was—"

"It won't go outside this room. Besides, Asa Mast needs a good kissing. He's needed it for a while."

"Really?" Anna struggled to find her voice. She glanced down and was relieved to see that Asa had fallen back asleep.

"*Jah*, but that's not my story to tell. It's his."

"Oh."

"So, he's sick, is he? Well, he can just stay here until he recovers. I know that you have to go back tonight. One of the boys can drive you into town; the roads should be passable soon. We've heard the snow plows for the last hour."

Anna felt her world dissolving as the reality of her leaving struck with force. It wasn't the two hours' distance that bothered her, nor was it any concern about courting with someone from a different community—her *aenti* Ruth had left home when she'd married. No, it was something more—an inherent understanding of the man lying in the bed. She felt in her heart that if she ever saw him again, he'd be a polite, distant Amish man, far removed from the wonder and the intimacy of the births and the storm and his fevered kiss. Something else held him, she sensed, and that something would be enough to keep him hidden and reserved and lost from her forever.

Mrs. Stolis cleared her throat. "I wanted to give you something—for helping me and Mary."

"It's not necessary."

"It's necessary to me. Stop your moping and look here."

Anna broke from her thoughts and realized the older

woman held a heavy, folded quilt over her thin, outstretched arm.

"Help me spread it out."

"*Ach*, I can't." Anna shook her head.

"Hurry on; it weighs a ton."

They each took one set of the folded ends, and Anna walked backward until the quilt was revealed in all of its glory. Her eyes filled with tears.

"Do you know the pattern?" Mrs. Stolis asked.

Anna swallowed as she gazed at the rich red and green colors against a background of white. The flowers were clustered across the quilt, their wealth of stitchery evident in the outlines of the petals and the double-hued leaves.

"*Jah*, Christmas Roses."

"So it is, and my wedding quilt it was." Mrs. Stolis sniffed once. "It belongs to you now, because you reminded me of what it was like when Henry was alive—of who I was then. And now"—she glanced meaningfully toward the bed—"perhaps it will give you some insight into who you might really be."

Anna chose to ignore the confusing reference. "I can't take it. I mean, I'm so honored, but this belongs to your family—to Mary and Luke and the baby, or to your daughters."

"It's mine and mine to give, so now accept it with good grace as you should from your elder." The older woman walked forward and pushed the quilt into her arms.

Anna gave her a misty smile. "*Danki*. I'll treasure it."

Mrs. Stolis gave a brisk nod. "*Gut.* Now I'll leave you to your—nursing care. Come down when you're ready to leave."

Anna hugged the quilt and felt joy fill her, as if she were being embraced by all the women who'd labored over the beautiful quilt in preparation for a bride. Finally, she laid it in a chair and went upstairs to check on Mary and the baby. She found them dozing in peaceful repose, Christian looking cherubic in the crook of Mary's arm. Anna checked her respirations and did other small chores, then tiptoed from the room.

She went back down to the second floor to check Asa's breathing once more. She secretly wished that he'd wake again, but he slept on. So she sank down into the rocking chair, which held the quilt, and turned sideways toward a window looking out on the snow-laden fields below. Despite the fire in the now warm room, ice crystals splayed in dramatic detail across the windowpane as she felt the first pull of sleep wash over her. She realized that she needed a nap or she'd be crying all the way up the mountains to her home. So, gathering the heavy folds of the cedar-scented quilt about her, she laid her head back and drifted to sleep.

Her training awakened her at Asa's slightest move, and she rubbed her eyes as she realized he was murmuring with fever. She left the quilt in the chair and went to the bed to lay a hand on his brow when his words made her freeze.

"Jennifer," he pleaded. "Jennifer—think . . . our baby . . . please . . ."

Anna drew back as if she'd been struck. She stared down at him as he continued to cry out, and she felt sick to her stomach. She'd lain in his arms less than two hours ago, and now he was crying out for another woman . . . and their baby. A tear escaped and made its way down her cheek as she realized she knew nothing about this man. Nothing but one night. She'd been a fool to be dreaming, she told herself as she stuffed items back into her bag. She could think of nothing but fleeing the room, the house, and going home as soon as possible. She didn't turn to look at him when she grasped the knob of the door because he'd said the name again. Jennifer.

She swiped at her face and fled down the stairs, stopping only for a moment on the bottom step to pinch her cheeks and take a deep breath. There was no reason for any of the Stolises to know of her crying. She did not want anything to be said to Asa Mast when he awoke fully that might make him think he'd gained any interest in her heart. She would leave nothing behind that would allow him to feel he'd had a good joke on a simple, round midwife, and she crushed the tiny voice inside that told her he was not that kind of man.

She lifted her head and stepped into the kitchen area, finding Mrs. Stolis at the stove.

"I want to thank you for everything and to remind you to have Mary and the baby follow up with *Aenti* Ruth tomorrow, but I think, if it's convenient, that I'd better head back to town."

Mrs. Stolis gave her a speculative look. "Hmm . . . if that's what you really want. I thought you might stay for the meal."

"No ma'am . . . *Danki*."

"And how is Asa Mast?"

Anna drew a steadying breath. "Stable. I'm sure he'll recover well."

"I've no doubt he will. Did you have a chance to say your goodbyes to the man?"

"He . . . was sound asleep."

"Uh-huh. Abel's feeling well enough to drive you in. Abel? Take the midwife back into town to *Frau* Ruth's. She's in a hurry to go."

Anna flushed as the young Amish man put on his coat and hat. "I'll bring the buggy around quick."

Mrs. Stolis surprised Anna by embracing her, and the rest of the family called their thanks and good wishes as she soon found herself being trotted across plowed roads in the blinding glare of sunshine on snow.

SIX

Abel Stolis wasted no time helping Anna down, and she thanked him as he left her, standing alone, on *Aenti* Ruth's porch. She pushed aside the image of Asa's handsome face as he stood in the same spot last night while she felt for the house key in her bag.

Even Bottle's feline greeting did nothing to make her feel less alone as she dropped her bag and wearily went to make up the fire. As she knelt, staring into the low flames, she told herself that *Derr Herr* had a purpose in this, even if it was only to give her memories that, in time, she might be able to reflect on without hurting. She sighed aloud, then curled up on the hearth rug with Bottle beside her and fell into a deep sleep.

She awoke, disoriented, to find that daylight had fled, the windows were darkened, and someone was pounding on the front door. She rose stiffly and glanced at her brooch watch while she hurried to open the door. Six o'clock. She'd slept the day away, and now she prayed that it was *Aenti* Ruth and not another delivery. She swept the door open as she rubbed her eyes, then stopped dead when she saw Asa leaning against the doorjamb in his hat and coat with a brown bag in his arm. He exhaled and coughed when he saw her.

"I was terrified you'd left already; it would have been a long drive to Pine Creek tonight."

"*Jah?*" she queried, her heart pounding. Then unbidden worry for him took over. "You're going to catch pneumonia; come in out of the cold—please." She wrapped her arms around herself and went to poke the fire, trying to ignore his slow steps as he dropped into a chair.

"What do you want?"

He sighed and took his hat off, setting the brown bag on the floor. "You. I want you, Anna Stolis."

She pushed aside the surge of tearful pleasure his words produced and stayed stiff and still away from him.

"And I suppose you want Jennifer too?"

He lifted his fever-flushed face to hers, and she saw absolute pain in his eyes, as if she'd struck him a blow. But he took a deep breath and shook his head.

"No, but I did once—when I was eighteen."

Anna felt as if the floor had fallen out from under her, but she still couldn't move, mesmerized by the raw emotion in his face.

"Jennifer was the most beautiful girl I'd ever seen, *Englisch* or Amish."

Anna's heart sank and she hugged her generous curves more tightly against his words.

"It was my *rumschpringe*, and I saw her at a fall festival in town. It was like . . . like I saw the moon for the first time, or a star—so beautiful, but so distant. She was Amish, two years older than me and from a different community, but I didn't care. More than that, she was attracted to me because I was raised conservatively. And she was pulled by the unusual, the things she hadn't experienced."

He looked into the flames of the fire, and Anna saw the taut misery in the lines of his face as he went on.

"I bought a car so I could be with her whenever and wherever I wanted, and I ignored all the warnings from my friends, the little revelations that her exterior beauty might not match who she was inside. I was just so caught up." He looked squarely at Anna. "She became pregnant. It was, for me, a gift—a blessing. I wanted to marry her, and she agreed. But even though I'd drifted so far from how I'd been raised, I wanted to go and confess before the community. I wanted the baby to have security. But Jennifer wanted to leave the Amish. She wanted the *Englisch* world; she always had, and I knew that—" His voice broke. "Weeks went by; things didn't get better."

He swiped his large hand across his eyes. "One night I picked her up and she was wearing *Englisch* clothes. She told me that she'd found someone else who was going to help her, take care of her. She was going to meet him that night. I begged her—it was our baby. She told me to get over it." He swallowed hard. "We were in my car and arguing. I was driving . . . and then a pickup truck crossed the lane and hit us head-on. Jennifer—the baby—were both killed instantly. I walked away without a scratch." He put his head down into his hands. "The pickup driver was drunk; he wasn't hurt either."

Anna held her breath, tears slipping down her cheeks as he went on.

"The drunk driver went to prison; I went home. I told only my *mamm* and *daed* about the baby. They . . . forgave me somehow. In time I confessed before our church and her church for my anger in arguing with her while driving, my responsibility for buying and driving a car in the first place, and the way all of that contributed to her death. But I could never speak of the baby, of that incredible loss. And I was"—his voice dripped with irony—"forgiven and baptized and permitted to join the church."

He looked up. "But how could I really go on with a life that included a wife or children, babies, when I was responsible for that baby, that girl, no matter what her choices were? Inside, I've never truly forgiven myself or believed that *Derr Herr* has forgiven me, I guess, until last night."

Anna licked at a tear that crossed the corner of her mouth. "Last night?" she whispered.

He nodded, rising to come and stand before her. "Last

317

night, *Derr Herr* allowed me to experience again, and again, and again, the renewal of life—through you. It was like he was telling me over and over that he forgives me, that I could think of—and dream of—a new life."

Anna could feel the warmth of his body radiating toward her with his nearness, but she had to ask, had to know.

"Do you still love her?"

"No."

"How . . . do you know?"

"Because I was a boy, selfish and blind, who was in love with the idea of her, what I wanted to make her in my mind. I couldn't see past my own self and what I wanted to even know her as a real person, beyond what she looked like."

Anna gave him a steady look. "Well, you'll find no beauty here, no illusion of it either."

He drew a hoarse breath and reached out to lay his hands on her taut shoulders. "*Ach*, Anna, do you even see yourself? Do you know what you are?"

She lifted her chin. "I know who I am, what I'm capable of with *Derr Herr*'s help."

He nodded, smiling through his tears. "*Jah*, you are strong, like tempered steel. But there are other parts of you—" He bent and pressed his warm mouth near her small ear. "A tender heart, a gentle spirit." She shivered and caught hold of his dark coat as he began to press damp kisses along the line of her neck. "A beloved wife . . . a waiting mother . . . a lifetime of beautiful—"

"*Ach*, Asa." She took a deep breath. He looked down at her, and she lifted her capable hands to his broad shoulders. "I don't know how you can know so much about me. It is as if there are all those women waiting inside of me, but I've never thought, never dreamed—until last night—that it was the Lord's plan for me to become any of them. Not until you."

He bent his head and would have kissed her, but she pressed her hands to his flushed cheeks and wiped at the tears that clung to his thick eyelashes. He turned his head and kissed the inside of her palm.

"Asa, I want you to know—I'm so sorry about Jennifer, about the baby. I know what it's like when *Derr Herr* chooses to take life, when a pregnancy doesn't end like you believe that it should."

He nodded against her hands as she went on.

"But you will be a *gut* father one day."

He gave her a secret, warm glance and she blushed as she realized how she must sound to him.

"Tell me, Anna Stolis." He smiled. "Is that a promise? Or a proposal?"

She pulled from him and covered her hot cheeks with her hands. "That didn't come out like I meant."

He laughed aloud and she thrilled at the rich, full sound. He caught her against him and stepped backward until he dropped into a comfortable chair, with her in his lap. She half struggled to rise but he held her still.

"Now just a minute, Doc. I've brought you something."

She ceased her playful struggle as he reached down and caught up the brown paper bag from the floor, putting it in her lap.

"Open it."

She looked in the bag, then cried out in glad surprise when she pulled out the heavy Christmas Roses quilt that Mrs. Stolis had given her but she'd left behind in her flight from the house.

Asa reached around her and began to open the folds of the quilt, gently enfolding them both in its warmth and beauty. Bottle jumped up onto Anna's lap and nestled to find a comfortable spot.

"I don't know what Mrs. Stolis must have thought when I ran out of there," Anna said as he found her hand.

"That good lady told me that, apparently, I talk a lot when I have a fever. She figured I'd mentioned Jennifer."

Anna nodded.

"She also said to ask you about a particular nursing style you seem to have perfected to soothe your male fever victims. She said that it might catch you the flu one day."

"*Ach*, that woman!"

He cradled her close. "To tell the truth, I don't really feel all that well just yet. Care to show me?"

And she did.

DISCUSSION QUESTIONS

1. Asa and Anna's relationship is formed by a spontaneous meeting that is, in retrospect, clearly arranged by God. What "chance meetings" have you had in your own life that have revealed God's presence to you?

2. Asa's past is redeemed in a unique way through the experiences of the night. How has God turned your past mistakes into healing or wholeness in the present?

3. Anna's character is one of self-reliance and personal resourcefulness until she discovers a love that allows her to lean on another for support. What relationships in your life provide you with the greatest support?

4. How does the symbolism of "new birth" play out in the story on levels beyond the actual deliveries?

From bestselling authors in the Amish genre come three sweet stories centered around Amish traditions and the possibility of romance.

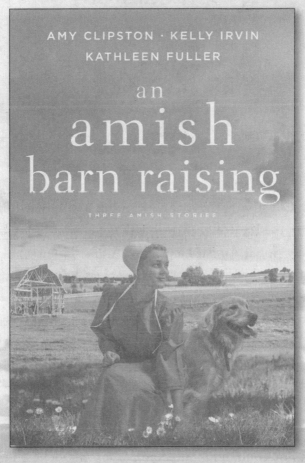

Coming April 2021

Available in print, e-book, and audio

ABOUT THE AUTHORS

AMY CLIPSTON

Photo by: Dan Davis Photography

Amy Clipston is the award-winning and bestselling author of the Kauffman Amish Bakery, Hearts of Lancaster Grand Hotel, Amish Heirloom, Amish Homestead, and Amish Marketplace series. Her novels have hit multiple bestseller lists including CBD, CBA, and ECPA. Amy holds a degree in communication from Virginia Wesleyan University and works full-time for the City of Charlotte, NC. Amy lives in North Carolina with her husband, two sons, and five spoiled rotten cats.

Website: AmyClipston.com
BookBub: bookbub.com/authors/amy-clipston
Facebook: @AmyClipstonBooks
Twitter: @AmyClipston
Instagram: @amy_clipston

SHELLEY SHEPARD GRAY

Photo by: The New Studio

Shelley Shepard Gray is a *New York Times* and *USA TODAY* bestselling author, a finalist for the American Christian Fiction Writers prestigious Carol Award, and a two-time HOLT Medallion winner. She lives in southern Ohio, where she writes full-time, bakes too much, and can often be found walking her dachshunds on her town's bike trail.

Website: ShelleyShepardGray.com
Facebook: @ShelleyShepardGray
Twitter: @ShelleySGray

KELLY LONG

Kelly Long is a nationally bestselling author of Amish fiction who enjoys studying the Appalachian Amish in particular. Kelly was raised in North Central Pennsylvania, and her dad's friendship with the Amish helped shape Kelly's earliest memories of the culture. Today, she lives in Hershey, Pennsylvania, with her three children and is a great proponent of autism spectrum and mental health needs.

Facebook: @Fans-of-Kelly-Long
Twitter: @KellyLongAmish